HAUNTED

A SPELLBOUND REGENCY BOOK THREE

LUCY LEROUX

Haunted © 2022 Lucy Leroux

❀ Created with Vellum

TITLES BY LUCY LEROUX

The Singular Obsession Series
Making Her His
Confiscating Charlie, A Singular Obsession Novelette
Calen's Captive
Stolen Angel
The Roman's Woman
Save Me, A Singular Obsession Novella
Take Me, A Singular Obsession Prequel Novella
Trick's Trap
Peyton's Price

The Spellbound Regency Series
The Hex, A Free Spellbound Regency Short
Cursed
Black Widow
Haunted

The Rogues and Rescuers Series
Codename Romeo
The Mercenary Next Door
Knight Takes Queen
The Millionaire's Mechanic
Burned Deep - Coming Soon

Writing As L.B. Gilbert
The Elementals Saga
Discordia, A Free Elementals Story
Fire
Air
Water

Earth

A Shifter's Claim
Kin Selection
Eat You Up
Tooth and Nail
The When Witch and the Wolf

Charmed Legacy Cursed Angel Watchtowers
Forsaken

CREDITS

Cover Design by Robin Harper
  http://www.wickedbydesigncovers.com

Editing by Jason Letts
  https://imbueediting.com/

CHAPTER 1

The phantom touch brushed along the length of her legs, urging her to part her knees. A sense of heat bloomed within that took her breath away as he softly caressed the silky skin of her inner thighs.

But she was too inexperienced for this. She twisted away from the compelling caress, squeezing her legs shut with a gasp of both regret and embarrassment.

The deep, throaty voice laughed softly. "So modest. You'll soon shed those inhibitions...once you realize the truth."

The words echoed as if bouncing off the walls of her still-dreaming mind.

"What is the truth?" she asked breathlessly, opening her eyes a crack.

"That you're *mine*."

Helena Garibaldi flinched, sitting up as the dream faded. Bright sunlight poured through the window. It woke her more effectively than being doused with water would. Such a vivid, scintillating dream couldn't continue in the light of day. That man and his voice belonged to the dark.

She pushed off the covers and walked to the window, throwing it open to let the cold morning air cool her overheated body. She ran her teeth over her lower lip then abruptly stopped. They felt too sensitive, as if someone had been kissing her only moments before. Her breasts were also sore...as well as other places.

Heat suffused her cheeks. It was getting worse.

The voice had been with her all her life. He even had a name, although she wasn't allowed to use it. Her mother had cautioned her to never think of the voice as a person.

"Perhaps he was one once," her mother Isobel crooned, holding her in her arms after an unnerving episode when she was five years old. "But he is not one now. Using his name will only give him strength and power over you. If he appears again, you must not speak to him. Don't acknowledge his presence. Act as if he isn't there, and in time the apparition will fade."

But Helena hadn't ignored him. He'd been so hurt when she tried that she hadn't been able to stand firm the way her mother wished. Instead, she had lied about her friend. Because that's what he called himself, her friend.

One of Helena's earliest memories had been of running through the greenhouse with the spirit. He had been her constant companion, someone who understood that she was different and didn't shun her for it. The spirit had played with her when no one else would.

Helena hadn't been like other children growing up. Uncanny things happened around her. Candles would flare too high. Birds of prey nested on her windowsill on three different occasions. Plants that had no business blooming in winter would suddenly spring to life if she spent too much time in their vicinity.

One of the worst things had to do with the animals. For a few years, every dying animal in the house or the woods would seek her out in their final moments. At eleven years old, she had been woken in the middle of the night by one of her father's hounds climbing into bed with her.

The poor beast had been attacked by a predator in the woods. It crawled into the house and up two flights of stairs to die in her bed. Her father had thought she'd been attacked when she woke up screaming, covered in blood. It had taken him hours to accept that there was no assailant. By then the entire estate had been searched from end to end, because she'd been too hysterical to explain about the poor beast, which she'd pushed off of her and to the far end of the bed.

Very few of the estate's children wanted to play with her after that. Not that many ever had. Being the daughter of the *Conte*, the estate workers discouraged their sons and daughters from playing with her out of an overblown respect for her station in life, and their nearest neighbors did not have children close in age.

Truthfully, her parents wouldn't have cared if she played with the estate's children. Her mother had been a mere governess when she met her father, and she was very democratic in her views. Neither parent was overly concerned with maintaining the dignity of their station. But the estate workers remembered her grandfather Aldo too well. When he was the *Conte*, every protocol and tradition was strictly observed—including the one where the nobleman bedded his female servants.

It was an open secret that her brother Tomas was not her brother at all. By blood, he was her uncle, her grandfather's by-blow, the product of an affair with a maid. But in all the ways that mattered, he was her overprotective brother who watched over her whether she liked it or not.

Tomas had also been telling her to ignore the voice most of her life. Helena tried, forcing it to go silent for months at a time, but he always came back. And she always let him. She couldn't help it.

Aside from her brother, the spirit was her only friend, a companion only a handful of years older than she was. But now that she was a full-grown woman, he was something else. Something darker. More demanding.

The spirit was...lonely. He never said so, but Helena knew. The older she grew, the stronger the connection between them became. Lately, it was almost as if she was experiencing his feelings as if they were her own. That frightened her, so she'd resumed her efforts to keep him at bay during the day.

She hadn't realized how vulnerable she would be at night.

He started appearing in her dreams. She couldn't quite see him, but while dreaming she was startled to learn she could *feel* his touch.

When he began to take liberties, she hadn't understood what was happening, not until it was too late. She had been seduced by slow degrees. Guilt warred with shame until she was stretched too thin, turning brittle. A stiff wind could shatter her if she didn't take care.

This has to stop. It felt as if she was standing at a precipice, lured by his voice. He was trying to coax her over the edge into madness with his touch. And she was almost ready to plunge in headfirst. Why else had she started retiring to her bedchamber so early every night?

Helena gave herself a hard shake. She had to dress. The coolness of the morning wouldn't last, and she had many herbs to gather in the neighboring hills today before her mother went into labor.

The end of her mother's confinement was drawing near. Isobel was expecting twins. Helena knew they were boys, the long-sought male heirs to her father's house.

She and Tomas were not in line to inherit the estate—she because of her gender and Tomas because of his illegitimacy.

For many years it had appeared that the estate would pass to a cousin. Her parents had tried for more children over the years. However, unlike her mother's first pregnancy, those that followed had been difficult and fraught with complications. There had been two miscarriages.

Her mother didn't like to discuss those terrible losses. For a long time, Helena had assumed her parents had given up, ensuring she would remain their only child by blood. That was until the unexpected happened. Late last year her mother had shared her joyful news.

Helena had mixed feelings when she found out her mother was with child again, but any misgivings faded the farther the pregnancy progressed. Now, with the due date only weeks away she was sanguine about the prospect of being an older sister and helping her mother with the babes.

The last hurdle was the delivery. Helena had been preparing for months. As a young, unmarried woman, she wasn't supposed to know the details of childbirth, but her mother was the region's most prominent healer. Though there were many midwives in the area, Isobel had been called upon to assist many births in the past. Technically, Helena hadn't been allowed inside those birthing chambers, but she had always been an inquisitive child. She had learned enough to help her mother and was determined to do so again.

Helena had been scouring the hillsides for a few weeks, gathering the herbs, plants, and wildflowers her mother used to help expectant mothers through the difficult process of bringing new life into the world. There was the added benefit that her mother's healing supplies would be well-stocked when she rose from childbed to resume her work.

No time to waste. Helena donned a simple day dress and hurried to the greenhouse that was her mother's special domain. Despite her advanced pregnancy, the Contessa insisted on remaining active until the last possible moment. But today her mother's usually agile form was less than graceful, as her added bulk made it difficult for her to walk.

Isobel smiled up at the daughter who'd grown taller than her as she made her through the neat but crowded room. "There you are," she said, the slightest trace of a Scottish burr overlaying her perfectly pronounced Italian. "Have you seen the Lactucarium pots I planted last week? I left them here on this table."

Helena's cheeks became flushed. "I'm sorry. I'm afraid the seeds sprouted already. The flowers have bloomed. I set them aside."

"Oh," her mother said, blinking before smiling reassuringly. "No matter. I'm sure we can still harvest the leaves."

"But the plant is more potent before it blooms. My apologies, mother," Helena added with a sigh, feeling every one of her one-and-twenty years like a weight she had to drag behind her. Once again, her gift had complicated what should have been a simple matter.

Isobel patted her hand before moving her hand to absently massage her lower back. "You mustn't worry, my darling. The ones we preserved last fortnight will do."

5

"You've told me dozens of times that fresh leaves harvested before the plant blooms are the most efficacious," Helena said. "The Lactucarium grows all over the hills east of the lake. I will pick more this afternoon. I was going to gather some of the lake plants in any case."

Her mother cupped a hand over her cheek. "If you insist, but do me a favor. If you don't find them close at hand, come back. Your brothers' arrival is almost upon us and I may need you."

"Of course," she promised, leaning into her mother's touch.

Isobel bustled to another table, but her gait was closer to a goose's waddle than her usual graceful glide. Helena glanced down. Her mother's feet were bare.

The Contessa grinned as if delighted by the observation. "I'm afraid none of my shoes fit at the moment. My feet have swollen to the point the maid can't lace most of them."

Helena leaned over to kiss her mother, patting her rounded stomach to include her brothers in the caress. "Why don't I ask the servants to prepare you a nice, warm bath? Not too hot. You can soak your feet and back."

"Don't fuss, my darling. I'm perfectly well." Isobel was already consulting her notes. "There's so much to do before your brothers arrive."

Helena took the notebook from her mother's hand. "Nevertheless, I want you to let me take care of this. You need to rest while it's still possible."

She didn't need to tell her mother there wouldn't be many opportunities for that after her brothers arrived. Isobel knew.

Her mother threw an arm around her, relenting. "What would I do without you?"

She squeezed her back, leaning her head on her shoulder. Helena let her mind go blank, savoring the simple moment of peace and quiet.

"He's back, isn't he?"

Startled at the unexpected comment, Helena shifted away to look into her mother's face. Isobel's hazel-green eyes, the exact same shade as hers, rested on her face. As usual, they saw too much.

Isobel sighed, and her eyes clouded over. "When I was pregnant with you, I was convinced you were going to be a son. I could feel a male presence hovering. But it wasn't you I sensed."

Helena's heart squeezed a little at the revelation. "You never mentioned that before."

Her mother's lips tightened. "Acknowledging a spirit gives them power. At first, I believed he was harmless. When you were a child, I sensed him now and again. My mother could commune with spirits. It was a gift she wisely ignored, and inevitably the spirits faded from her life. They always do. They're strongest when they first cross over and last a few years at most."

"I know." Her great-grandmother Helena's journals said the same. Her namesake had kept extensive records and journals. Isobel had inherited those and other books on healing and spell craft, books Helena had spent her whole life studying.

It didn't surprise her that her spirit did not conform to the wisdom in those books. She had always known he was special. Exceptional even. She'd held that knowledge close to her heart, secretly pleased that was the case. Helena hadn't wanted to let her friend go.

"Please don't worry. Everything is fine," she lied, affixing a benign smile on her face.

"Helena…" her mother began, her misgivings clear on her face.

"I'm going to get Martina to prepare the soaking tub. Then I'll summon father to help you upstairs. I want to get out to the lake before the heat becomes unbearable." She turned on her heel and headed for the door.

"Take Tomas with you!" her mother called after her.

But Tomas was occupied helping the Conte with the horses. One of the foals was having trouble, and there was no one better than her brother to help. When it came to horses, Tomas was gifted, both as a rider and caretaker.

Helena took care of the work in the greenhouse first, waiting as long as she could for Tomas's escort but gave up in the late afternoon. She struck out with her baskets on her own, determined to gather the plants and seeds she needed.

The worst of the heat was over, but Helena was still uncomfortable in her light muslin dress. Thankfully, a cool breeze occasionally wafted off the lake. She would catch it in brief gusts, but it was better than nothing.

Alas, there was no Lactucarium near the house.

Pursing her lips, Helena hiked up her skirts and started for the other side of the lake, stopping first to splash water on the sleeves of her dress and a little on her neck. It helped for a short while, but by the time she made it to the far shore, she was sweating and breathing faster.

There was no wild Lactucarium at the lake's edge. Wiping her brow on a handkerchief, she wandered farther up into the hills. She finally found what she needed and more at the bottom of a shady incline.

Humming softly, Helena busied herself filling her basket. In addition to the Lactucarium, she found two other plants used regularly in healing work.

The sun had already dipped below the surrounding hills when she felt something brush against her hand.

"*Helena*," the spirit whispered. His breath puffed against her ear almost as if he was standing next to her. She shivered.

"Go away," she hummed under her breath, working on digging up the roots.

This variant of Lactucarium was difficult to cultivate in the greenhouse, but Helena was determined to try. *If only my curse worked when I wanted it to.* If they could grow their own in the greenhouse, it would help in winter when it was scarce on the hills.

"*Helena*," the spirit repeated, more sharply this time. "*You need to run.*"

"What?" she straightened up with a frown.

A snapping twig told her she wasn't alone anymore. Spinning in a circle, she saw them. Three unfamiliar men with dirt-streaked faces and coarse unkempt clothing. They'd crept up on her so quietly she hadn't heard them.

One of them was holding the second basket, tossing the plants out as he looked for valuables, but she was too startled to scold him. Helena stood, rooted to the spot like a rabbit in the sights of a hunter. Their air of menace was unmistakable.

"When do we need to deliver her?" the shortest of the men asked the tallest.

Dark-haired and flat-faced, the leader narrowed his eyes at her, probably wondering why she wasn't running away. "He said tonight, but what he doesn't know won't hurt him. We can afford to have a little fun."

The spirit's voice was quieter now, his voice the merest hint of a whisper. *"I said run."*

An unseen force pushed her—hard—breaking her shocked stupor. Obeying, she dropped the basket, sprinting in the direction of the lake.

CHAPTER 2

*H*elena burst through the underbrush, fear driving her forward. She was running faster than she ever had, but it wasn't enough.

They caught her before she cleared the tree line. One of them covered her mouth roughly, grabbing her from behind.

The stench of acrid sweat and stale beer filled her nostrils as he forced her to the ground. Struggling she jerked away, rapping her head hard against an unseen rock .

Dazed, Helena tried to sit up and grab the stone to defend herself. But gritty hands pushed her back down.

"If she's not still a virgin when you hand her over there will be hell to pay," one of the men snapped.

"I know that. Just hold her arms," the man weighing her down said while moving to grab her face. His fraying trousers were already undone. He tried to pry her mouth open with one hand.

No. Her pulse pounded in her ears, and she tried to scream, but it came out strangled and breathless—too quiet to be heard across the lake.

"That one'll bite your *pisello* off," his shorter friend warned.

"Then turn her over," the leader grunted, shoving at her shoulders.

Helena was pushed face down in the grass. His bulk was crushing the air from her lungs. She clawed at the ground, trying to pull herself out from under the man, but she couldn't get him off. He was too big.

Tears filled her eyes. Her mouth opened in a soundless scream, but in that instant the weight pressing her down abruptly disappeared. Out of nowhere, a piercing whistle filled her ears, nearly deafening her. It was so loud she could barely hear the men shouting.

The air was roaring. She rolled over, squinting against the whipping wind.

The scene that met her eyes was so startling and unexpected that she had to blink to make sure it was real. One of the men—the leader who grabbed her—was lying on the ground, his sightless eyes gaping at the sky. His shirt front was drenched in blood.

The second man was floating, suspended over the ground by an unseen force. The horrible sounds he made indicated he was being choked.

"*Witch.*"

Helena turned, surprised to discover the third man right there but skittering back on his heels. His face was twisted, an echo of the horror she was just beginning to feel.

He pointed at her. "*Puttana* witch. Let him go."

"I'm not..."

The wind drowned out her voice. A gash opened on the suspended man's throat. It was as if an invisible blade had sliced his neck open. Blood sprayed everywhere, splashing her skirts and the sleeves of her dress.

Stupefied, she stared at her trembling fingers. Flecks of dark-red blood dotted her skin. Helena found her voice with sudden force. She started screaming.

"*Helena.*" She twisted her neck to the left. That wasn't the spirit.

Tomas cleared the hill, running toward her. Her third attacker turned, intending to flee, but her brother caught him by the collar and yanked him back with his powerful arms.

The man's strangled shout was cut short when Tomas slammed his head against a tree trunk. The villain crumpled to the ground.

He turned to her, his eyes wild. His face blanched at the sight of the two bloody bodies. "What did you do?"

Trembling she shook her head. "I didn't. It wasn't me."

The wind gusted past her toward the lake. Then it stopped, leaving a stiletto-sharp silence in its wake.

"Go home."

Tomas started, looking around him. "Who was that?"

Helena's lips parted. Her brother had heard *him*. The spirit had never been audible to anyone else before. She and Tomas stared at each other in shock. Then his face grew firm.

"Come now," he said, taking her by arm and propelling her to the lake. "We can't allow anyone to see you."

Helena glanced down at her skirt. The blood was bright against the pale yellow muslin. "They'll think I'm a murderess."

The local magistrate would arrest her. She would hang.

"It's more than that." Tomas glanced over his shoulder, but the bodies were long gone. "Those deaths don't look natural. That and you are too weak to make those cuts. They'll suspect witchcraft if you don't change before you go see mother."

"Mother?" she echoed blankly.

Tomas met her troubled eyes, his expression stark. "The baby is coming, but there's something wrong."

Her hand flew up in confusion and protest. Tomas grabbed it before it touched her face. *"Don't.* You'll smear yourself in blood."

Helena stopped short, pulling on his sleeve. "Tomas, the baskets!"

Everyone on the estate would recognize them. They were made with a distinctive weave only she and her mother used.

Tomas swore aloud and slipped off his coat. "I will return for them, but you have to hold this over yourself to hide those stains."

"What about the third man? Is he dead?"

"He better hope he is," Tomas growled. "But if not, he probably won't remember what happened. People who suffer blows to the head frequently don't, and I made sure to strike with as much force as I could muster."

Still shaking, Helena nodded, taking the coat. "Tomas, did you really hear him?"

He stopped, his eyes wide. "Yes, your ghost killed them."

She shook her head, wrapping the fine linen coat around herself. "He *saved* me."

Helena wanted to tell him what the ruffians had said. Someone had hired them to abduct her, but Tomas was long gone. He'd run after the baskets.

Turning, Helena hurried to the house, sticking to the trees to avoid being seen. As soon as she snuck into the house she heard it, her mother's distant scream echoing through the halls.

HELENA CLUTCHED ISOBEL'S HAND, heedless of her clothes and what she had to do. Her mother was in too much pain. She had to go to her without delay.

"What happened?" Isobel gasped. Her face was red, her hair plastered to her head with sweat. Blood stained the sheets below her legs.

"Shh," Helena hushed, giving the elderly midwife a meaningful glance.

"Have you been hurt?" Her mother's eyes fixed on the dark stains on her dress.

"Tomas and I are fine," Helena said. "I'm more concerned with you."

Her mother stared at her as if she was crazy. "What happened?"

"We'll discuss it later," she murmured, feeling her mother's stomach. She didn't know how she knew, but she could tell one of the twins was in danger. Something was wrong. Her mother knew it as well.

"I think one of your brothers is dying," Isobel whispered, tears glinting in the low light.

"*No.*" Helena shook her head. "We can save him. We can save them both."

Isobel took a deep breath and nodded. "Give me that towel," she said.

Helena frowned. "Those have been used. Let me ask the maid for a clean one."

Her mother's lips tightened. "I said *that* one."

Brow creased, she handed one of the soiled and bloody towels to her mother. Isobel waited until the mid-wives' back was turned before wiping the front of Helena's gown with the bloody towel.

"I will save all of my children."

Helena took a deep breath, tears stinging her eyes. "I…"

Isobel squeezed her hand. "Go take those towels to the maids and ask the cook to boil more water."

In other words, she needed to make sure she was seen carrying the bloody towels. "I'll get the extracts we prepared as well."

"Good." Isobel winced as another contraction racked her body. When it was over, her head fell back onto the pillow in exhaustion. "Go now."

Nodding mechanically, Helena hurried away with her bloody burden.

The delivery took hours. It was arduous and painful to watch. Helena had mopped her mother's brow and held her hand, supervising as the midwife applied the various extracts and tinctures they had made.

Her brothers arrived sometime near dawn, both healthy and perfect.

Isobel hadn't fared as well. The delivery had been difficult. She had lost a lot of blood. Nevertheless, instinct told Helena she would make a full recovery. It would take time, but her mother would be fine.

Exhausted, Helena kissed her mother's sleeping brow. The Conte had already visited, meeting his sons and heirs for the first time. He had lingered as long as he could until the estate manager had called him away.

She left the bedroom, her steps uncoordinated and halting from having knelt next to her mother for so long.

"Helena, come here." Her father hailed her from the door of his study. She walked inside, surprised to find a crowd.

Like her, her father was rumpled and disheveled from being up all night. Tomas stood next to him, his arms crossed over his chest in a defensive post.

Her hands fluttered, her stomach dropping as she recognized one of the men. Andrea Ricci was the local magistrate.

The bodies had been discovered.

CHAPTER 3

The dead men had been found by one of the estate's tenant farmers. He'd been in the company of his youngest daughter. Helena could only imagine the little girl's fear and confusion at this moment.

"I explained how my clothes became soiled," Helena told the audience for the third time. "It's my mother's blood. She just delivered twins."

Her father, Matteo, the seventh Conte Garibaldi de Santa Fiora stood next to her seat, putting his hand on her shoulder in a silent show of support.

The magistrate paced in front of her like a judge who'd already pronounced his sentence.

"A young unmarried woman assisting with a delivery?" The man didn't have to hide his incredulity.

"My daughter has assisted her mother in her healing practice for years. You know that," the Conte said, his voice bristling.

"But a birthing? The very idea…"

Helena straightened her spine. The magistrate was not known for his open-mindedness or understanding nature. "My mother needed me. There were complications with the birthing. She was in a lot of pain. Thankfully, she came through it, and all is well now."

"All of that is beside the point," Ricci said, his peremptory tone bordering on offensive.

They had known the magistrate for years. Andrea Ricci and her father were not friends, but he had never been adversarial before. *Well, he's never investigated a murder on our property before either.*

Her father drew himself up. "And what is your point? These men were trespassing on my land. What the hell were they even doing here?"

"That's what I'm trying to determine. The intruders were not shot, as one would do with poachers. But these men had their throats slit, which means murder."

"Again, no member of the family was on that side of the lake today." The Conte drew himself up, poking Andrea in the chest. "These baseless accusations are an insult to me and my family."

"I'm afraid they are not baseless." Ricci paced in front of her, staring down the bridge of his nose. "The bodies were lying next to piles of flowers and grasses. It's widely known that your wife and daughters collect these weeds to make medicines."

"Helena is a gentlewoman. She would never hurt a living soul."

Ricci pivoted to look at her brother. "Actually, I think it's much more likely that Tomas here did the killing,"

Helena leaned forward in her chair. "*What?*"

Tomas was a suspect? She clutched the arms of the chair, unable to hide her dismay.

Ricci inclined his head. "It would have taken a very strong man to kill these two men. Tell me, Tomas, do you carry a blade?"

Two men. Helena leaned back, schooling her features in an attempt to mask her fear. So the third villain had escaped...

Was that why Ricci was here? Had the surviving blackguard gone to the magistrate?

Calm down. That was unlikely. The man would have been incriminating himself, admitting someone had hired him to abduct her.

Tomas scowled at Ricci. "Of course I do, a sword. But I don't carry it on my person in my own home. I didn't kill anyone. I remained close to the manor all day. I have done so all week. We all knew mother's time was drawing near. I wanted to be near in case she needed anything."

He gestured to his chest. "Also, there is the fact I haven't changed my clothing since this morning. My valet can confirm this. The entire family and most of the servants have been awake all night waiting until my mother and brothers were out of danger. As you can see my clothing is rumpled but unstained. None of us have had the opportunity to sleep, let alone bathe or change."

Ricci stepped closer to him, peering at his clothing. The shirt Tomas was wearing under his gold and tan waistcoat was a light-blue hue. Any stain would have been visible, but there wasn't a speck of blood. *Thank the lord the man he fought hadn't bled on him.*

"I did go gather some herbs in the afternoon," Helena volunteered. "But only very close to the house. I also wished to stay near in case my mother began her labor. I have no idea why there were piles of discarded wildflowers. We are hardly alone in our use of them. Perhaps one of the estate's tenants decided to make them into a tea. They are frequently picked for that purpose."

Ricci rocked back on his heels. His eyes were narrow on Helena's face as if he was willing for her to break down and confess all. "I will have to speak to the servants to confirm all of this."

Her father straightened his coat authoritatively. "I will allow that if only to end this preposterous line of questioning. I fully expect a quick resolution to this matter—I personally suspect three or more vagabonds trespassed and had a falling out. But it happened on *my* land, so I will pursue my own answers. If there are more such trespassers, then my family and tenants may be at risk."

Ricci nodded. "I would expect no less."

A few moments later, the magistrate left the room, presumably to question the servants.

"This has been a bizarre day, but I promise that years from now we won't recall this part." Her father leaned over to stroke her hair, the love he had for her apparent despite his suspicion over the state of her clothes.

She hadn't had time to explain what happened to him, but she didn't need to. He was her papa.

"You're exhausted," he said. "Why don't I help you upstairs?"

Tomas stepped forward. "I'll do that. Why don't you see which maids are still awake and send them up with hot water? Helena needs to bathe before she can sleep."

Her father nodded, scrubbing his face. There were dark circles under his eyes. Now that Ricci had left the room, his fatigue was showing.

Helena got to her feet, swaying despite herself. Tomas rushed to her side, taking her arm. But she wasn't ready to leave.

"You're correct, papa. Today should be a joyous day—or rather a joyous night. I'm sorry this terrible thing is marring it."

"Not your fault, *piccola*." The Conte's smile was weak but genuine. "All will be well in the morning, but I think it best if you stay in the house for the next few days. In the meantime, all of the grounds will be searched."

He stepped forward to stroke her hair. "I'm afraid today's events mean no collecting on the far side without an escort—not ever again."

Her father's words were protective, but she knew he was the one who needed reassurance. But she couldn't throw her arms around him. Her dress was too filthy.

Instead, she nodded and let Tomas lead her away. They were on the stairs when he stopped her. "Did you tell mother what happened?"

"Shh. Ricci is still here somewhere, questioning our servants."

"But..."

She gripped his arm. "Meet me tomorrow in the library. We'll talk then."

Tomas's dark eyes bored into hers, but after a moment his head jerked down in an abrupt nod. They continued to her bedroom door, where her lady's maid was preparing her much-needed bath.

CHAPTER 4

*H*elena pulled out the dusty atlas, almost slipping off the ladder when the heavy volume upset her balance. Catching herself, she descended, taking care to move cautiously. It wouldn't do to injure herself now, not when there was such a long journey ahead of her.

She put the atlas with the other maps and travel guides she'd gathered from her parents' library. Tomas found her there in the early afternoon.

"I'm sorry. I didn't mean to sleep as long as I did," he said, sitting down at the table across from her.

"Judging from the dark smudges under your eyes, it was no more restful than mine."

Tomas rubbed his face. "I didn't fall asleep till well after sun-up. Clearly, you did not attempt sleep at all."

Helena shook her head. "I couldn't."

She had lain in bed for several hours staring at the ceiling as she fought to comprehend what had happened. How could her spirit have killed those men? When had he grown so strong?

"Did you eat anything?" Tomas was frowning at her.

"Yes," she lied. Every time she contemplated breaking her fast, she saw those bloody bodies in her mind. Just thinking about it made her stomach churn. She'd already been sick once this morning.

Tomas nodded. Helena wasn't in the habit of lying to him, so he accepted her at her word.

"The magistrate finished questioning all of the house servants yesterday. I believe he and his men will continue with the estate's tenants today."

"Do you think they'll find the third man?" The anxiety of that was twisting her in knots.

"I doubt it. Unless he's a half-wit he's long gone. Did you recognize him?"

She looked up at him through her lashes. "No...but he was sent here."

Tomas leaned closer, his eyes widening. "What?"

Helena needlessly rearranged the volumes in front of her. "The man who grabbed me mentioned it before he...before. He said someone hired him. They were supposed to take me and deliver me to someone—I don't know who. They never said his name. But those men decided to hurt me first."

"Those men were trying to abduct you?" Tomas grabbed her hand. "Helena, why didn't you tell me this before?"

She lifted a shoulder and sighed. "There was no time. Mama needed me."

Tomas leaned back. "I'm sorry. Those men should have never laid a hand on you. If I'd seen them, I would have killed them myself."

Helena shivered. "I'm glad you didn't have to."

She didn't want her brother to take a life. Tomas was a good man. Helena had never doubted his strength, but the act of killing would have deeply affected him.

Murder stained the soul. She knew that because this was not the first time she had witnessed it.

Helena pushed back the memories of the black witch who had come hunting when she was a child. An innocent servant had died after getting in their way. But her mother had saved her.

Today something else had.

Tomas frowned. "I'm still trying to understand what happened out there. The voice I heard... was *his* voice, wasn't it? Your spirit."

Wordlessly, she nodded. "He has grown stronger."

"Strong enough to kill?" The fear and worry in his face and the line of his shoulders was so unfamiliar. Her strong older brother feared *nothing*.

Helena put her face in her hands. "I don't understand how this can be. The fact that you could hear him would be proof enough that he's not a normal ghost, but what he did to those men..."

She broke off with a shudder.

Tomas crossed his arms. "He's English."

"Yes."

He sat back in his chair with a thump. "I always assumed he was Italian. I never imagined you were being haunted by a *foreigner*."

A startled laugh escaped. "You say that as if his background was the most bizarre detail in this madness."

"As far as I'm concerned, it almost is. Shouldn't your ghost be a countryman?" Tomas sounded offended that this was not the case. "Why didn't you ever mention he had an accent?"

She couldn't help but smile. "I suppose because I've grown so accustomed to him after all this time. His personality and nature are almost as familiar to me as my own. Nothing about him seems strange to me anymore. That fact he was English was simply a part of him, an indelible and intrinsic fact."

Helena broke off, wrapping her arms around her.

"Is that what these are for?" Tomas gestured to the atlas and maps in front of them. "Are you trying to discover where he is from?"

"No." Helena shook her head. "I already know where he's from."

Tomas's head drew back. "How?"

She shrugged. "Because he told me. I even know his name."

Staggering, Tomas gripped the sides of his chair. "What?"

"He is called Lucien, and he grew up in a castle outside of a tiny village called the Devil's Slide."

"Oh." Tomas blinked, nonplussed.

Helena pulled one of the most likely volumes toward her. "I've even seen snippets of the castle in my dreams. It's very old with a large pleasure garden overgrown with weeds. There's a lake nearby as well—not a grand one like Bolsena. Smaller, and the water looks cold and dark. It's a dreary and desolate place."

She held up one of the maps. "I'm searching for the town. It must be small because it does not appear in the larger maps of England."

Tomas nodded, taking the atlas from her. "Maybe we should ask mother. She lived in England for many years before she met father. Perhaps she's heard of it."

"*No.*" Helena's response was immediate and abrupt.

He grimaced. "Why not?"

She took a deep breath, but her throat thickened, making it difficult to speak.

"Helena, what aren't you telling me?"

"I have to leave."

Tomas's brow creased. "I don't understand."

Helena leaned forward. "I *cannot* stay here."

Tomas gripped her hand. A militant light appeared in his eyes. "We will find the man who paid those villains to take you. As long as I'm alive, no harm will come to you. I swear it."

Her eyes watered unbidden. "That isn't why I have to go." She buried a hand in her hair, heedless of her maid's intricate coiffure.

"Over the years, I've read everything I could on the nature of spirits and ghosts. Just days ago Mother confirmed what I discovered —a normal spirit should have weakened and faded over time. Mine has done the opposite. He is stronger than he's ever been."

Tomas looked sick, his eyes distant. "Yes, that much is obvious."

Helena shook her head. "Nothing about him fits the lore. When I was a child, he was only a few years older than me. But now he's a man. He's aged as I have, and he can manipulate objects and move *people*. Now he can be heard by someone without a drop of witch's blood in their veins."

Tomas snorted.

"I'm sorry." They didn't discuss her and Isobel's nature too often, but when they did, they tried to be forthright and direct.

"Don't apologize. I'm quite content not having to see what you see." He drummed his hand on the table. "And I believed some ghosts *could* move objects."

"Poltergeists," she agreed. "But all of our books say the same thing. A poltergeist haunting is of short duration, months at most before they burn out. And as far as I can tell, they can only affect objects around them in a burst—pushing books or vases off shelves. Blunted force. Spectral phenomenon of that nature is frightening but doesn't compare to what happened in the hills."

Her brother's hands rose. "The man was floating off the ground. It looked as if his throat was being slit."

"But there was no blade," she said. "Even a poltergeist would not be capable of such a feat."

He was silent for a moment. "You have convinced me. Your apparition is…unique. But that doesn't mean you have to leave your home and your family."

"That's exactly what it means!" Helena burst out. Startled by her own vehemence, she subsided, looking down at her hands.

"I used to believe he was my friend," she said in a low voice. "He's kept me company, played with me. But now that I know what he's capable of, I can't sit idly by. I have to do something to end his visitations."

"You want to end them?" Tomas pursed his lips for a moment. "But he was protecting you. The spirit saved you."

She gripped the edge of the table. Tomas didn't understand. "And what happens if he decides I'm in danger again? Or if someone insults me? What if—heaven forbid—I argue with you or one of our parents? He could hurt you or them."

Her voice dropped to a ragged whisper. "He might even kill one of you."

Tomas winced, running his finger along the edge of the table. "All right. I understand your fear. How do we stop it?"

I have no idea. But she didn't say so aloud. "I need to go to England. I need to find him."

His lips pulled down. "You've lost me again."

Helena stood, wringing her hands. "I've given this a great deal of thought. I can see only two possibilities. The first is that my spirit is a murder victim. He was killed before his time, and his body has not been laid to rest on sanctified ground. If we find him and bury him, then he should be able to cross over and go…wherever it is spirits go."

Where that was, no one knew. The accounts of people who had crossed over and returned were unreliable at best.

"What's the second possibility?"

"It's a variation of the first. That he died a natural death before his time and left behind unfinished business, something so compelling that he attached himself to me in an effort to try and resolve it."

"If that's the case, why hasn't he mentioned it before? I know he speaks to you. I believe you said he was the one that told you to drop my favorite boots into the lake."

She blushed. That had been years ago when her friend was full of mischief. "Perhaps he doesn't remember that there is an issue to resolve. I don't think spirits retain all the details of their former lives. Mine often refused to answer direct questions. He is willful."

There was a long silence as Tomas absorbed that. He was quiet so long Helena resumed her work, poring over maps and atlases of the English countryside.

I often ride to a place called Jacob's Ladder. It takes over an hour, even on my fastest stallion. I sometimes climb up the rocks to a stone cairn at the top. I add my stone to the pile. There's not a soul for miles. The view of the valley below is worth the effort.

"Can I help?" Her brother was still frowning, but he was sitting up now. He'd accepted what she'd told him.

Helena pushed one of the books toward her brother. "Look along the coast, but not at the ocean's edge. I think we are looking for a small town twenty to thirty miles inland."

He nodded, and they both resumed their search. After a half-hour, Tomas raised his head. "I think I found it."

He extended a traveler's guide to the western coast of England. There was a small but detailed map including the distant town of

Manchester. Miles away to the southeast a tiny dot was marked "Devil's Slide."

She took the book from his hands, her heart thrumming like a bird's wing. "You *did* find it."

Helena had searched for the town on her father's globes and major atlases on and off for years. When she didn't find it, part of her had been relieved. It made it easier to pretend it wasn't real, that her spirit was weaving stories and creating novel details for his or her own entertainment.

Seeing that name in print made her realize she had been fooling herself for some time. The spirit hadn't fabricated anything he'd told her.

Tomas took the book back, comparing the small map to other more detailed charts of the region. "I think we should sail there. I know it is not apparent from the maps, but it will be much faster than going overland through France."

Helena's lips parted. Tomas looked up, scowling. "What? You didn't think I'd let you go alone without a proper escort, did you?"

Her heart swelled, and the relief almost made her feel weak. "But you have so many duties here…"

Tomas was her father's right hand. Despite employing a competent estate manager, Tomas was responsible for the well-being of the tenants, their housing, and the harvest. Plus, he had his own studies and interests, including his own horse-breeding enterprise.

Tomas even had friends, unlike her.

He scoffed. "My principal duty is to ensure the safety of our family. If you say we have to go to England to do that, then that is what we will do."

Worried, Helena's lip trembled. "Mother and father will try to stop us."

"Which is why we aren't telling them." He stood, retrieving the pen and inkwell from their mother's desk. "Of course, we should wait a few days until Ricci finishes his investigation. We don't want to look like suspects fleeing the law."

Helena didn't think a few days would be sufficient to allay the magistrate's suspicions, but she wasn't prepared to argue with her brother. Now that she had decided to go, she felt a pressing need to get underway. The next few days were going to be torture.

She took her seat, intending to help her brother plan their journey when a thought struck her.

"Tomas, what about the man behind the kidnapping? We don't even know who he is."

He looked up from the map he was studying. "I'm aware. However, I have a few thoughts on the subject. But this trip must take priority. Don't you agree?"

She hesitated then nodded in agreement. "As long as you think mama and papa will be safe in our absence."

"I do, but we won't take chances. We'll tell them everything in our note. Father will take the proper precautions. He won't let anything happen to mother or the new babes."

The twins. Helena's heart hurt to know she would be leaving her tiny brothers when they were so fragile and vulnerable. But the danger to her family was greater if she stayed…

Mollified, she murmured her agreement before picking up the journal with a map. She ran her finger over the small lettering. *Devil's Slide.* Being born into a noble family meant Helena had been fortunate to travel through some of Italy, but this ominously named hamlet may as well have been on the moon.

As frightened as she was, she was more concerned about what she would find. Something told her that whatever happened to her spirit —how Lucien's death had come about—was worse than anything she could imagine.

CHAPTER 5

The sea voyage to the English port of Plymouth was not as arduous as Helena initially supposed. Every sailor aboard the ship remarked on the calm sea and favorable winds.

"We'll make port a full two days ahead of schedule," the captain had told Tomas with a broad grin. It was good news, but for Helena the trip didn't end soon enough. Life aboard the *Anne Sella* was enervating and claustrophobic.

Helena was accustomed to a life full of activity. She enjoyed helping her mother and the heady whirl of their small but active social circle. The enforced passivity of the crossing gave her too much time to think. She desperately wanted the voyage to end, almost as much as she dreaded what she might find.

Helena was also wracked with guilt. She hated abandoning her mother after such a difficult birthing, but she and Tomas had stayed long enough for her to be certain Isobel and both her brothers would be well.

"We'll only be parted for a short while," Tomas assured her repeatedly.

Mother and father have over a score of servants to help, she reminded herself. She hoped her detailed letter explaining their quest and promising to take every precaution would be enough to keep them from going mad with worry.

England was beautiful but odd. Despite arriving at the height of summer, it wasn't as warm as her native Italy. To her eye, the rolling hillsides were wilder, not as beautiful or welcoming as those she'd grown up in. But the stony peaks were impressive and awe-inspiring.

Tomas had been thrilled to learn that they could cut their travel time down significantly by riding on the recently inaugurated Liverpool to Manchester rail line. From there they would hire a private coach to take them to Stockport and on to Hayfield.

Helena had heard that passengers were now able to ride trains in England, but she hadn't imagined she would have the opportunity to board one.

Tomas was almost frenetic in his excitement. They stood on the platform together staring at the massive engine belching black smoke. A long line of passenger and freight cars was attached to it.

Her brother's curious eyes took in everything. He pulled out a small leather-bound notebook and began to rapidly sketch the engine.

"Imagine a rail line from Viterbo to Rome," Tomas murmured as he drew. "When we return home, I want to speak to father about the efforts to build a railway line. I think we should invest."

Helena frowned, coughing as the wind blew a cloud of sooty smoke over their heads. "I'm sure it will be a convenient mode of conveyance, but personally I won't enjoy seeing the rails cutting through the hillsides. It's also much dirtier than I thought it would be."

"I think you'll grow to appreciate it more afterward," he warned her with a grin. "Because once we reach Manchester we'll be obliged to continue by carriage for the remainder of the voyage. It will be a long and arduous journey, much more so than our leisurely trips around Bolsena. Only then will you able to draw a true comparison."

Loath to admit he was right, she demurred, "Let's come away. This smoke is intolerable."

A few more steps and the air was clearer but the wind was just as sharp. It whipped over her, and she closed her eyes, reaching out for her brother.

Her fingers brushed against Tomas's light wool coat. She began to speak but stopped as a frisson rolled down her spine. Startled, she opened her eyes, surprised to see that her brother had wandered to the edge of the platform. He was bent over and examining the massive wheels under the engine, taking copious notes...which meant the coat she was touching belonged to someone else.

Withdrawing her hand, Helena shifted to the side. She nearly fell over backward when she met the icy blue eyes of the man standing far too close to her. Her first wild thought was that her ghost had found her, but she didn't have time to do anything except gasp before his hand shot out, steadying her.

"My apologies. I didn't mean to startle you." The stranger's voice was smooth and cultured with a distinctive cadence that was blessedly unfamiliar.

Her foolish idea was wrong. Her spirit hadn't materialized on the platform simply because she'd set foot on his native soil.

"That's quite all right," she replied in English, straightening, and pulling away until the man's hold fell away.

Though the man had a pleasing countenance, his paleness was startling in the bright sunlight. She inclined her head and began to turn away, but the stranger stepped in time with her.

"That's a very interesting accent. Are you Italian by chance?"

Helena hesitated. She wasn't accustomed to speaking to young men in passing, not without a formal introduction and her father or brother hovering nearby.

"You don't have to answer," he said quietly. "It's obvious that you are, but there's something more, a trace of something in your accent."

"My mother is Scottish," she admitted, her eyes flicking in Tomas's direction. He was still occupied with the engine, having found a conductor to question, but his head raised, meeting her eyes across the distance. When he saw the young man at her side, he excused himself and began to hurry back.

"I see. That explains your excellent English," the stranger said. He glanced down at the ticket in her hand. "It seems we are headed in the same direction. Perhaps we will meet again."

She frowned. Why did that seem like he was making a promise?

"*Helena.*" Tomas hurried toward her, dodging around other passengers and porters. It was almost time for the train's scheduled departure, and the platform was growing crowded.

She turned around and frowned. The pale stranger had disappeared. Tomas reached her side moments later. "Who was that?"

Helena shrugged. "A fellow traveler."

Tomas grunted noncommittally, scowling over his shoulder where the stranger had stood, but then the train whistle shrieked. Helena winced, putting a hand to her ears, but Tomas grinned, his infectious enthusiasm returning. "It's time. Let's go find our seats."

CHAPTER 6

*E*very innkeeper and stablemaster between Disley and Hayfield tried to dissuade Tomas from taking Helena to the Devil's Slide.

It began as gentle remonstrances, where the person in question, usually a man whose services Tomas had just engaged, would frown when they learned where they were going. Then they would suggest another, far more picturesque destination. The warnings grew in severity the closer they got to their goal.

The last one, delivered by ancient ostler at the Crown and Rose coaching inn had been particularly memorable. "No one goes to Devil's Slide. 'Tis an evil place," he pronounced in appropriately sepulchral tones.

He leaned closer—presumably enjoying the novelty of an attentive audience. "The woods are full of unnatural beasts that hunt the unwary down like dogs. People who wander there don't come back."

"Leave the visitors be," the coachman had interrupted as he pulled their rented carriage to a stop in front of them. The coins they had paid were gripped tightly in his fist. "Everyone knows the stories 'bout the Slide and the demon duke are claptrap."

"The demon duke?" Tomas repeated, his thick black brow raising in question. He and Helena exchanged glances in the dusty courtyard.

"That's what everyone calls the Duke of Blackmore," the skeptical coachman replied. "They say he bargains with the devil and feeds on the blood of unwary maidens. Bunch of nonsense."

"Then why do so many people go missing there?" the ostler shot back, but his arguments died. He doffed his cap at them, muttering under his breath an admonishment to her brother to sleep with one eye open.

Helena had initially dismissed the conversation and the other warnings as idle gossip, efforts of the local populace to entertain themselves with sinister tales of the macabre. However, all those ominous and dire prognostications came back full force the moment she and Tomas arrived in the tiny village of Devil's Slide.

At mid-afternoon, the center of town seemed dark, as if the bright summer sun was filtered through a layer of smoky glass despite the fact there wasn't a cloud in the sky.

Even Tomas noted the oppressive atmosphere. "It would be one thing if this were London or Manchester with all those furnaces and chimneys blowing soot and smoke everywhere," he observed, squinting at the cluster of buildings that comprised the heart of town. "But this sky defies explanation."

Helena agreed but held her tongue.

The village had a single main thoroughfare. She could make out signs for a baker and a butcher, but none for an inn. They were dismayed to learn Devil's Slide was too small to sustain one. However, the helpful coachman told them that the town's few guests typically stayed in rooms above the pub.

Tomas took one look at the exterior of the Bucket of Blood and decided against staying there.

"I'm sure the name is facetious," she told him, squinting at the quaint thatched building.

"I don't care," he insisted, instead making arrangements to take up residence in an empty cottage outside of the village that was to let named after the merchant who built it, Hapley House.

Their first few days were a mad scramble to hire staff and set up an impromptu household in the wilds of the Peak District.

The accommodation they found was a two-story dwelling a ten-minute walk from the village proper. It was a spacious dwelling meant for a large family, but Tomas preferred it to the cramped quarters that were the alternative closer to town. Despite the typical small-town antipathy toward foreigners, her brother managed to secure day help in short order.

"I can't say I'm too surprised given the wages we're offering," Tomas said after he secured a slightly sour-faced woman named Sally to be their cook and a gap-toothed girl named Judy as a maid. "I don't think the Devil's Slide is too prosperous. Too many rumors about the demon duke, I expect."

Helena considered that. "What if they're not rumors? What if the duke has earned his sinister reputation?"

Tomas sniffed and then sneezed. Judy's industrious work cleaning and airing out the rooms had stirred a fair amount of dust. "Are you suggesting he may have been responsible for your spirit? Do you think he murdered the lad we're looking for?"

She sighed, sitting on one of the threadbare settees. "We know nothing of the man, so it's too soon to say. However, given the way everyone carries on about him, I can't help but think we need to learn more about the master of Blackwater Castle."

"In other words, our plans have not altered at all," Tomas said, crossing his arms. "Yes, that's very helpful."

The tone of brotherly condescension rankled her. Helena picked up a pillow and threw it at him, satisfied when the resulting cloud of dust sent him into a coughing fit.

Later that night, Helena was glad for Tomas's arm as he escorted her inside the taproom at the Bucket of Blood.

Given the size of the town, it was unsurprising that all conversation among the locals died the moment they walked in the door. Helena pasted a smile on her face, ignoring the curious and suspicious looks cast their way. The same thing had happened in most of the inns they had frequented in the course of their journey. It was inevitable.

Their style of dress and the way she wore her hair immediately marked them as outsiders.

However, this silence was of a decidedly different quality than others they had previously experienced. While they had been objects of curiosity along the stage route, here the looks they received were almost hostile.

Tomas, supremely unruffled as always, guided her to an empty table.

"They're certainly embracing the macabre in this little hamlet, aren't they?" she murmured in Italian as they sat down.

"Don't let this reception affect you. It's simply an odd and depressing little town," her brother assured her. "We can begin our inquiries here. These people must know a lot about Blackwater Castle."

Helena glanced at the assembled patrons, trying not to appear nervous. There were over a dozen men and women seated at wooden tables scattered around the room. Despite the fact that it was summer, a fire was burning at the other end of the room, presumably to combat the inexplicable chill in the air.

It was almost as if the looming castle in the distance cast a pall over the surrounding area, bleeding away the sun and warmth it was due in mid-summer.

"I'm not certain these people will be willing to speak to us," she said, keeping a bland smile on her face.

"It will be fine. You just have to find the right person. Every community has a gossip."

Tomas almost beamed when a middle-aged giant appeared at the threshold of the kitchen, a towel slung over his shoulder. Despite a bushy beard swiftly going grey and his large stature, the innkeeper's open countenance was a refreshing change from the other inhabitants of the room, who openly stared at them with thinly veiled suspicion.

"That's our man," Tomas said in a murmur.

The stranger approached wearing a welcoming expression on his round face.

"You must be the foreign couple who let the old Hapley House," he said, introducing himself as Harold, the Bucket's proprietor.

Helena blinked a few times. She had been so used to being known as Tomas's little sister that she forgot they didn't resemble each other at all.

The man mistook her surprise for something else. "We don't see too many visitors in these parts. Everyone has heard of your arrival. The entire village is talking about it."

"My name is Tomas Garibaldi. This is my sister Helena," Tomas volunteered before handing over his card as if he were paying a call.

The man blinked in surprise but took the card with parted lips. He held the thick paper stock by the fingertips, seemingly afraid to soil it.

"What can I do for you, Mr. Garibaldi?" Harold asked, making a valiant effort not to mangle their family name and utterly failing.

Tomas inclined his head formally, requesting a meal before describing their fictional plans to tour the local ruins.

"Not many of those to speak of," Harold said after relaying their meal request to a young girl who resembled him so strongly she had to be his daughter.

Helena put a hand on Tomas's arm.

"My brother is being his usual modest self," she said, speaking for the first time. Her clear and well-modulated English could be heard in every corner of the room as the entire taproom stopped to listen to their conversation.

"We are here to research his latest project," Helena said, improvising on the spot. "My brother is well-known for his gothic horror novels in our homeland and now he intends to set one in the English countryside."

"Gothic novels?" Harold echoed.

"Yes, the kind filled with apparitions and spectral phenomena. They're usually set in mysterious castles and the like," she said, nudging Tomas when he shot her a skeptical glance.

"Play along," she leaned in to whisper in Italian.

Harry wrinkled his nose. "The sort of novel that Mrs. Radcliff writes?"

Tomas nodded, though his lip curled up at the corner sourly. "Yes, are you familiar with her work?"

The man's face shuttered. "No, we don't have much use for that sort of entertainment here."

Her sense of direction had not adapted to the new environs, but she thought he glanced away in the direction of Blackwater Castle.

"We were naturally intrigued when we heard there was a large and ancient castle in the vicinity," Helena said, feigning enthusiasm. "Does the current master allow visitors to tour the grounds?"

Harold looked crestfallen. "'Fraid you won't have much luck there. His Grace hasn't entertained in years, and never when the old duke's wife is abroad. She sometimes has a few small gatherings—house parties and the like. But unless they are invited by the Dowager Duchess, strangers don't set foot on the Devil's Hold."

"The Devil's Hold?"

"That's what folk in these parts call the castle, on account of His Grace's nickname—the demon duke." He leaned forward conspiratorially. "Not that anyone would dare use either of those names to his face of course. Although, when they would have the chance, I'd be hard-pressed to say. His Grace never leaves the estate."

Helena tried to hide her dismay. "Perhaps the duke could be induced to allow a short visit? A place called the Devil's Hold would be very inspirational for a novel. I would hate to think we came all this way for naught."

"We could always start with the church or hall of records," Tomas interjected. "We could learn about the history of the area before approaching His Grace."

Helena twisted around to look at him. "But we need to see the graveyard."

She understood her brother's need for caution, but after the long voyage to their destination, she couldn't let one of her spirit's descendants put her off because he didn't enjoy socializing.

"The *graveyard?*" Harold laughed. "My you're a brave one, aren't you? But I guess the two of you do that sort of thing all the time in your travels."

"Yes, she is, and we do," Tomas muttered. He took a deep breath and relaxed in his chair, affecting a casual air. "Helena, we just arrived. We can afford to take our time and learn all we can before we take any definitive steps. You know I prefer to research my novels extensively before I begin to write."

"Yes, of course." Muting her annoyance, she turned back to Harold with a bright smile. "Is the Blackwater family large?"

"Blackwater is the estate and title—the family name is St. Germaine. And no, the current duke is the only one left."

"He has no heir?" Tomas was only half-interested. Harold's daughter had appeared with their meal. Her brother's attention was on his oversized slice of venison pie that contrary to expectation smelled lovely.

"Never been married," Harold informed them. "But there's still plenty of time for that. I don't think the rumors are true."

"What rumors are you referring to?" Tomas asked before stuffing a large forkful of pie in his mouth.

Harold waved expansively. "That the duke can't marry because of his bargain with old Scratch."

"Old who?" She and Tomas looked at one another. It was an unfamiliar term to both of them.

Harold bent over, checking around to see who was listening. "Old scratch is Lucifer himself," he said in a low voice. "The folk around here say the duke made a pact with him. The reason why changes depending on who you ask. It's all nonsense of course. The family do tend to grow a tad eccentric in old age, mind you, but I'm one of those who knew His Grace as a boy. He used to come here when he was a lad before he got sent away to school."

He turned, pointing to the long oak bar next to the kitchen door. "When old Harry—that was my father—ran the place, His Grace would come in and sit right there in that seat to have a pint. They'd discuss all the local news and doings in the nearby villages. The duke would always tip his hat to him and my mother when he took his leave. He was a fine lad."

Helena leaned toward him solicitously. "How old was His Grace?"

38

"About fifteen or sixteen and already the duke. His father died in a riding accident when he was ten or so."

"So, he lost his parent at a young age?" Helena asked, the wheels in her mind turning. Could the old duke be her spirit?

For some reason that didn't feel right.

"Yes, but he was in better hands with the current Duchess, his stepmother. She raised him as if he were her own. She's a fine lady— traveling the continent now, but she'll be back."

"Then, His Grace is the only resident at the castle?" Tomas asked.

"Except for the staff."

"He must be lonely," Helena mused, wondering how they were going to appeal to a recluse.

"By choice," Harold said. "But then there aren't many who share his interests. The demon duke is the scholarly sort. According to the castle staff he spends his days conducting endless experiments. Of course, that just makes people more suspicious."

Helena was puzzled. "You seem very fond of him despite his with-drawal from society."

"I suppose I am," Harold beamed as if he'd needed someone to point this out.

"Then why do you call him the demon duke?"

"Oh, that." Harold wiped his hands on his apron. "It's nothing. A bit of a holdover from the previous duke, God rest his soul. Just a little play on his given name, which was Damon. Silly really, but it's what they called him."

"I see," Helena said. "And is the current duke named after his father?"

"No, the current duke is named after his maternal grandfather, who was French. He was christened Lucien. Lucien St. Germain."

CHAPTER 7

*S*he burst into the cottage with Tomas hot on her heels.
"Helena, it doesn't mean anything. Lucien is obviously a
family name."

She spun on her heel as he closed the cottage door behind him.
"You heard what Harold said. The name was handed from his mother's side of the family. There haven't been any other St. Germaines
christened Lucien. His father was called Damon."

"So, he's the only Lucien Harold knows of!" Tomas protested,
setting down his hat on the table. "But Harold's not that old. Your
Lucien has probably been dead for a century or more. There could be
half a dozen others."

She pulled out a chair and sat down. "No, there can't be. Dear God,
I'm just beginning to understand."

Tomas threw up his arms. "Understand what? You're talking
nonsense."

Helena's eyes filled with tears. She shook her head, her mind
spinning.

Chastened, Tomas put his hand on her shoulder and pressed his
case further. "We came all this way to lay a murdered man to rest."

She looked down at her hands trying to find the right words. "

That's just it. I'm not sure we are anymore."

"*Helena*," Tomas sighed. "Be reasonable."

She held up a hand. "That's exactly what I'm doing. Look at the evidence."

He scrubbed his face with his hands. "I am—what little we have. For all we know your spirit may not be a member of the St. Germain family at all. He may be the child of a servant or a tenant of the grounds. According to Harry, it's a vast holding."

She shook her head. "The spirit is too well-read and knowledge-able for either of those possibilities. Don't forget I've spoken to him at length over the years. And in that time, he's changed."

"How?"

Her hands twisted together in her lap. "In the woods, you heard his voice for the first time. It was that of a grown man. Would you agree?"

"Yes," Tomas grunted.

Helena leaned forward and met his eyes. "But when I was a child, so was he."

Tomas frowned. "It wasn't always a grown man?"

"No." She leaned forward. "I told you this in Modena. Don't you remember? He used to *play* with me."

Helena silently berated herself for not having seen it before. "I don't remember a time when he wasn't with me. At first, he watched over me, hovering in the periphery. I remember feeling secure and safe whenever he was there because he was bigger and seemed so knowledgeable."

She broke off and covered her mouth with trembling fingers. "I should have realized the truth long ago. Spirits of the dead are frozen in time, unchanging from the moment of their demise. This one grew from a boy to a man. He was a few years older than you when he first appeared, but if he was a spirit you should have overtaken him in a few years. But you didn't. Instead, he matured with us, aging as we aged..."

Tomas was skeptical. "I'm having difficulties crediting that your spirit is actually some flesh and blood man—a duke of all things."

Helena slumped forward, her exhaustion a heavy weight trying to pull her down to the floor. "Logic would agree with you, but what if it's true?"

He sighed and settled in the chair opposite her. "I suppose Harold could be wrong about the darker rumors being fiction. Perhaps the duke does traffic with demons."

Her stomach tightened, but such a possibility was beginning to look more and more likely. "You think the duke is what mama calls a *stragone*—a male witch."

"If he is, then our task is simple." Tomas stood and began to pace. "We will force him to leave you alone."

"Simple?" she echoed. The few bites of dinner she had managed to swallow swirled in her stomach unpleasantly.

Tomas leaned forward to squeeze her hand. "You barely touched your meal at the pub. I concede that was probably wise on your part. If I see another boiled vegetable, I will toss the dish into the nearest ditch."

He stood and disappeared into the cottage's kitchen, returning moments later with a wedge of yellow cheese and a loaf of bread. "Eat some of this and then go straight to bed."

"I don't think I can."

"Just a few bites," he coaxed.

Too tired to argue, Helena ate mechanically before trudging up the stairs to her bedchamber. She undressed and slipped into a thin lawn nightgown, contemplating her reflection in the cloudy looking-glass on the dresser for a long while.

Could it be that her ghost was a living man? If he was then why had he been silent since the lake?

The noise of the front door opening and closing suggested Tomas was equally preoccupied. Should she offer him a tonic to help him sleep? For that matter why didn't she take one? Sleep would continue to elude her otherwise.

"To you my ghost," she whispered as she lifted the vial to her lips. Helena had a very strong feeling she was going to need her wits about her if she was going to beard the lion in his den.

Pity that she had blithely walked into it. *Foolish, ignorant lamb.*

CHAPTER 8

*L*ucien St. Germaine, the thirteenth Duke of Blackwater sat deeper in his leather armchair, staring broodingly at the fire. He lifted a glass to his lips. A bottle of claret sat on a nearby table. It was almost empty, but you wouldn't have guessed he'd managed the feat on his own from his starkly sober state.

It was far too difficult to drink himself numb these days. Not with claret in any case. He needed to find something stronger, perhaps a bottle from that case of French brandy he'd been saving. If only he could remember where he had left it...

Pity that my fantasy world took such a melodramatic turn.

Lucien closed his eyes, trying to recapture the fragile essence of those dreams. But he could recapture only the faintest wisps of sensation. Without sleep to refresh and strengthen his memory, it was the most he could hold onto. But after that last nightmare, his dreamworld felt...tainted.

There was little point to sleep in any case. *She* had stopped visiting his dreams. He wondered if it was for good this time.

It's for the best.

He needed to focus on the here and now, on the needs of the estate and its people, not some phantom female. Lucien had many duties he'd been neglecting. True, some would be difficult to carry out in his current condition, but there were others that were manageable, even when soused. He'd been doing a desultory job of maintaining the castle grounds and surrounding farmland, at best.

He really should walk the grounds and see what most urgently needed repair. *No, best not.* Lockton, his ancient estate manager, might die of shock. He'd be better served pensioning off the old man and promoting his junior estate agent. And he would. Eventually.

In the meantime, Lucien would have to find some other diversion to occupy his time.

There was always that other matter his stepmother Jocelyn mentioned in every one of her letters. But finding a woman to marry who could compare to his fantasies might prove impossible.

That doesn't change the fact you have a nursery to fill. His father's last words were about duty. Lucien had a duchy to preserve for future generations. *Or... I could let the blasted St. Germaine line die with me.*

He snorted. Now there was an idea guaranteed to make his illustrious ancestors turn over in their elaborately carved crypts.

A slight scuffing noise interrupted his reverie. Lucien smacked his lips together. The alcohol had dulled his senses more than he'd believed, else he would have noted the intruder before his sanctuary was breached.

It was a man. The heavy tread gave him away. The intruder was behind him, somewhere near the door, but instinct told Lucien he hadn't come from that direction. No, this man had entered through the third-story window, which meant he had entered the castle, found the balcony on the second floor, and scaled the narrow ledge underneath the window.

Without turning his head, Lucien reached for the bottle of claret, pouring some into his glass. "I have to commend you on your skill. I don't know how you made it past the dogs. They should have sent up an alert the moment you cleared the tree line."

Not to mention the other security measures his father had scattered around the castle. The average man shouldn't have been able to get past them. Perhaps one of the villagers had gotten lucky. *Or you were too drunk to maintain the little traps properly.*

Unfortunately, that was far more likely.

Lucien held up the bottle waving it at the stranger. "Come join me, but if you wish to partake, you'll have to get your own glass," he said with a languid wave toward the sideboard containing the extra tumblers.

This was met with a long silence. Apparently, his visitor wasn't interested in sharing a late-night drink.

The stranger appeared at his side in front of the second armchair. He was a young man, at least four or five years his junior. His clothing was simple compared to Lucien's out-of-date wardrobe, but the cloth and stitching were of the highest quality. Definitely not something he purchased in the village.

The corner of Lucien's mouth lifted when he saw the pistol in the man's hand. It was pointed at his heart. "Let me guess. You've come here to right a grievous wrong."

"That is correct." The man's voice was surprisingly steady. And heavily accented. This was no village youth. The man wasn't even English. But Lucien didn't know any Italians. Not outside his dreams anyway.

He laughed. "I'll be damned…you're a foreigner. You must have come all the way from London for this."

The young man narrowed his eyes. "And what do you believe *this* is?"

Lucien shrugged negligently. "I assume you've been hired by Leonard's family to hasten my untimely demise."

The barest trace of a frown crossed the man's face. "Leonard?"

Lucien lifted his glass, taking a small sip of wine. "He's a distant cousin. Next in line for the duchy."

One heavy eyebrow rose. "And you think this Leonard is trying to kill you?"

"Given that he is ten years old, I would sooner suspect his mother. She's the ambitious sort. Also, mean as a pit viper."

A muscle in the man's jaw flexed. "Leonard is not why I'm here. I came to make you undo the curse you cast."

Lucien leaned back, crossing his legs. This was more familiar territory, although being accosted by a foreigner was still a novelty. "I see. Let me guess...did a family member fall sick today? Were they struck down by some inexplicable and sudden illness?"

The man held the gun steady. Only the slight pursing of his lips indicated that he was listening.

"No?" Lucien scratched his head. "Then perhaps it was a sudden spate of bad luck? Did your crops fail? Livestock lost? Did your cow birth a calf with two heads? Or was it something more biblical in nature...a swarm of locusts perhaps?"

The man tilted his head. "Have the villagers blamed you for such things in the past?"

He grinned. "All that and more. Would you expect any less from a man who bargains with Satan?"

The Italian's wonderfully melodic baritone flattened. "Superstitious nonsense. The devil doesn't exist."

Lucien frowned. "This wine must be more potent than I credited. I thought you said you were here to have me lift a curse."

"I am."

"And yet..." He trailed off expectantly.

"I don't care about the random events the inhabitants of this backwater blame on you. I only care about my sister." The man lifted the gun higher. "Release her."

"Well, now..." Lucien leaned forward. "Truthfully, this isn't the first time I've been accused of kidnapping a young maiden or two, but I'm afraid there is no female locked in the dungeon. You are welcome to search, of course. But I must warn you the castle is old and quite large, with many twisting passages and hidden rooms. Be prepared to spend a few days in your quest."

The man scowled. "Helena isn't locked in your dungeon."

Lucien blinked. For a moment he sat there, stupefied. Belatedly, a bolt of energy shot through him, straightening his spine.

He gripped the arms of his chair. *"What did you say?"* he whispered.

The man unclenched his jaw. "You heard me."

"Your sister's name is *Helena*," he said hoarsely.

The man nodded sharply, but the pistol wavered.

"No, this can't be right," Lucien muttered giving his head a shake in an effort to clear it. He only succeeded in making the room whirl around him.

Helena was a figment of his imagination, a creation spun out of the loneliness of his youth. True, she had sometimes felt more alive and vibrant than the people around him, but she wasn't *real*. It wasn't possible.

And yet this man claimed to be her brother. Lucien leaned forward, a fascinated expression on his face. "Are you *Tomas*?"

The man's head drew back in surprise, but just as quickly his mouth firmed. He raised the pistol higher.

"I am he," the Italian said in a low voice. "My sister and I traveled all the way from our home in Viterbo to this unfortunate little hamlet for one reason—to force you to leave her alone. Cease bedeviling her dreams. People already shun her for her differences. And stop killing those who threaten her. That's *my* duty."

For a moment Lucien stared, rooted to his seat. He wasn't aware he had stopped breathing until his lungs began to burn. Heedless of the gun, he scrambled to his feet as Tomas's words penetrated his claret-clouded haze.

His head whirled, but he fought the sensation, grasping the man with both hands. "Helena is *here*? In the Devil's Slide?"

The Italian stepped back, his lips parting in surprise as Lucien clutched his coat. Fortunately for him, Helena's brother was more disciplined than him. He didn't fire the pistol, despite the fact the barrel was now pressed against his shoulder, only inches from his heart.

"Where *is* she?"

Tomas's nose wrinkled, but he finally lowered his arm, slipping the pistol into the pocket of his greatcoat. "You cast your curse while on another continent. You can end it without an audience with her."

Lucien laughed, the sound high and tinged with something like hysteria. "This isn't happening. I'm asleep again."

But why would you dream about Tomas? His sister was a much more pleasant subject for his nocturnal fantasies.

And yet it was Tomas standing here in his library. Not to mention the fact the heat coming off the young Italian's body was warmer than the fire in the hearth.

No, his mind wasn't fabricating this encounter in his sleep. The Italian was flesh and blood, and Lucien was holding his coat. This was no dream...which meant Helena wasn't one either.

He turned burning eyes to his guest. "I have to see her."

"No, you don't." The Italian was adamant, but he didn't need Tomas to tell him where she was.

Lucien had lived in the Devil's Slide all his life. Despite how locals felt about him, he knew the village and the surrounding land like the back of his hand. The nearest inn was in Hayfield, almost twenty leagues away. That meant Tomas had taken rooms at the Bucket, or he'd let a house or cottage in the vicinity.

It's not the pub. As his sister's escort, Tomas wouldn't feel secure staying at a common pub.

Lucien owned all of the houses and cottages between his estate and the village proper. If Tomas had rented one of the vacant properties near the castle, his estate manager would have alerted him. And those inside the village had been occupied by the same families for generations.

That only left a few possibilities. The most likely of these being a cottage that bordered the eastern edge of his estate or the one just at the edge of the village.

It isn't the one at the edge of the village. Tomas would want privacy for himself and Helena, and the one on his eastern border was larger —a merchant's home that had stood empty for a few years after the family had decided to move closer to London.

Feeling lightheaded and giddy, he grinned, throwing his arms around Tomas. He embraced him fiercely before letting go, sprinting out of the room before the Italian could change his mind about shooting him.

Lucien had a dream to run to ground.

CHAPTER 9

*T*omas chased after the mad Englishman through the castle grounds, but the devil flew as if he was on wings. He lost his quarry before he cleared the woods. Not that he needed a map to know where he had gone. Obviously, St. Germain had guessed where they were staying.

He knew the land. *That was the only reason you lost him*, Tomas reassured himself, but fear and concern propelled him forward despite the sharp stitch in his side.

The fact the man had known his and Helena's name was damning, but it didn't mean he was the demon acolyte the villagers claimed him to be. Nevertheless, his doubts had been erased. St. Germain was most definitely a *stragone*.

Tomas was no stranger to the supernatural. Though his adoptive mother had downplayed her gifts, he had always known what she was. Matteo, the brother who had raised him had never tried to hide his wife's uncanny nature, and he'd explained how they met—an abbreviated version that left out many details but was an explanation nonetheless.

And Tomas adored Isobel. She was a wonderful mother, a kind and generous soul who took in her husband's bastard brother and claimed him as her own. The fact that she was a witch paled in consequence compared to that. Tomas had never been afraid of that otherness, not even when little Helena had started showing signs of the same strange abilities.

However, it was infinitely more unnerving to recognize that otherness in the eyes of a stranger—a man he suspected of great and terrible deeds.

He couldn't allow that man anywhere near his sister.

Pumping his legs, Tomas stumbled over a tree root. He caught himself on the slim trunk of a birch tree to keep from falling, lungs heaving. He had badly miscalculated by going to see the damn demon duke, a mistake further compounded when the blasted man got away from him.

The servants he had hired, a maid and a cook, lived in the village. They arrived early in the morning and departed shortly after serving supper. That meant Helena was alone, sleeping in her bed in an empty cottage. His foolish blunder had left her unprotected.

Catching his breath, Tomas resumed running again—the cottage was just over the hill.

He reached the open doorway moments later. St. Germaine hadn't bothered to close it when he broke inside. Tomas wouldn't ask himself until much later how he'd managed to unfasten the heavy lock without breaking it.

Winded, he reached the stairway, taking the steps two at a time. Helena's bedchamber door was also standing open. There was enough light from the glowing coals for him to see them.

His sister was lying in bed, her eyes closed. The duke was kneeling next to her, studying her sleeping face as if fascinated.

"*Helena.*" St. Germain breathed her name, reaching out to caress her, but he hesitated before his fingers touched her cheek.

Tomas rushed over, hauling the man to his feet. "Don't you dare touch her, you ghoul!"

"You're going to wake her," the man whispered with a grunt, trying and failing to break his hold. "What is your profession in Italy? Are you a damn bricklayer?"

Tomas grunted, struggling to keep his grip. St. Germain was a few inches taller and wider than him across the shoulders with a powerful build.

He fenced and Matteo had taught him to box, but given the breadth of the muscles under his hands the demon duke was also a sportsman of some kind, not an idle nobleman.

In a fight, Tomas might not win. It depended on how well-trained his opponent was.

"Get out of here," Tomas hissed, trying to haul the man to the door. Thankfully, Helena was a very deep sleeper. She didn't stir. "For God's sake, you've broken into a woman's bedchamber in the *middle of the night*."

Apparently, the demon duke wasn't beyond the pale yet. He allowed himself to be dragged to the hallway.

"Is Helena ill?" St. Germain put his hands on his hips. "That amount of noise should have woken her."

Tomas released him, pushing him toward the stairs. "She's exhausted," he snapped. "It was a very long journey, and until we arrived her dreams were constantly plagued by *you*. Naturally, she's been fighting sleep."

He could see the man wanted to protest, but his lips pressed together firmly. St. Germaine inhaled audibly. "I haven't...visited with her for weeks."

The admission hung in the air between them.

"So, she was right?" We didn't harry off to another continent on a wild goose chase. *You* are the spirit that's been haunting my sister since she was a child."

A hint of a smirk appeared on the devil duke's face. "As you can see, I am very much alive. I'm no spirit or shade."

"Then...*how?*"

Tomas didn't have to explain what he meant. St. Germain comprehended his question perfectly. But he chose not to answer.

He crossed his arms. "Bring her to me in the morning."

Tomas scowled. "Absolutely not. I came here to find a way to be rid of you. I'm not going to serve up my sister like some sort of sacrificial offering."

St. Germaine's face hardened. "I would never harm Helena."

The sincerity in the harshly whispered words was compelling, but Tomas wasn't about to take any chances with his sister's safety.

He stared at him, trying to see past the man's unruffled facade. "Until tonight you didn't even know she existed, did you? You thought she was a dream or a vision, like she believed you were a ghost."

There was a long silence as the duke studied him, but the bastard refused to admit even that much. Prying answers out of him—truthful ones—wasn't going to happen in the upstairs hallway in the middle of the night. Another tact was necessary.

"Let my sister sleep. I will call on you in the morning."

St. Germain inclined his head the tiniest of fractions. "Will you bring Helena?"

"*No.*"

The duke parted his lips to protest, but Tomas held up his hand. "Not yet. We must speak first."

"Very well," St. Germain said grudgingly. "I will tell my staff to expect you."

Tomas watched him leave from the top of the stairs. He didn't relax until St. Germaine had left the cottage.

CHAPTER 10

*H*elena bent over the cramped writing desk in the office, trying to make out the closely set words on the page. She was attempting to decipher a journal her parents had acquired early in their marriage that had belonged to a famous witch from Andorra, the tiny principality nestled between Spain and France.

The diary was several hundred years old, with ink so faded the words were barely legible. Simultaneously translating it to English and Italian was an arduous task, but it helped take her mind off her current predicament.

Tomas was lying to her.

He had never done that before. Then again, they had never been in this position before.

For the last few days, Tomas has disappeared after breakfast. She suspected he was trying to find out more about the Duke of Blackwater and his estate, but since that night at the pub he refused to discuss the matter.

Last night, Tomas had returned to the cottage well after dinner, leaving her to dine on a miserable meal of boiled meat and potatoes on her own. Helena's nose wrinkled at the memory. She'd been hopeful that breakfast would be an improvement since their cook

Sally was the baker's eldest daughter. Regrettably, her expectations had been too high. The bread was the only passable item. It didn't help that Helena wasn't fond of kippers. She didn't understand how anyone could eat fish so early in the morning.

There was also the fact that without Tomas's escort she wasn't at liberty to go anywhere in town.

We should have hired a companion in addition to a maid and cook. Then at least Helena would have been able to venture out to the market and perhaps pay a visit to the small church in town. She wasn't as confident that they had any records of note there, but at least she would be out and about being seen by the local populace. In her opinion, that was an important first step to winning their confidence.

As it was, Helena had to make do with their maid Judy. The girl was fifteen and eager to share everything she'd heard about the Devil's Hold and its mysterious master. However, Helena soon found it necessary to cut short her helper's eager narrative as the stories grew more fanciful.

"They say the demon duke wears a collar of teeth around his neck and keeps massive wolves to guard him while he sleeps," Judy said, her voice dropping as if she were repeating a closely held secret. She was dusting the near-empty bookshelves at the time, and quite poorly at that.

Helena, who'd grown skeptical of the increasingly lurid details set down her quill. "Human teeth?"

"Aye, miss." Judy's big brown eyes widened impressively. "But they're all small. My cousin says it's because they come from little children."

Despite her dubiousness about the claims, Helena's stomach fluttered. The ostler's dire warning reverberated in her mind. "And have any children gone missing in the vicinity?"

"Well, no." The maid lowered her feathered duster, visibly crestfallen when faced with the inconvenience of facts. But she perked up as inspiration struck. "The demon duke must order them from London like he does his fine boots. But last year old Mr. Miggins did vanish in the woods. So did the widow Abshire. Also a few years back a couple of soldiers coming from the war made camp there. No one saw hide nor hair of them after those first few days."

Helena nodded sagely, pretending to be impressed before thanking Judy and suggesting she help Sally in the kitchen.

The soldiers had most likely been passing through before returning home to their own parishes. As for the old man and woman, the poor things *had* probably met an untimely end in the woods, no doubt as the result of an accident.

It was hardly the scores of missing souls the ostler at the Crown and Rose had implied, but numbers were fluid things the farther a rumor traveled.

Helena raised her head when she heard crunching footsteps on the gravel path leading to the door. A tentative knock followed. Judy shot past her, almost running in her eagerness to get to the door. Helena bit her lip to keep from laughing, but her amusement turned to concern when the girl squealed in alarm after a few moments of hushed conversation.

Rushing to the entrance, she blinked as Judy turned from the door with a strange parcel in her hand.

Judy was so flushed she resembled a boiled lobster. "My lady, this just came for you! From the castle!"

Helena frowned. "The Devil's Hold?"

"Yes! And it's from the demon duke himself. His coachman told me so."

She stared, her mouth open as Judy set the parcel on the foyer table and pushed it toward her.

Uncertain what to do, Helena unlaced the strings wrapping the object. Thick slices of starched paper fell away in quarters, revealing a stunning plant in a jade pot.

"My word," Helena breathed, circling the table to admire the strange flowers. There were three blood-red blooms so dark they were almost black.

"Those are the devil's roses!" Judy exclaimed. "They only grow at the castle. I never thought I'd see one."

"In fact, this is an orchid," Helena corrected her. "I imagine they don't grow wild. In this climate, it would only flourish in a greenhouse."

She reached out to stroke a velvety petal. "My mother used to cultivate them, although I've never seen one in this particular shade."

"There's a note," Judy squeaked.

Helena suppressed a wince as the exclamation vibrated in her ear. Judy was a dear girl, but her voice could climb to unbearable heights when she was excited.

Breathing deep, Helena snatched the little white card fastened to one of the long stems with a piece of twine. She turned away to keep the missive from the maid's prying eyes.

Helena,
I'm counting the days until we meet again.
Tell your brother I won't wait much longer.
-L

"What does it say, my lady?" Judy whispered, her sense of drama finally suited to the occasion.

Helena folded the note, frowning at the flowers. "It tells me that my brother owes me an explanation."

TOMAS TIPTOED INTO THE KITCHEN, surefooted even in the dark. His night vision was excellent, so he had no need for a taper. As soon as he found something to eat, he would retire. He had to rise very early to avoid his sister.

Light flared from the small table where the servants ate. He covered his sensitive eyes until they adjusted to the lantern Helena had lit.

"*Tomas.*"

Groaning, he stopped his hand halfway to the breadbox.

She walked up to him, hands on her hips. "I don't believe you. Where have you been all this time?"

"Err...many places."

Helena's foot began to tap, a sure sign of her irritation. "Including Blackwater Castle?"

He briefly considered lying, but Helena snatched his arm, marching him into the salon she was using as an office. A spectacular orchid specimen was sitting on her desk.

"You've seen him," she accused.

Tomas gritted his teeth. Damn the blasted duke. "I have," he admitted after a long minute. "I went to confront him after our interview with Harold at the Bucket."

Her lips parted. "I don't believe this. How could you do something so egotistical and foolhardy!"

Tomas scowled. "I went to force him to leave you alone. How was that egotistical?"

"It was pure Garibaldi arrogance to go without me," she ground out. "Tomas, I love you, but you're not *gifted*. He could have hurt you."

She broke off to put her hands over her face. "Good lord, Judy told me he keeps wolfhounds. They could have torn you apart."

"They're normal hounds," Tomas scoffed. "Nor am I so inept that I can't avoid the various snares set to capture unwary intruders around the castle—all ordinary. Nothing magical."

He stood up and paced, stung when he saw her blink rapidly. "Besides, the duke isn't about to harm me. Not that he wouldn't consign me to Hades if it suited him. However, at the moment he's concerned with making a good impression."

Helena sat down on the poorly padded settee. She picked at her skirts. "D-does he...?"

Tomas nodded shortly. "He knows who we are. The bastard didn't bother to deny it."

"Then he's definitely not a spirit." It wasn't so much a question as a stunned statement of fact.

He sat down next to her, taking her hand in both of his. "St. Germaine admitted to visiting with you, but that was the only admission he made."

"*Visiting*? Is that what he called it?"

"Yes. For what it's worth, I think he was just as surprised to learn you and I were flesh and blood as we were to learn that of him."

Tomas was quiet for a long moment. "There's one other thing. He wants to meet you."

Helena's lashes fluttered. "Well, that's hardly a surprise."

He crossed his arms, looking down his nose at her. "I went alone to make certain that didn't happen. I don't want you to meet him."

His sister's expression was touched with condescension. "Tomas, that isn't practical. I need to see the man. We're living at the edge of his estate for pity's sake. How can we possibly avoid him?"

"It will be a simple enough matter if you never leave the house," he declared. "I doubt His Grace will come calling."

Helena snorted.

"*What?*"

"You saw the orchids he sent." She smiled that annoying little smile women employed when they were amused at something a man said in all seriousness.

"Judy the maid almost had a fit of the vapors," Helena continued. "She kept carrying on about the demon duke coming to carry me away. I'm sure the entire village has heard about his gift. These orchids were cultivated by the Duchess of Blackwater herself. They don't grow anywhere else."

Tomas stood up to examine the unusual blooms. "They're flowers...They are *just* flowers, correct?"

"Yes, of course they are," Helena huffed. "But they came with a note. I don't think His Grace intends on waiting very long for an introduction."

"Well, he damn well better wait."

If the blasted man had been serious about meeting his sister, he would have agreed to undo his spell or whatever it was he did to visit Helena in her dreams. Instead, the scoundrel had listened to Tomas threaten and harangue him for the better part of the morning, wearing an inscrutable little smirk the entire time.

In that the duke and his sister were alike. *Smug witches.*

When Tomas had tired of berating the *stragone*, he'd taken a turn listening. St. Germain had attempted to persuade him to escort Helena to dinner at the castle. When it was clear neither of them was ever going to give way, Tomas had left. He'd wandered the woods, riding along the border of the estate in an effort to become familiar with the area.

When it had grown dark, Tomas had gone to the Bucket of Blood for dinner and a pint. He'd met another visitor to the area too, a young divinity student researching the origins of his mother's family. The pale blonde man had proven to be excellent company, especially after Harold had convinced the scholar to sample his finest ale.

Tomas had hoped to stay away long enough for Helena to retire to bed, but his sister was as stubborn as he was.

The flowers hadn't helped. "I should have known that arrogant bastard wouldn't wait," he muttered. Not after he saw her.

In his brotherly opinion, Helena was too attractive for her own good. He and his father the Conte had a devil of a time keeping the fortune hunters away. One of them had been behind the kidnapping attempt. He was sure of it. But his father would have to be the one to unearth that particular miscreant. Tomas had his own to deal with.

He glared at the orchids. "It would have to be something wholly unsuitable for a young lady."

"They're *orchids*, Tomas," Helena chided.

Scowling, he rounded on his sister. "He should have sent peonies or some such thing. Those are the kind of flowers you give to an unmarried girl."

He could tell Helena was trying not to laugh at him. "Judy said those orchids are a special creation of his mother, the duchess. Of course, the girl believes they're a strange type of rose so perhaps she is not the most reliable source of information."

"The current duchess is his stepmother," he corrected. "His own mother died in childbirth."

"Oh. How sad for him." His sister looked stricken. Tomas wanted to swear. Only a few details and already she was softening toward the interfering son of a bitch.

He tsked. "Damn it, Helena, this man is not to be pitied. He's a *stragone* of unknown abilities."

His sister rolled his eyes. "I don't think they'll be unknown for very long."

With that parting shot, she rose, retiring to bed.

Tomas went to the sideboard, muttering as he poured himself a soothing glass of the Amaro he'd brought with him from home.

"I knew I should have listened to Harold and stayed for another round," he told the stove.

CHAPTER 11

*H*elena stirred in bed as the cover shifted down, exposing her body to the cool night air. The bedroom had been quite warm when she retired so she'd chosen her thinnest night rail to sleep in, but she was regretting the choice now as she shivered in the dark.

Reluctantly waking, she reached out to pull the quilt back over herself but stopped short when her hand struck something warm and pliable. Bolting upright, she snatched the sheet and pulled it up to her chin.

Was that a...? The object she had struck was a hand. There was a person standing over her.

"Tomas? Is that you?" Helena mumbled.

She caught a tiny scuffing sound as if someone was backing away. She licked her lips, her mind spinning as another possibility occurred to her. *"Lucien?"* she whispered.

Had her spirit turned nobleman decided to pay her another midnight visit? But why wasn't he saying anything? He'd never been reticent before.

Oh god. It was very faint, but she could just make harsh breathing from the darkened corner near the door. It was not the demon duke visiting her dreams. For one, she wasn't asleep.

There was an intruder in her room.

No sooner had she come to the realization than the culprit decided to make a run for it. The dark shape pounded to the door, passing through a shaft of moonlight in front of the door. The only details Helena could make out were a dark coat and cap covering a tangle of hair.

A strangled scream escaped her as the intruder threw open the door. His retreating footsteps could be heard reverberating through the entire cottage.

"Helena!" Tomas burst into her room, pulling on his clothes.

"Someone was in here," she gasped.

The front door slammed shut downstairs. Tomas stumbled to the window before turning on his heel to run after the intruder.

Shaking from head to foot, Helena pulled on her wrapper. She lit a taper and hurried downstairs, waiting for her brother by the front door.

He returned a few minutes later. "I lost him in the woods," he panted, his chest heaving from the sudden exertion.

His hands reached for her, coming to rest on her shoulders. "Did you see him? Was it St. Germain?"

Her fingers fluttered to the collar of her wrap. "I don't know."

LUCIEN BRUSHED Aristotle's coat with rapid, sure strokes. It had been a bruising ride, but he still had too much pent-up energy to spare.

"Charlie, saddle Diogenes," he ordered his groom.

"Are ye going to take him out as well, Your Grace?" Charlie asked, squinting at him in the bright sunlight.

"Yes. He needs the exercise too," he said, bending to massage the horse's front leg. He didn't want his prized stallion to stiffen up.

Charlie relayed the order to one of his subordinates before hurrying back over.

"I can finish that up, yer grace. Your visitor looks a mite impatient."

He turned, his heart squeezing. Was it Helena? Had she finally come to see him?

His excitement subsided as he saw it was just Tomas, running up the lane.

"Perhaps you should saddle Heraclitus as well."

If he was going to have to listen to Tomas make more excuses about why he couldn't introduce him to Helena, he may as well use the time productively.

Tomas may not be keen to ride around his estate so Lucien could survey the southern border of his property, but at least the obstinate Italian would see how large the property was. As Helena's only family in the vicinity, it wouldn't hurt to impress Tomas with the size of his wealth and holdings.

Lucien hailed the Italian, about to call out a friendly greeting when Tomas stalked down the center of the barn. He bent to pick up one of the currycombs he used to loosen dirt on the horse's coat, throwing it at him with force.

The comb bounced off his chest. Catching it on the rebound, he looked down at the dirt marring the front of his waistcoat. "What the devil—"

Tomas bent to pick up a feed bucket. It missed his head by inches.

"You said you were going to wait for a proper introduction," he shouted. His accent was so thick he could scarcely make out the words.

Lucien threw down the brush. "And I have," he growled, jaw tight. "Rather patiently under the circumstances, I might add."

Tomas strode forward until his face was only inches away. "Then what the hell were you up to last night?"

"Last night?" What the devil was Tomas talking about? Had the Italian gone mad?

Tomas leaned in, looking over his shoulder to make sure no one could hear him. He needn't have worried. Lucien's grooms had made themselves scarce when the first brush went flying.

"Don't pretend you don't know what I'm referring to."

Lucien leveled a supercilious glare. He brushed the dirt with a slow, deliberate movement. "I haven't the faintest clue what you are ranting about."

"You were in Helena's room last night."

Lucien's lips parted. He racked his brain, trying his best to remember a dream state visitation, but for the life of him he couldn't recall anything—and he always remembered a dream with Helena in it.

He shook his head, confused. A flare of something he could only call jealousy flared to life in his breast. "I didn't sleep till dawn. If Helena dreamed about someone else, it wasn't me."

Tomas drew back in confusion. "I don't believe you. Who else could it have been?"

Lucien stilled, disquiet pooling in his gut. "Are you saying that there was an actual intruder in Helena's bedchamber last night?"

The Italian narrowed his eyes at him. "It wasn't a dream this time. We both saw him. But she woke up and he ran out of the cottage as if the hounds of hell were in pursuit."

Lucien swore under his breath, grabbing Tomas's coat by the lapel. "Is Helena all right? Was she harmed? Did he touch her?"

Tomas knocked his hand away. His expression was chastised. "She's fine. She had a terrible fright is all."

He took a deep breath, willing the burning coil of anger and anxiety to dissipate. But it wouldn't until he saw her. "Charlie!"

His head groom appeared, leading Diogenes by the bit. Lucien strode over and took the reins, mounting the horse in a fluid movement.

"Excuse me, Tomas, but I'm not willing to take your word on this matter. You can stuff your proper introduction. I'm going to see Helena now."

He turned the horse toward the stable's double doors, riding away before Tomas could stop him.

∾

Diogenes thundered to a stop in front of Hadley cottage. Lucien jumped off the horse, tossing the reins into the bushes next to the front door.

Pounding on the door, he waited impatiently for it to open. As soon as it did, he pushed back the startled tweeny.

"Where is your mistress?" he demanded.

The girl gaped at him, one hand still on the door. Her brown eyes were as wide as saucers. When she didn't move, he scowled at her. "Answer me, girl. Where is your mistress?"

To his dismay, the girl let loose a startled exclamation before keeling over, falling to the floor in a dead faint.

"Bloody hell," he muttered, looking around for help.

"'Scuse me," an indignant voice broke in. "Judy, what is going on 'ere?"

A matronly woman appeared from the direction of the kitchen, wiping her hands on the apron tied around her waist. She hurried over at the sight of the girl sprawled out at his feet.

"What—" The woman lifted accusing eyes to him, but the words died on her tongue as she recognized him.

Unfortunately, this servant was likewise struck dumb by the sight of him. Lucien suppressed a groan. Normally he was philosophical about his less than savory reputation, but this was ridiculous.

"Take care of that for me," he said, waving down at the unconscious servant. "Where is Miss Garibaldi?"

Wordlessly, the cook pointed to the hall with a shaky hand. Dismissing the unfortunate pair, Lucien headed to the back of the house.

He paused in front of the door where Hadley senior had kept his office, waiting for his heart to stop racing.

What is wrong with you? He was behaving as if there was something dangerous beyond the door. *It's nothing like that—just your future.*

Lucien threw the door open far too hard. It banged against the wall and bounced back. Exhaling, he stopped it with his foot and looked up to see if the woman of his dreams had witnessed his clumsy entrance.

And that was a resounding yes. She had seen everything.

Straightening, Lucien froze and stared as the daylight streaming from the window revealed every detail he'd missed in her room a few nights ago.

Helena was standing at the window, one arm wrapped around her middle, the other frozen halfway to her face.

Lucien tried to make himself step forward and found, much to his surprise, that he couldn't. It was as if he was pinned to the spot by Helena's more green-than-gold gaze. Unable to move, he clutched the door, drinking in the sight of her.

Her hair was dark auburn, but there were glints of gold mixed into its depths like the embers of a fire. Those hazel eyes were an endless pool of swirling color, a deep well he could easily get lost in. The dusty rose-tinted gown complemented her creamy complexion, making her skin glow in the afternoon light despite the shadows gathered under her eyes.

I was not prepared for this. The sight of this flesh and blood woman was like being jolted with an electricity machine.

Helena's bare fingers floated, hovering a few inches from her sensuous mouth. He could feel himself swelling, wanting desperately to bring them to his own mouth to lick and taste.

He didn't remember being released from his stupor, but suddenly he was there standing inches away from her.

Helena's deep pink lips parted. She opened and closed her mouth a few times but couldn't seem to find words any better than he could. Tentatively, her hand raised, reaching out and stopping a hairsbreadth away from touching him.

Lucien held his breath, covering her hand with his to push her fingers against his cheek.

A rush of heat coursed through him.

She felt it too. Her lush lips, the deepest shade of pink he'd seen on a woman not wearing rouge, allowed a quivering breath to escape.

His breeches grew unbearably tight.

The blood was rushing in his ears, roaring so loud he almost didn't notice the preternatural sweep of air that rushed around him. The light flashed orange as if sunset had come early.

Gasping, Helena stepped back, looking around them with wild eyes.

"*No*. Don't let go," he rasped, grasping her hand in his.

Her eyes flared at the sound of his voice. "It *is* you," she whispered.

"You didn't recognize me?" he laughed.

She shook her head. "No."

"Oh." Crestfallen, he let go.

Helena's cheeks were suffused with color. "But I know your voice," she said in a hesitant voice.

Lucien wanted to close his eyes in relief, but he didn't want to miss a second of her company.

"And I know yours." He would recognize it anywhere—low and throaty with hints of honey. Like Tomas, Helena spoke with an accent, but he found hers far more melodic and enticing.

"That's not all I know," he said, moving his hand to her cheek. "Do you remember this?"

He stroked her, running his hands down the vulnerable satin of her neck until his hand cupped the back of her head. Her lashes fluttered as he pulled her closer. Inclining his head, he pressed his forehead to hers as her breathing shortened, becoming faster and faster. The feeling between them intensified.

His lips grazed her flushed cheek, but she broke the spell by pulling away a few inches. "This is madness. I don't even know you."

Lucien laughed again, feeling uncharacteristically giddy. "Well, if you don't, then no one does."

Helena was straining against his hold. Reluctantly, he released her, allowing her to beat a strategic retreat behind the settee. He sobered when he saw her caution, remembering what had brought him here.

"My apologies for descending on you in this fashion. Please allow me to make the introduction your brother was so reluctant to undertake." He backed up a step and bowed deeply. "My name is Lucien Alexander Edgeworth St. Germain, the thirteenth Duke of Blackwater. And I am at your service."

Helena watched him wide-eyed, then her lips quirked. She dipped into a graceful curtsy. "Lady Helena Garibaldi."

He stepped closer to her, unable to help himself. "You've adopted the English manner for introductions."

"My mother was a governess in this country for many years. She was working in my paternal great-uncle's household in Northumberland when my father, the Conte Garibaldi de Santa Fiora came to visit. They were married a few weeks later."

Lucien blinked, edging closer. "I hadn't realized. I should have guessed that you had strong ties to this country. Your grasp of the English language was always excellent."

Measuring the shrinking distance between them, she bit her lip, backing away another step. "Though she became fluent in Italian, my mother always spoke English in our home in addition to French."

He nodded, fascinated. This small detail explained so much. Helena's proficiency with his mother tongue had been one of the many reasons he'd believed she wasn't real. How else could he explain the fact she lived in Italy but understood every word he'd said as a youth? He certainly couldn't speak Italian, although he had looked up certain curse words once he was older. As well as words for a few other acts...

Some of the things you shared with her were not fit for such dainty ears... Unbidden, a flush crept up his neck. The impulse to pick her up and ravish her on the nearest bed was outweighed by his desire to wrap her up in cotton wool. He wanted to lock her up in the tower at the castle—for her own safety, of course.

"Your brother came to the Hold and told me about your intruder. You must have been terribly frightened." Lucien reached out, but Helena shied away from his outstretched hand.

He masked his disappointment badly. "Do you believe it was me in your bedchamber last night?" he asked, his voice hoarse.

The world stopped as she hesitated. She shook her head, and he could suddenly breathe again. "*Good.*"

Hoofbeats pounded outside, and he sighed. "It seems our time is up."

An unnamed emotion flickered across her face. Lucien thought it might be disappointment, but that could have been wishful thinking on his part.

"That took him less time than I thought it would," he murmured as Tomas ran into the room, disheveled and out of breath.

"Let me guess," he said. "Charlie saddled Socrates for you."

"No. It was Parmenides." Tomas paused, his chest still heaving. "He's a fine mount," the Italian added grudgingly.

Lucien inclined his head. He used to take pride in his discerning eye for bloodstock before his most recent fit of melancholia. "Consider him yours for the duration of your stay."

Tomas appeared mollified for all of one instant, but Lucien's next words wiped all goodwill from his expression.

"I was just extending an invitation to your sister," he lied. "Until last night's intruder is caught, the two of you should come and stay at the Hold."

"*What?*" Tomas sputtered.

Lucien didn't look at him. He kept his eye on Helena's carefully composed face. If he didn't know any better, he would have guessed she was trying not to laugh—hopefully at her brother.

"This cottage is not safe enough for Helena," he said, staring straight at her.

Tomas moved into his field of vision, his expression thunderous. "That's Lady Garibaldi to you. And I find this invitation terribly convenient under the circumstances. I'm not convinced it wasn't you in her room last night. It wouldn't be the f—"

Tomas broke off, biting his tongue before letting slip the details of Lucien's one and only nocturnal visit.

"I told you it wasn't me," he growled. "My word is usually more than sufficient. However, since you are a stranger to these parts, I'm willing to overlook the aspersion to my honor."

Tomas glared at him, but before he could think of another caustic reply Helena took her brother's arm. "Now that I have met His Grace, I can say with absolute certainty that he is not the man who trespassed last night. I saw the intruder clearly in the moonlight as he was running out the door."

"Only from the back." Tomas pointed out with a growl.

"It was enough," she said with a meaningful widening of her incredible eyes. "His Grace is far too tall to be the man I saw."

For a moment that took the wind out of Tomas's sails, but he quickly recovered. "That hardly signifies. It could have been any of his staff—the man has a score of men and boys working in those stables."

"For the love of…" Lucien trailed off as Helena turned to look at him.

"Breeding horses is one of my passions," he explained helpfully before taking a look at her up and down. "In fact, I have the daintiest little mare that would make an excellent mount for you. Do you ride?"

Her eyes danced. "I do, but—"

"She is not going riding with you," Tomas interrupted.

"Then a short stroll, perhaps. There's a pretty path running along the edge of the woods just beyond the kitchen garden."

"No!" Tomas threw his hands in the air, exasperated.

"*Tomas,*" Helena admonished. "Now is our chance to get answers," she added in Italian in a low voice. To his surprise, he understood every word.

Perhaps I picked up more Italian than I believed.

Her brother's mutinous expression would have been comical under other circumstances. Lucien prepared himself for a long and drawn-out argument, but the irritated Italian surprised him.

"*Fine.*" Tomas inclined his head at his sister before turning to him. He narrowed his eyes. "Stay in eyesight of the house. I'll be watching from the windows."

CHAPTER 12

*H*elena progressed her way along the walking path carefully, acutely conscious of the steely muscles beneath the fine cloth of the duke's sleeve under her hand.

She couldn't take her eyes off him. As beautiful as Lucifer himself, the demon duke was almost a head taller than her. He was also superbly fit, with shoulders broad enough to make his tailor demand a premium to outfit him.

Her gaze lingered on his dark hair and eyes. And that mouth...

Heaven help her, she was going to disgrace herself if she didn't stop staring. Not that she was alone in her distraction. The duke couldn't seem to tear his gaze from her either.

She stopped. "Your Grace—"

"Call me Lucien, please."

The familiar dark-velvet voice sent a shiver down her spine. Hearing it in broad daylight seemed wrong. Blushing, she laughed a touch nervously. "I don't think I can."

"Helena, today may be the first time we've laid eyes on each other, but we are hardly strangers."

This was the single most bizarre experience of her life. "I don't know what we are, but I am very pleased you are not dead, Your Grace."

"So am I…" He laughed aloud, then he stopped in the middle of the path. "Helena, if I had known you were real, I would have come for you. You have to believe that."

Her lips parted, uncertain what to say. Thankfully, he seemed to understand. He resumed walking, keeping a hand over hers as if to discourage her from breaking away.

"Incidentally, I never thought you were a phantom or specter."

Her brows rose. "Then what did you believe I was?"

His mouth twisted humorlessly. "Proof of my madness."

Helena couldn't hide her astonishment. "You believed yourself mad?"

Lucien's smile grew wry. "You've been in the Slide long enough to have heard the rumors. My father died too early to show signs of it, but the way the stories go most of the Dukes of Blackwater succumb to their eccentricities in their old age."

He shook his head and shrugged. "With that legacy hanging over my head, I thought I was simply precocious."

Helena considered her next words carefully. "You are not mad. But I cannot explain the things you can do."

His lips parting derisively. "I'm afraid I can't either."

"Then your soul wandering isn't intentional?"

He blinked. "Soul wandering?"

"That's how it's been described in some of my mother's books."

The duke frowned. "What kind of books are these?"

Oh, dear. Was Tomas wrong? Did Lucien not know anything about the true nature of his affliction? Her heart squeezed tightly in her chest. *What if he doesn't believe in witchcraft?*

If that was the case, she couldn't confide in him. Terrible things happened to witches and other practitioners of the occult arts. Despite the strange nature of their acquaintance, she didn't know this man.

Dear Lord, had she dragged Tomas from one danger to another?

Helena took a step away, but the duke wouldn't let her go. His face clouded. "Helena, what's wrong?"

She ran her teeth over her lower lip. His eyes fastened on the small movement, glazing over.

"I need to know what is happening." Helena touched his arm with her fan. "How did this tie between us develop?"

The duke winced. "Since you were supposed to be a figment of my imagination, I'm afraid I've never questioned our connection. But I'd be lying if I said I regretted it."

He looked behind her in the direction of the house, craning his neck to see the windows. Taking her hand, he pulled her along the path until they came to rest by a clump of trees that marked the start of the forest.

Spinning her in his arms, he crowded her against the trunk of a thick elm tree.

"Your Grace, we shouldn't." Her voice was so breathless she could scarcely manage the words.

Lucien leaned closer until his legs were pressing against her skirts. His head bent down, nuzzling her cheek. "They can't see us from the house."

His breath fanned across her neck, sending a wave of sensation down her body. Why was there no air in this benighted hamlet?

"I didn't come here for this," she whispered, unable to stop herself from resting her hands on his chest. She told herself it was to check his progress, but she knew the instant she touched him that it was a mistake. The feel of such hard and sinewy muscle, so warm despite the layers of fabric between them, was intoxicating.

"And yet here you are," he murmured. Lucien lowered his head, giving her ample time to stop him.

Please, please. Helena's hands fluttered, but she didn't attempt to stop him. She couldn't.

He began by teasing her with the lightest of caresses. The gossamer brush increased in pressure slowly, letting her become accustomed to his heat. His lips were softer than they appeared.

And then he deepened the kiss, and she forgot her own name. The world stood still as his mouth robbed her of all sense, pulses of pleasure weakening her limbs.

"Helena, touch me," he urged, between sipping kisses.

"*Your Grace,*" she squeaked, breaking the connection.

"It's Lucien." His mouth moved to her neck, tasting her skin with a little murmur of satisfaction.

Gripping his arms, she threw her head back. The sky above them began to spin. Flames of desire licked at the tips of her breasts and between her legs, a slippery elixir began to flow. In her mind she was back in her bed back home, writhing in his embrace.

She may as well have been naked in his arms. Her gown and chemise were little defense against a storm of this intensity.

Groaning, Lucien shifted closer, taking her mouth again. His tongue pressed against the seam of her lips, coaxing her into parting them. One taste and Helena knew she was lost.

This was a dimension her dreams and waking visitations had been missing. The way her body would react to the flavor of his mouth and the faint scent of salt and sandalwood on his skin had been an unknown factor, like the missing ingredient to a spell.

If she had known what it would do to her, she would have run in the other direction. Being alone with him was madness. But it was far too late to try and escape.

A whimper escaped her as his tongue stroked hers. She broke away with a gasp. "Are you supposed to do that?" she asked incredulously.

Her ignorance amused him into a chuckle. "Oh, Helena love, we are going to have such fun together."

His mouth came down on hers again, tilting experimentally until he found the angle that made her want to press every inch of their bodies together.

Her back was pressing against the tree trunk now and she was grateful. She needed the support to remain upright.

Lucien was murmuring her name. Then air began to swirl up her legs and thighs where it had business being.

"Your grace?" Her voice was shaking.

One of his hands was tight against the back of her waist, holding her to him. The other was stroking up her leg like it was taking ownership.

That is what he's doing, she thought. And God help her, she was letting him.

Strong fingers pulled open the tie of her drawers, then drifted further down to delve through the short silky hair that shielded her secrets. He tugged on it gently, startling her into breaking the kiss.

"For the love of…" Lucien groaned as he traced her seam, seemingly delighted by the slick wetness. "You're so sweet and hot against my fingers," he mumbled, sounding as if she'd given him the greatest gift. "So right."

Helpless, Helena clutched at his shoulders as he circled the nub before pinching it lightly. She trembled in the circle of his arms, the small quake moving down her body.

His breath was hot in her ear. "Don't worry. I won't leave you unsatisfied. All I want in return is for you to say my name. Just that."

What came out was a whimper, and he laughed, one of his fingers breaching her entrance.

"That's close enough, love," he said as he began to stroke inside, simultaneously pressing his palm against her nub. Memories of dreams half-remembered filled her head, and her hips began to rise and fell, meeting his industrious fingers.

Then she broke, her body contracting only to fly apart in a desperate release.

He swallowed her cries with his mouth, his hands supporting her as she slowly recovered, each piece of her coalescing to make someone new. Someone different.

She pulled her head back, trying to find words when he lifted his hand. His eyes were looking directly into hers as he sucked on the tips of his fingers, the ones covered in her essence.

It was like a match thrown on dry tinder. She watched him, openmouthed in stunned immobility, which was a blessing really because she was mere moments from leaping on him to do unspeakable and unladylike things.

"Damn," Lucien swore, his head lifting with a scowl. In the distance, she could hear her brother calling her name.

The duke swore under his breath. "I know these woods better than anyone. Believe me when I say I can get us so lost no one would ever find us."

Still drunk on sensation, Helena blinked, trying her best to gather her scattered senses. She pushed her skirts down and adjusted the bodice of her gown with a blush. Lucien hadn't succeeded in undoing the row of tiny buttons, but he'd made a valiant effort.

Pushing the duke away, she raised shaky hands to her face. "I can't. I must give a care for my reputation, Your Grace."

Lucien raised a brow. "I assure you that isn't going to be a problem."

Helena couldn't believe her ears. "How can you say that?"

"*Helena!*" Tomas was shouting now.

She bit her lip again and he almost lunged for her. "I really must go now," she laughed, holding him at bay with a raised hand.

"Very well, allow me to escort you back." He reached out, adjusting her coiffure with a quick flick before offering his arm.

"We didn't discuss our mutual problem," she said, quickening her steps to keep up with his long-legged stride. The house was fast approaching.

He shrugged. "The way I see it, we don't have one."

Helena tugged him to a stop. "The lake *was* a problem."

The duke opened his mouth. A thousand emotions flickered across his face, but when he caught her watching his expression shuttered. "Why don't we discuss that some other time? I think I've pushed your brother to his limits."

She turned to find Tomas standing in the kitchen garden, waiting with his arms crossed. He was staring daggers at the duke.

Lucien took her hand, bending to press a kiss against her the back of her hand. "I will call on you tomorrow. And the day after…and the day after that," he said in a voice loud enough for Tomas to hear.

Helena took in the mutinous line of her brother's mouth and

grimaced. "Perhaps that might be a bit excessive. Why don't you call again in a few days?"

Lucien's eyes fixed on her face, flaring dark fire. "*Tomorrow*. Even your brother would agree—we have much to discuss."

Pivoting to Tomas, Lucien's features altered like quicksilver. He grinned wickedly, waving with irrepressible cheer as he took his leave. A moment later they heard the pounding of hoofbeats begin and recede into the distance.

Helena took a long, shuddering breath. Her skin tingled, and her lips were exquisitely sensitive. Dear God, what was she going to do?

Tomas joined her in the garden, taking in her state with a judgmental frown. "You're fortunate that mother and father aren't here to see the state of your gown."

Embarrassed, she glanced down at her skirts. They were crumpled, and her face felt hot. She was probably blushing, her lips kiss-bruised.

"I should change before the servants see me." If Judy caught a glimpse of her, it would be all over the village like wildfire.

Seizing on the excuse, she hurried past Tomas without further conversation, but he wouldn't have been her brother if he could resist having the last word.

"That man is a menace, Helena. You better learn his secrets fast, so we can go home before your reputation is in tatters—although it may be too late for that."

Her shoulders hunched as if he'd struck her physically, but she didn't stop moving until she was safe in her room.

Instinct told her that Lucien St. Germain wouldn't keep any secrets from her. However, the price she paid to learn them might be very high indeed.

CHAPTER 13

 o one was more surprised than Helena when the demon duke came courting. After his first unannounced visit, he began to make regular calls to Hapley House, typically arriving in the mid-afternoon and bearing gifts.

On one such occasion, His Grace arrived with an armload of aromatic flowers he claimed to have picked himself. The next afternoon it was a box of sweet confections, a creation from his chef at the castle. Another day he arrived with a freshly embroidered handkerchief bearing her initials and edged in French lace.

Tomas put a stop to the gift-giving when the duke presented her with a lovely chestnut mare with the most delicate conformation and sweetly intelligent eyes.

"Absolutely not," he'd thundered at the hapless groom who'd delivered it, sending him and the horse away with many Italian curses and a great deal of hand-waving.

Helena held back her mirth from her vantage point by the door until the lad had disappeared down the lane.

"Who does that man think he is?" Tomas stared after the departed horse with undisguised longing.

A duke with unlimited funds, who having discovered I am real now believes I belong to him.

Helena pasted a smile on her face. Tomas didn't require an answer. Instead, she gave him a commiserating pat on the arm. "It was a very fine mare."

His face softened. "It was, wasn't it?" Heaving a heavy sigh, Tomas trudged indoors.

Her brother's love of horseflesh made returning the beautiful creature quite painful for him—a detail that delighted the duke to no end.

"He thinks returning Hypatia means he has to do the same for Parmenides," Lucien confided to her on his next visit with a devastating grin. "Tomas doesn't know I'd give him the bloody horse for five minutes alone with you."

"We aren't precisely alone." Helena glanced at the door of the salon meaningfully.

Her brother insisted on leaving it open for the duration of the duke's call. Every few minutes he would walk past the threshold, stopping to glare at the man before continuing on, only to return every few minutes on a regular circuit.

Torn between amusement over her brother's hyper-vigilance and anxiety over sitting with her dreams made flesh, she smoothed her skirts for the third time.

"Are all your horses named after Greek philosophers?" she asked, grateful that her voice sounded normal to her ears.

His Grace was uncomfortably handsome today. He was impeccably styled in matching hunter green breeches and a matching frock coat so fitted she couldn't stop measuring the width of his shoulders with her eyes. This matched a waistcoat of lighter green worked through with gold thread. His glossy top hat sat on the nearby table.

The colors of his ensemble were muted compared to those of her native Italy, but they set off Lucien's hair and coloring. Brighter colors would have clashed with his dark perfection.

"Yes," Lucien replied, his striking countenance warming. "I became interested in the classics after a little bird told me a story about Aristides and how he had animals living inside his house."

He smiled, becoming impossibly more attractive. "I moved one of

79

my ponies into my bedroom that night, much to my stepmother Joce-lyn's dismay."

Helena stopped short with her teacup halfway to her lips. He meant her. She had been that little bird. She had no idea the story made such an impression.

"*Oh*." Her lashes fluttered, and she suppressed a giggle. "That wasn't precisely the message I meant to convey. I seem to recall it was a parable on the value of education. I believe I shared it shortly after you told me you tossed your mathematics texts out the window to avoid your tutor's lesson."

"Well, it worked, in a roundabout fashion." His grin was almost indecent. It could have melted snow. Then his eyes dimmed and grew distant as if he was remembering an unpleasant memory.

Helena frowned, recalling why she had brought up the story in that long-ago conversation. "You were upset about leaving school," she said in a low voice.

He blinked, all expression leaching from his expression. "That's right."

They stared at each other. He huffed and leaned back, clearly conflicted. "I sometimes forget I have no secrets from you."

Helena wished that were true. *You will not get a better opportunity than this.* "Your Grace," she began.

"*Lucien*," he corrected, elongating the syllables. Whatever disagreeable recollection had been on his mind was gone. The way he was looking at her now, it was as if he could see through her gown.

Heat rushed to her cheeks. "Your Grace—" she repeated firmly, stopping herself when Judy came in pushing an overloaded tea trolley.

It was not the first time Judy had served tea to the demon duke, which was why Helena hurried to stand and help her.

She reached out just in time to catch a precariously balanced plate of scones and check the cart, arresting its progress before the young maid could run it into the duke's shins—again.

Judy, flustered, picked up the teapot and made the mistake of looking into Lucien's amused face. One glance was all it took for the unfortunate maid to freeze, her mouth gaping, the teapot forgotten in her hands.

Sensing disaster, Helena took the heavy porcelain pot from her unresisting hands. "Why don't I pour, dear?"

Judy didn't respond. She continued to stare at Lucien as if she half-expected him to sprout horns and a tail. Sighing, Helena excused the girl with a less than subtle nudge out the door.

Lucien's eyes were dancing. Helena didn't miss the ornery gleam in his eyes. "I hope you're satisfied with yourself," she said, handing him a cup.

"Pardon?" He batted his thick black lashes at her.

"Don't play the innocent. I know you enjoyed that," she scolded him. "You take perverse pleasure in terrifying people."

"I don't have the slightest idea what you're talking about," he said with an air of injured innocence. The beguiling sincerity of his expression nearly made her laugh aloud. The man had the devil's own charm.

Making an effort to control her misguided mirth, she sat down across from him. He looked so out of place in the salon.

The delicate peach wallpaper and settee fabric was too bland for her tastes, but she couldn't fault the furnishings or decor. Despite his stylish waistcoat and snugly cut breeches, Lucien St. Germain more closely resembled a plundering Viking than a modern-day nobleman. He would be more at home in a throne room or a medieval keep than a fashionably appointed drawing-room.

Lucien set down the teacup and picked up a biscuit. He chewed it appreciatively. "These are good."

"It's one of the few things Sally does well," she shared conspiratorially.

"Sally?"

Helena stirred sugar into her teacup. "Our cook. She's the baker's daughter."

"I see." He flashed her a tempting smile. "I happen to have an excellent chef at the castle. I imported her entire family from France after the war. Her son is my valet. You and Tomas should join me for dinner tomorrow night. I can safely promise it's the best meal in the county."

Helena set down her own cup and took a deep breath. "I'll consider it…if you tell me why you left school."

His expression hardened, but it was the work of a moment. After a beat, he shrugged. "I usually don't discuss that time, but this is not a typical situation. You may as well know it all. My father had passed away in a riding accident earlier that year and I was…in poor health. My stepmother decided it would be best if I convalesced at home."

"Oh, I'm so sorry," she said, startled to hear that he had ever suffered from any ailment more serious than a cold. He looked so fit now. *So very fit…*

"I'm afraid my sickly constitution continued well into adulthood."

Helena's expression must have betrayed her surprise, because Lucien nodded as if to dispel her disbelief. Words of protest—mainly compliments on his obvious vigor and vitality—bubbled to her lips, but an ingrained sense of propriety prevented her from voicing these aloud.

"I think I should explain my affliction," he said with a sigh. "It began when I was a child. I would be at play until suddenly I wasn't there. My mind, or perhaps a better word for it would be my spirit, wasn't there anymore."

The blood drained from her face. Could it be? *Oh no.*

He reached out to take her hand. "I never had the words to describe what was happening to me, so we called it what the many physicians my father and later my stepmother consulted said. We called them my 'spells.' I much prefer your term—*soul wandering*. Not that the sawbones ever realized what was really happening. No one did. My stories were so fanciful Jocelyn believed I was fabricating them or recalling dreams. She would give me tonic after tonic, some of her own creation. Eventually, I put a stop to it."

By self-medicating with spirits, she guessed. An unfamiliar mix of sympathy and guilt tightened her stomach.

"As a child and young man, the spells would strike me down at random," he continued. "Unfortunately, normal life wasn't possible as long as I suffered from them. I couldn't continue at school. The teachers and other pupils never knew how to react when I grew unresponsive. They would shove smelling salts into my face to no avail. When I succumbed to a fit at the top of a staircase in my dormitory and almost tumbled down them, Jocelyn decided—very sensibly might I add—that I continue my education at home. She hired a series of tutors with a wide range of specialties. I daresay that lot provided a finer education than Eton possibly could have."

Helena's lips trembled. "Lucien, I'm so sorry."

"For what?" There was no resentment in his face. "For finally giving me answers to the questions I've been asking since boyhood?"

How could he be so casual? So matter of fact? Even after confining himself to the Devil's Hold, he would have been oppressed. Without control of his visitations, he wouldn't have been able to freely move about the estate. He would have required constant supervision.

She wiped the corner of her eye with her gloved hand. "This strange affliction has ruled your life, and I can't help but feel responsible."

"Hardly," he scoffed.

"But—"

A hint of a smile played at the corners of his mouth. "May I ask you something? There was nothing you did to—what did you call it? To summon a wandering soul to your side?"

"What? *No.*"

"Then you didn't do or say anything to force me to your side?"

"No, of course not," she said indignantly. "The very idea!"

He held up his hands in surrender. "I am simply making the point that you had no more control than I did."

Helena looked down and shook her head. "That's very generous of you. I'm not sure I would feel the same in your position, but then I experienced the, er, visitation very differently from you."

"I want to know everything about that."

She studied him. He was breathtakingly handsome and so damaged. Every instinct told her to take him into her arms, but she knew if she did she'd never escape them.

Helena took a deep breath. "There is a reason I believed you were a spirit. I would be doing my lessons or playing in the greenhouse and the skin on the back of my neck would prickle. I'd turn my head and there you'd be. I couldn't see you, but I knew you were there. And then you would speak. I could hear your voice clear as day."

"But you never saw me?"

"No. I would glimpse snatches of your features in dreams but nothing more. If I had passed you on the street, I would have never known you."

"Unless I spoke."

"Yes, your voice possesses a distinctive timbre and depth," she acknowledged with a blush.

He watched her with that unwavering intensity that made her feel like a doe in the sights of a hunter. "I would have known you anywhere," he murmured.

Her brows puckered. "Because you could see me?"

"Yes. Not clearly of course. My vision during my soul wandering was hazy as if it were obscured by a veil or a gossamer weave, but over time I saw enough."

As if tied by a thread, they leaned closer to each other. "What did you see?"

"My mind learned to combine all those small observations to puzzle out the lines of your face, to divine the shifting landscape of color in your eyes and measure the lush curve of your...lips."

Her breath caught. Under the light muslin of her bodice, the buds of her breasts tightened as warmth flooded her body.

His words reverberated in her ears, that husky midnight velvet quality that was so characteristic of him strengthening. "Mercifully, as I grew older the haphazard nature of my spells changed. I was able to resist succumbing when I was awake. Consequently, I only surrendered when asleep. And I soon learned that presented some very real and surprising advantages."

Her cheeks flamed as she remembered the heated embraces of her dreams. Helena mentally cursed herself for leaving her fan upstairs.

"I, um…" Tongue-tied, she blinked, wondering what on Earth she could say in response. "Then it was never intentional?"

"Well…not in the beginning. For the last few months, I retired to bed at an absurdly early hour. Sometimes the sun was still up."

Helena burst out laughing, surreptitiously fanning herself with her hand. "But you never attempted to, er, wander while awake?"

Lucien leaned back in his chair. "On purpose? No, I cannot say that I ever did. But I've never been one for experimentation. That was a peculiar idiosyncrasy of St. Germain's of generations past."

Her brow creased. "What does that mean?"

He shrugged. "I come from a long line of dabblers. The dukes of the Devil's Hold pursued many esoteric interests, enough for more than one of them to earn themselves the title of mad alchemist. Even my father—a distressingly practical penny-pincher—threw hundreds, perhaps thousands of pounds away on his passion, the study of electricity. He even built his own electricity machine. It's in the attic."

The duke picked up his teacup and took another hearty swallow. "I do admit that I too briefly succumbed to the lure. The equipment was sitting there gathering dust after all. But I never had the same zeal for it that my father did."

The same could not be said for the wider family. He regaled her with anecdotes of all the ancestors and present-day relatives who shared the St. Germaine tendency for scholarly obsession.

"Even my mother, my father's first wife, Christien, my mother, was seduced by the mysteries of botanical experimentation. She grew all sorts of rare and precious herbs and flowers. My stepmother Jocelyn shared her botanical enthusiasm for a time but has largely abandoned those studies in favor of collecting illuminated manuscripts. That's one of the reasons she decided to tour the continent. Perhaps, if dinner with me is unappealing, you would like to pay a call on her. I'm sure I can pry her away from her manuscripts long enough to show you the gardens."

"Oh." Helena was a little startled. "I thought your stepmother was still traveling abroad."

"She returned a few months ago, but she hasn't made her return widely known just yet." He leaned back on the settee with an indulgent smile. "Jocelyn has a tendency to shut herself away with her spoils after one of her trips. She is a serious scholar and likes to barricade herself in her private salon studying her new acquisitions for several months after her return. Only once the appeal of her books wanes does she dive back into the social whirl."

"I see," she murmured, registering the enthusiasm in his voice when he spoke of his stepmother. He was obviously fond of her. It appeared he bore no ill will toward the woman who poured "tonic after tonic" down his throat.

Helena resisted the urge to stroke him. Touching was a growing temptation. "And you? What is your passion?"

"Besides your lovely self?" A smile touched his eyes, but he looked away to contemplate the bland furnishings. "Without the freedom to travel, I devoted myself to my lands. Most of my studies have been restricted to agricultural matters—trying to improve crop yields and the like. Or at least they were. I admit my interests in breeding horses have taken most of my time the last few years."

"The few I've seen have been fine specimens." Her brother's heavy step alerted her to his presence outside the door. She waited for him to move on before continuing. "Tomas would never say so aloud, but he's very impressed with your stock. And those orchids you sent were lovely. I understand your mother cultivated them."

He nodded, and she paused trying to find the right words. "It sounds as if you have many diverse and interesting branches in your family tree. Were there any who had a genuine interest in the occult?"

Helena strived to keep her tone casual, but she couldn't fool him. His eyes flared, searching her face.

"There have always been rumors of course," Lucien said, equally carefully. "Some to the effect that my grandfather dabbled in the black arts. As I said, they called him an alchemist, but he wasn't the first. The villagers are always quick to point their fingers in the direction of the castle whenever something unfortunate befalls a member of the populace."

"That hardly seems fair."

Lucien brushed her sympathy aside. "Don't concern yourself for my sake. I'm accustomed to the stares. And the fearsome reputation helps in some cases. Poachers and vagrants steer clear of the estate. Speaking of which, I've been making several improvements that I'm sure Tomas would be interested in seeing. Perhaps you would like to accompany him? Did I mention that my chef makes a delightful veal dish...unless you prefer pigeon?"

"I would love to tour the castle," she said, relenting.

"What?" Tomas stomped into the room. From his expression, it was clear that he had been eavesdropping for some time.

"Perfect!" Lucien rose, ignoring the interruption. "I'll expect you tomorrow for luncheon. Then we can tour the grounds and follow it up with dinner."

Aware he only had moments, he swept out before her brother could protest. When he was gone, Tomas rounded on her. "Oh, stop," she scolded. "You know we need to visit the castle eventually."

"I have visited," he sniffed.

"Well, I haven't," she retorted. "And the fact you went without me is still a stone under my saddle. We need answers."

Tomas crossed his arms. "I thought that was what you were doing closeted with the man all afternoon—getting answers. If you weren't achieving that objective then what, pray tell, have you been doing all this time?"

She rose to close the door so the servants wouldn't overhear. "I suspect that the duke has no understanding of his legacy. He acknowledges the history of witchcraft in his bloodline without explicitly stating it, mostly—and I believe this to be true—he has no idea he's a *stragone*."

Tomas wrinkled his nose. "How can he not know? He's been soul wandering for most of his life."

Helena swept out a hand. "With no inkling of how it works. He only recently gained the ability to restrict his visitations to his sleep."

She grasped her elbows, pulling them in tighter as she walked up the window, studying the tree line. The Devil's Hold was on the other side of the forest but from this window, she could see some of the turrets above the trees.

Helena worried her lip, thinking. "I need to take a closer look at the greenhouse and the library at the Devil's Hold. Do you think I can persuade His Grace to show them to me on the tour?"

Tomas joined her at the window, scowling at the distant castle. "I think he'd shave himself bare and dance a jig if you suggested it."

"Stop pouting," she chided. "He's promised us an excellent meal prepared by his French chef."

Mollified, Tomas relented. "Well, that's something at least. If I see another hunk of colorless boiled meat on my plate it will be too soon."

CHAPTER 14

*B*lackwater Castle was a bustling place. From the industrious maids wiping down every surface inside and out—including the vast smoky windows—to the gardeners buzzing in the garden like bees, it seemed as if there was industrious activity everywhere.

Helena and her brother had already toured the parapets of the castle proper with the duke. She had wanted to walk the extensive ramparts as well but was disappointed to learn that these were in a state of disrepair and would be unsafe to walk on.

"But they're on my list of repairs. For you, I'll move them near the top," Lucien had said with a droll wink that raised her brother's hackles. However, this was followed by an hour-long visit to the stables, which restored Tomas's good humor.

Lucien's collection of equines was superb. He had over a dozen prize specimens, each one more beautiful than the last.

Tomas nearly teared up when he was invited to inspect a giant bay named Anaxagoras. "His conformation is excellent," he said in Italian, staring at the departing horse the way a lovesick poet mooned over his muse. They were only able to tear him away with the promise of a four-course luncheon.

The meal was an elaborate event. The duke knew this was his best hand, and he played it flawlessly. Delicate slices of beef and veal were paired with fresh vegetables from the garden and served with a cream-based sauce that made her want to lick her plate. Tomas pretended to be unaffected by the meal, despite eating roughly his own weight in pastry-coated duck and sugared fruit.

This was followed by a tour of the orchard, where her brother promptly stole an apple.

"Tomas, that isn't ripe yet," she chided. Her brother shrugged and bit into the crisp flesh, chewing loudly.

"My apologies Your Grace," she said. "He has been subsisting on boiled meat too long."

The duke laughed. "If it entices you to come back, he can eat the whole damn orchard."

"*Tomas,*" she scolded when Lucien stepped away to greet his estate manager, who'd hailed him. "I cannot credit that you are *still* hungry. We spent nearly an hour and a half at the table thanks to your insistence on having second and third helpings. You can't possibly tell me that you didn't have your fill?"

"That was the first decent meal we've had since we arrived in town. You can't blame me for lingering a bit."

"Well, I do. Especially since we've seen so little of the castle."

"You mean you haven't seen the library or greenhouse. And this castle is too bloody large for a few hours visit—"

"Then she should definitely stay longer." The duke apologized for the interruption as he returned to join them. "My junior estate manager has been after me to implement certain improvements to the property for some time. I think he believes I'll change my mind so he's taking advantage to get everything done at once. We took on extra staff for the summer, including a few builders and stonemasons. The Hold is overdue for necessary renovations."

Tomas's head drew back. "Why would you balk at improvements? It's a landholder's duty to develop and better his lands."

Lucien's mouth twisted. "You sound remarkably like my father. Pity he rarely practiced what he preached. He was far more interested in his experiments than the crops. I told myself I would be different, but I confess the last few years I've allowed the state of the Hold to fall by the wayside."

"And what is responsible for your sudden change of heart?" Helena asked, lifting her parasol to shield herself from the sun. She gestured to the frenetic activity, concerned for the men's health. "Wouldn't these improvements be more efficient in the spring before it grows so warm?"

"Probably," Lucien conceded. "But in the spring my mind was…elsewhere."

Helena averted her gaze, not trusting herself to look at him. His nightly visitations had begun in the spring.

She hurried ahead so Tomas wouldn't see her flushed face. "I'm sure your men appreciate having some activity after a long dormant period, regardless of the season, though it might be prudent to serve them some sort of refreshment, so they don't succumb to the heat."

He smiled at her. "I've already arranged it with my steward, but I'm pleased that you've taken a special interest in the welfare of the Hold's residents."

"Any person of conscience would be equally concerned," Tomas interrupted repressively. "My sister's concern is not particularly noteworthy."

Helena suppressed the urge to bat her brother with her reticule. She didn't need to ask what was wrong with him. Tomas hated the idea that she was becoming invested in Blackwater Castle and its master.

"Of course," Lucien said, looking over his shoulder with a gleam in his eyes. He offered her his arm. "What would you like to see next?"

"The greenhouse," Helena said with what she hoped was casual ease.

Lucien cocked his head at her. "How did I know you were going to say that?"

She waved at the distant glass and iron structure. "I confess I'm terribly curious to see more of those orchids you sent me, along with whatever else your mother cultivated."

Helena tried to recall what he had told her about Christien during his visitations. There hadn't been much. Her phantom had spoken of his family very rarely. In fact, she could only recall him mentioning them a handful of times. He had been far more interested in her life.

He offered her his arm and led them to the large greenhouse nestled against one wall of the keep. "My mother was gifted when it came to plants. I don't really remember her, but my father would often say she could grow anything. Jocelyn ordered the orchid cultivar be maintained indefinitely, so it will be one of the estate's unique perquisites."

Up close, the structure was much larger than she'd originally supposed. It branched out into a T-shaped structure with three wings jutting out from a larger circular dome.

Helena stepped inside, her breath catching. From the exterior, she would have never guessed that the sprawling structure was home to Nirvana.

Lush, greenery-filled raised banks edged in stone lined the building. They were filled with plants and trees of every description, including several exotic varieties Helena had only seen in books. In the center was a series of long tables holding potted plants, home to a veritable rainbow of flowers.

"This is remarkable," she said, aware that she was gaping like a child on their first visit to a pleasure garden.

Lucien nodded. "I believe my father used the same architect who designed the pavilion at Kew Gardens. He built this greenhouse for my mother. When it came to impressing Christien and her family, no expense was spared. His second wife was somewhat less fortunate," he added dryly. "Her wedding gift was a new carriage. He also had one of the rooms adjoining her chambers redone, converting it into a private library."

"From what you've told me, that sounds like the ideal gift for her."

He shrugged. "It would have been had he bothered to fill it with books. He claimed it was presented to her empty because he didn't know her tastes. I think he didn't want to be bothered to learn them."

Helena's lashes fluttered. Lucien noticed. "Is something wrong?"

She turned, giving her brother a pointed look. Tomas coughed and stepped away, wandering down the path a bit to give them the illusion of privacy.

"It's nothing."

"Helena," he cajoled.

She took a deep breath. Why was this so difficult? She never had trouble speaking to him when she thought he was a spirit.

Of course, Helena had no idea he was so overwhelmingly masculine back then. Just looking at him was enough to make her heart hold its breath, if such as thing were possible.

"I suppose I was not expecting such a personal confidence," she confessed.

"There's no need for reticence," he said, leaning in to whisper. "The two of us, we have no secrets—only things still unsaid."

Helena could feel her cheeks blazing under his hungry, focused gaze. It almost looked as if he was going to pounce on her then and there. Quivering, she decided to change the subject.

She pointed to the pipes running along the walls. Her mother's greenhouse had a similar system of hot water pipes for the winter months, but it was nowhere near this elaborate. "It should be blazing hot in here. I take it these don't just help heat the space in winter. Do they also cool?"

"Yes," he answered, giving her a look that clearly articulated her reprieve was temporary. "The greenhouse is situated to take advantage of what light the keep is capable of getting. The shades on the ceiling are only needed in high summer. Pipes with cold and hot running water are used to regulate the temperature during the cooler weather of autumn and winter. There's a dedicated boiler to supply them."

"What an impressively efficient design. How do you keep the water cold in the summer months?"

The duke guided them down the wide corridor between the raised beds, explaining how the cold pipes drew from an underground stream, one of several that fed Blackwater lake. He then showed them to the other wings, one filled with fruit-bearing trees, bushes, and vines.

While many of the herbs growing in the spice tables could be used in spell-work, some of the more obvious ingredients were missing.

"Most of the vegetables are grown in the kitchen gardens, which are extensive," the duke finished. "I'm happy to give you a tour of those as well."

He said this with an amused gleam in his eye.

"Perhaps another day," Tomas said repressively. "We've taken enough of your time already."

Lucien spun to face him. "It's no trouble. I want you both to become familiar with Blackwater Castle…intimately so."

His gaze transferred to Helena's face with those final words. Her face flamed. He was incorrigible.

Tomas was of a like mind. He looked like he was inches away from choking the life out of His Grace.

"Please consider this your home away from home. And any time you'd like to visit the stables, Tomas, you are more than welcome."

"That's a very generous offer. I, for one, would love to spend some time in the library," Helena said, taking her brother's arm and digging her fingers in for emphasis.

She smiled at her brother until he scowled and gave in. "Visiting the stables again would be delightful," Tomas said in tone suitable for a funeral. The last word was spat out like a curse.

Hiding an obvious laugh, Helena urged Tomas out the door before her brother exploded. They were only a few feet from the entrance when they were hailed by a feminine voice.

An older lady wearing a plum sateen gown that looked fresh and crisp despite the heat waved to them from the castle's main entrance.

Her face was that of a bright aging elf. Delicate but slightly pointed features were paired with deep lines and wrinkles around the eyes that suggested she laughed often. She was accompanied by a pale man in sober plain clothes who squinted and shielded his face from the bright sunlight.

"Brilliant." Lucien beamed. "I didn't think you'd meet my step-mother today, but it seems she has emerged from her cave early."

The woman walked over with light mincing steps, laughing at something the man said. "Lucien darling, I'd like you to meet someone."

Their groups met halfway. Lucien inclined his head at his step-mother. "Well, this is a day for introductions. I have some special guests I'd like you to meet. Allow me to introduce you to Lady Helena Garibaldi and her brother Tomas."

Smiling with genuine enthusiasm she curtsied, surprised when the Dowager Duchess came forward to take both her hands in her own. "You must be the Italians I've heard so much about. It's such a pleasure to have young people in the neighborhood again. Isn't it wonderful, Lucien?"

"It is," he said, his eyes never leaving Helena's face. And because he was looking at her so intently, everyone else did too.

Helena could feel her face redden. Combined with the afternoon heat, it felt as if she was going to burst into flames. To make matters worse, Lucien seemed amused by her discomfiture. *That's it.* She was going to have to strangle him.

After a moment she recovered enough to return the Dowager Duchess's kind greeting. When she was done, she turned to the woman's companion. Her eyes widened, and she took a step back when she recognized the man.

"*You,*" she said, blinking at the tall, pale man in somber clothes.

"Have you met?" Lucien's voice was noticeably cooler as he took in the newcomer, his gaze bouncing between them.

Tomas wore an almost identical expression. "You know my sister?" he barked.

"We met on the train platform." The man bowed over her hand. "Nigel Ellison. It's a pleasure to formally make your acquaintance. I've dined with your brother at the pub several times but had no idea you were his sister."

"I see. What a wonderful coincidence," Helena said with a genuine smile. It dimmed a touch when she saw a familiar-looking design on a pin affixed over the man's right breast.

"Yes," Lucien added flatly, his lack of enthusiasm apparent in the tightening of his facial muscles. "How fortuitous."

Nigel nodded and smiled as if he hadn't noticed the men's lack of enthusiasm. "Her grace has been kind enough to show me some of her illuminated manuscripts. It is a magnificent collection. Simply breathtaking."

Lucien grunted something polite as his stepmother preened, visibly delighted by the young scholar's praise.

"I've given our Italian visitors the run of the main library, mother. Perhaps they would enjoy seeing your collection as well."

"It would be my pleasure," the Dowager Duchess said, holding her hands together in front of her with a warm smile.

Helena thanked her, trying to work the conversation around to a specific time and date, but Tomas was already pulling her arm impatiently.

But she stood firm, giving him a pointed glare. "Excuse me, Mr. Ellison, may I ask where you got that pin? It's a very interesting design. From where does it hail?"

Nigel Ellison's pale lashes fluttered. He covered the pin for a moment before removing his hand. "I couldn't speak to its origins. It's a bit of a family heirloom, albeit not much of one. Just a trinket that has been passed down."

"Really?" She folded her hands together. Next to her Tomas straightened, alerted by her interest. "It appears new."

Mr. Ellison's smile did interesting things to his face. "Merely well cared for."

She tilted her head at him, wondering why her senses were on alert. Or she was until she glanced at the duke. His glowering appraisal of the scholar was no doubt at fault. His irritation so intense, he was practically shooting off sparks.

Tomas tugged on her arm again. Reluctantly she bade them good-bye, letting her brother escort them down the lane that would branch off into the path through the woods, the shortest route to their cottage.

"Why are you so insistent on leaving? Lucien was a minute away from giving us a tour of the library himself."

"I couldn't help it," Tomas hissed, walking them down the lane. "The way the man looks at you borders on the obscene. And in front of his mother no less."

Helena raised an eyebrow. "So, you'd rather he continue his visitations on the astral plane where you cannot see or hear him?"

"No!" Tomas looked as if he was close to a fit. He passed a hand through his hair, and she could see he was at the end of his tether.

"Why were you so interested in Ellison's pin?" he asked, abruptly changing the subject as they approached the main castle gates. The small dark lake outside looked almost inviting in this heat.

She shrugged, kicking out a leg to circulate air under her skirts. "The design seemed familiar, but I can't place it. I'm sure it's nothing."

Tomas grunted. Sighing, she reconciled herself to returning home without the answers they sought. She hadn't really expected to untangle this knot in one visit, had she?

Whatever this tie between her and Lucien was, it was as old as she was. Helena had no evidence of the fact, but in her heart, she knew he'd been with her since her first breath. Somehow the fates had seen fit to bind them together. Helena was only just beginning to understand why.

She was only half-listening to Tomas's continued complaints as her mind busily turned over every detail of their visit. But the sharp cry cut through her preoccupation like a knife.

Helena turned to see a nightmare tableau. Lucien was standing far in the distance, the horse he'd been handling rearing up on its hind legs. The hooves of its powerful front legs were inches away from his head.

And Lucien was just standing there. She was too far away to see his face, but his hands were slack at his sides, his shoulders slumped.

Something was terribly wrong.

The horse stamped down its legs, its hooves striking the ground hard enough to kick up dust. Maddened, it continued to stamp and jump, inches away from a frozen Lucien.

None of the grooms were in sight. They must have been inside the barn or out on the grounds exercising the horses outside the keep walls. Far in the distance, next to one of the entrances leading to the library and main gallery was a spot of purple. The Dowager Duchess had been going inside.

Helena couldn't make out the darker clothes of the scholar next to her. The old duchess was standing alone.

She took in all of that at a glance, horrified.

"Helena?"

Startled, she jerked her head to voice. It was the duke. She couldn't see him, but it was as if he was standing right next to her. Which meant he wasn't in his body.

He can't get away.

Helena screamed. She let go of Tomas's arm and began to run toward her duke's still form and the rampaging horse. But her skirts hampered her.

Fortunately, Tomas was not similarly encumbered. He shot past her, eating the distance between him and the horse with his longer legs. She kept running for the duke, shouting incoherently and gesturing for him to move despite knowing he couldn't react.

A body couldn't move without the mind.

Then Tomas succeeded in grabbing the reins of the maddened horse. All those years of managing her father's stables and bonding with the animals were condensed into the most fraught and terrifying minute of Helena's life.

Her brother used his bulk and muscle to forcefully pull the horse away from the duke. Tugging its head down to his, he began to murmur in soothing Italian.

The beast could not possibly comprehend the language, but it responded to Tomas's tone. The horse began to settle as she finally reached the duke at the same time as his groom.

Lucien hadn't moved an inch the entire time, not even when the horse's hoofs passed mere inches from his skull.

CHAPTER 15

"*H*ere." Tomas thrust a cup of tea into her hand.

"Thank you," Helena murmured, staring at the flames in the parlor fireplace.

They had been home for hours, but she couldn't stop thinking about the poor duke.

"Did you see his eyes?" Her brother threw himself in the wingback chair next to her. He sipped his own china cup, one she strongly suspected did not hold tea at all.

"I did."

The expression on Lucien's face was going to haunt her dreams. It had been so empty and lifeless. He'd simply stood here, slack-jawed until she'd touched him.

The aftermath of the incident with the horse had been hectic. She'd taken Lucien's face in her hands, and he'd roused, blinking at her in confusion and then dismay before he'd shaken his head and backed away. His stepmother had run up to him then, ushering him away before he'd fully recovered his senses.

The scholar had been nowhere in sight.

Tomas gulped down his tea and winced as it burned his throat on the way down. "Do you know what happened?"

"His soul wandered," she sighed.

"Believe it or not, I figured that part on my own," he said sarcastically. "But I thought he could manage it."

"So did he." Helena felt heartsick, remembering the expression on his face. "At least up to a point. But his ability seems to have slipped the reins."

Lucien had said as much—that he could restrict his soul wandering to his sleep. He could exert some measure of control. Or at least he could before they arrived in the Devil's Slide.

"What about the horse? What was wrong with it?" Lucien's mounts were too well-trained to suddenly behave as this one had, frothing and stamping out of nowhere.

"I'm still not certain," Tomas confessed. "It was almost as if it had been bitten by a hornet or a snake, but I saw no sign of a bite. And the grooms and I examined that animal from muzzle to tail afterward."

"It was no coincidence," she decided, rubbing her hands together. "I think some force maddened the horse at the same time as it ripped Lucien from his body."

Helena racked her brain trying to recall if she'd sensed anything. Perhaps there had been something—a change in pressure perhaps. But the entirety of her focus had been on Lucien. She shuddered, recalling the blankness of his eyes and how cold he'd been to the touch.

"Now you have the same look on your face as your benighted duke did after his rescue," Tomas sniped.

She set the cup down on the tea trolley. "I don't know why I believed this, but in my mind I thought that simply by meeting me the duke's problem would disappear."

Tomas paused with his teacup halfway to his lips. "He believed that as well, didn't he? That's why he appeared to be so…disappointed."

Her brother had a gift for understatement. Lucien's expression had been desolate.

Tomas leaned forward in his seat, sending a waft of strong spirits over her. "Well, take heart. His Grace will recover from this setback. As annoying as the man is, the duke is no fool. That affliction has been plaguing him his entire life. Meeting you in person is not going to solve the problem. Even you can't work miracles."

"No." Helena pursed her lips. "Yet somehow I think we were both expecting one."

Leaning over, she stole his cup and took a bracing sip.

"Dear lord, what is this?" She coughed and wiped her watering eyes.

"It's a local brew Harold from the Bucket gave me. Some kind of gin. I believe they infuse it with local wildflowers."

Helena's lip curled. "It is revolting."

Tomas grinned. "It really is, but beggars can't be choosers."

His smile subsided. "Truly, you can't blame yourself for the duke's affliction. Didn't you tell me it has plagued him since before you were born?"

"So he said, but his memories may not be clear on this point. He's scarcely older than I am."

Tomas scowled repressively. "The Duke is older than me, which makes him at least six years older than you."

"What point are you trying to make exactly?"

"He would be a terrible match for you. He's too old."

"Tomas," she groaned, putting a hand over her head at the bald-faced lie. "The man is in mortal peril. Can you please focus your attention on that instead of his suitability for marriage?"

"I never said he wanted to marry you," Tomas sniffed.

Helena suppressed the urge to throw something at her obstinate sibling. She rose to her feet. "Nothing has changed. We have to continue with our plans."

"Which is no plan at all."

"Untrue," she protested. "We must keep trying to learn everything about His Grace that we can. Perhaps there is something in the family history that explains all of this. In the meantime, I think you need to spend as much time as you can with him."

Her brother wrinkled his nose.

She leaned forward. "Tomas, please. Today showed us what happens when he is not in control of his faculties. He could have been seriously injured today, perhaps even killed. And there is no question of my keeping watch over him—the only way I'd be able to spend that much time in his company without causing a major scandal is if I married him."

Her brother slumped in his seat. "Don't worry. I'll protect your blasted duke for you."

She sighed and lifted her teacup, washing away the taste of the foul spirit with the weak brew.

"Thank you."

CHAPTER 16

"*I*f you don't pick up that chin, you will trip over it."

Lucien squinted against the early morning light at Tomas. The Italian had shown up this morning as his mount was being saddled.

Tomas had insisted on riding with him. Lucien knew the younger man wasn't accompanying him out of a genuine desire for his company. Not even his excellent bloodstock would be sufficient inducement for him to rise this early, judging from the jaw-cracking yawns he hadn't bothered to hide.

Tomas shrugged at his raised eyebrow. "It's what our mother used to say when one of us was pouting."

Lucien ignored that, focusing on the meandering path up the hills.

"So what did Helena promise you to act as my caretaker?" He prodded Aristotle over the rise. The Italian was back on Parmenides, the big bay he favored.

"Nothing. She asked and I agreed."

"Why?"

"Because she *is* my sister," Tomas scoffed. But then he caught up the reins too tightly, making the horse shy to the side.

"Loosen your grip," Lucien scowled. Tomas did so immediately, but he continued to glower after the Italian as he urged the mount ahead of him.

It had been a small miscalculation, but as aggravating as he was Tomas was a superb horseman. He would never mishandle a horse, even in such a minor manner.

"What is troubling you?" he asked, as Aristotle caught up to Parmenides.

Tomas shrugged. "I forgot you know better," he said curtly.

"What are you talking about?" Lucien was already irritated that he had to be grateful to the Italian for coming to see him today. He didn't need a surly caretaker on top of everything else.

Lucien hadn't had a spell in ages and lately only in his sleep. Visiting Helena had been such a pleasurable pastime that he'd almost convinced himself he was in control. He'd forgotten it had never been a choice.

But I would have chosen to visit her. Helena was his. And clearly, the fates agreed, or they would never have brought them together.

Although he did hate the loss of his independence. It was hell not being able to trust his own body. He would never complain to Helena of course, but Lucien despised needing a minder.

Tomas had been quiet for so long that Lucien had almost forgotten him until the Italian glared at him.

"Ah, yes," he said, recalling that the man was waiting for an answer. "This is the part where I insist that I don't have a bloody clue what you're talking about."

Tomas pulled Parmenides to a stop. "I meant the part where you knew I am not truly Helena's brother but instead her uncle."

Shocked, Lucien blinked and shook his head. "I didn't know. I can't recall Helena ever mentioning it."

His companion snorted. "Not even that time when I dipped her dolls in pitch?"

Lucien laughed. "I assure you she kept your secret despite that act of wanton destruction."

"It's not precisely a secret," Tomas said with a jerky shrug. "Isobel and my father attempted to claim I was legitimate, the product of

Isobel's previous marriage—one that didn't exist. However, too many people knew the truth. My real father, Aldo, the former Conte de Santa Fiora wasn't discreet. He had me out of wedlock with a maid who was his mistress for a few years. When she died he sent me to live with a tenant farmer until my older brother came for me."

"Your brother and his wife claimed you?" Lucien leaned back in the saddle, marveling silently when Tomas nodded.

In a world where illegitimacy had the power to damn him and keep him from inheriting even a penny, it was a noteworthy act. Yes, some noble families did provide for their bastard children, but few would have taken one into their home, raising the by-blows alongside their own children.

But he didn't say anything about that. Instead, he said, "They're unusual, aren't they?"

"Completely eccentric," Tomas admitted with a laugh. "But in a way that charms most everyone who meets them. Being wealthy and titled helps of course. Before their marriage, Isobel's otherworldly talents were a magnet for trouble. Her family was persecuted for the gifts that ran along the female line. I believe her aunt was killed for them. But she has my brother's protection now. They are an estimable couple, complementing each other in every way. And they're very fine parents. We have new brothers, by the way. Newborn twins...it was difficult to leave them."

"Yes. Helena mentioned them." She had been very concerned for their health and that of their mother, who had a history of difficult pregnancies. Lucien knew the guilt of not being there for her mother and new brothers weighed on her, but he was too selfish to suggest returning to Italy.

Tomas spoke a little more of the parents who raised him. Then he trailed off and Lucien chanced an impertinent and too-personal question. "Was it awkward welcoming the twins knowing they will inherit what you cannot?"

The Italian lifted a shoulder philosophically. "I've known I'm not in line to inherit most of my life, but my parents have been generous. The horse farm is my enterprise entirely—and with Matteo's help I've made it profitable. I daresay I'm better off than most second and third sons in England."

Lucien considered that. "I suppose you are at that. Being an only child, I've never considered the benefits of being a second son, but they are considerable—no pressure to marry and continue the family line, fewer responsibilities, no pesky estate management, etcetera."

"I do manage the estate."

"Oh," Lucien said, nonplussed.

"Only partially," Tomas admitted after a minute. "My father has an able manager, but we oversee his every move—Matteo wanted to make sure I would be able to spot a cheat if I ever decided to purchase my own lands."

The Italian gave him a sidelong glance, a familiar one. But Helena's were less sardonic. "He knew I would never accept a property that belonged to my real father—may his soul rot in hell."

"I take it the former Conte was not a warm and giving soul."

Tomas smiled again, but this time it was tinged with bitterness. "No. In fact, had it been up to him I'd be scratching out a living in a field. That was what he considered doing his duty by me—giving me to a tenant farmer to raise."

Lucien guided the horses under the stone-arch that led out of the orchard. Tomas had pulled alongside him when he spoke again. "I wasn't his only by-blow by any means. Isobel and Matteo tried to gather them all, but I was the only one who survived past infancy."

Lucien was fairly certain his father had no illegitimate children—the man's only mistress had been his love of experimentation, much to Jocelyn's distress.

"I think I will like your parents," he observed after a time.

"Well, they won't like you," his companion groused.

"Why the hell not?"

"You're an Englishman who thinks he has a claim to their daughter."

"I do have a claim," he sniffed. "The fates have decreed it so. Besides, I plan on marrying her. That should alleviate the worst of their fears."

Tomas laughed outright. "That only makes it worse. Matteo and Isobel would never want their daughter to marry an *Englishman*."

He spat the last word like a curse.

"How can they hate foreigners? Your adopted mother is Scottish for pity's sake. Surely my fortune and estates would be some comfort." The edge in his voice was unhidden.

The Conte di Santa Fiore was an illustrious and venerable earldom, but his title was one of the oldest in Britain.

"You can have ten bloody estates," Tomas announced dismissively. "It wouldn't matter because they are all in England. They would never want Helena to marry and settle so far away from them."

Damn. He hadn't considered Helena's ties to her parents or even to the brother who rode next to him now.

"I believe it's your turn for a personal confidence," Tomas said after he'd been quiet too long. "What can you tell me about yesterday?"

Lucien lifted a shoulder. "I was in my body and then I wasn't."

Tomas grunted when no more was forthcoming. "Care to elaborate?"

His memory was a little hazy, but he shared what he could—albeit grudgingly. "Since I could not induce you and your sister to stay longer, I decided to take Plato for a run before my estate manager hunted me down and chained me to my office chair. With all the improvements, he's been hounding me to go over the accounts twice. The groom had just gone back inside the barn, and mother and her visitor had wandered off somewhere."

He kept his eye on the path, making sure the horses didn't step in a hole, but he didn't need to worry. Both mounts were intelligent and surefooted. "Then my vision turned black. I thought I sensed your sister nearby. I even caught a glimpse of her—far closer than she should have been. This was followed by more darkness, and then Helena was there in front of me holding my face while my head felt like it was splitting."

He could still remember the heat of Helena's hands on his cheeks and the concern in her eyes before he'd stumbled back to his rooms with Jocelyn's help.

"Helena feels as if she let you down."

Lucien scowled. "The fault is not hers."

How could she think that? The problem lay with him. He was the damaged one.

Which begged the question—how could he expect a woman as beautiful and gifted as Helena to marry him? Did he really believe she was going to choose to spend her life saddled with some sort of metaphysical invalid?

Lucien didn't even feel comfortable traveling to his other estates, relying on his agents to report on their condition with accuracy and understanding.

If Helena married him, she'd be damning herself to the life he led, only worse. She'd be a virtual prisoner here in the Devil's Slide.

And she wouldn't even have the solace of her family nearby. All Helena would have was him.

And, damn it, deep down Lucien knew he was not enough.

"Yes, well, it would be easier for Helena to believe if she hadn't witnessed your sudden soul-wandering." Tomas's face darkened in what looked like sympathy. "I hadn't realized it could be like that—so violent."

Lucien tensed in the saddle. It had been that. He'd grown accustomed to the gentle slipping away that happened in his sleep. No, this had been a jarring experience, as if he'd been ripped out of his body. Fast and wrenching, but in a way that was too overwhelming to be called pain.

"It hasn't happened like that since I was a boy," he said with a frown. "Back then I succumbed with such regularity that I had to be accompanied everywhere on the estate. Most of the time I was unaware it had even occurred until afterward. I would wake up in strange places on the grounds, the library, the hothouse, the gardens. The servants grew accustomed to having to search for me. Any place deemed too dangerous had to be locked—not that it stopped me. I somehow managed to enter locked rooms without a key, or at least my body did. Even I never figured out how because my mind was thousands of miles away in the sunny hillsides of Lazio."

At least you went to her. When his soul had been forcibly vacated from his body it had followed his heart straight to Helena. Only yesterday the trip had been considerably shorter.

Tomas grunted. "My sister wants to help you solve this problem once in for all. She believes in fate too."

This was said as if someone had a knife to the man's throat.

The corner of Lucien's mouth turned up. As much as he hated being pitied, he wasn't about to reject help if it gave him an excuse to spend more time with Helena. "I'm not in a position to say no," he said magnanimously.

Tomas's look could have blistered damp wood, and he said, "Don't look so smug. I'm the one who drew the short straw. I'll be the one keeping you company while my sister explores your family history in your library."

Smile dimming, Lucien released a much put-upon sigh.

"It's not how I would wish to spend my time either," Tomas snapped.

"Well, that's some comfort," he said. "At least both of us will be miserable."

But even as he said it, Lucien realized it wasn't true.

Yes, he'd give anything for it to be Helena riding at his side instead of her brother. But having a friend was nothing to sneeze at.

CHAPTER 17

"*H*elena."

"Your Grace?" she mumbled, sleep reluctant to release her from its grasp.

He chuckled. "How many times have I told you to call me Lucien?"

Blinking sluggishly, Helena forced her eyes to focus. The duke was leaning over her—not his spirit. Him, the man. Flesh and blood. Very muscular, very warm and solid flesh…in her bedroom.

There was enough moonlight coming from the window for her to be certain.

Startled, she tried to rise, but he pressed her back down into the mattress. She pushed the sheet away, her arms reaching out instinctively. Suddenly he was lying on her, his limbs tangled with hers.

His weight was deliciously hot and provocative.

"What are you doing here?" she asked with a squeak as her body began to quicken, responding the way it always did in his presence. "If my brother catches you, he'll have your head."

Firm yet soft lips grazed her hairline. "Well, if you value anything above or below my neck I suggest you be very *very* quiet."

Helena stifled a giggle as his weight settled more heavily over her. He'd already removed his coat.

His head lowered back to hers. "I do apologize for the midnight call," he murmured between sipping kisses. "But thanks to Tomas, I've barely seen you this past week. You've been cloistered in the library looking through old diaries while I've been crisscrossing the estate with my manager, dragging your brother in tow like a fourteen-stone anchor, one who can't stop criticizing and offering advice like an old dowager aunt who thinks she's the country's leading expert in drainage and manure."

Helena snickered, and Lucien groaned, burying his face in her neck. "I finally talk myself into breaking into your bedchamber and end up babbling about manure."

Her silent chuckle sent a tremor through him that seemed to magnify and gain in strength until his body was trembling with suppressed need. His mouth covered hers, silky and warm despite the night coolness lingering on his cheeks.

He tasted of mint and spirits.

Despite her chuckle, Helena was nervous, expecting at any moment that her brother would burst through the door, most likely armed after their last intruder.

Strictly speaking, there was no way for the duke to be in her bedchamber. Every night before she went to bed, Helena and Tomas laid traps and snares at every entrance and window of the house. There was an additional circle of protection around the cottage itself. It was set to sound a bell directly in her and her brother's ears, a magical alarm mechanism taught to them by their mother.

Yet Lucien had evaded these security measures with little to no effort. She was going to have to ask him how he did that.

Then his lips trailed down her neck, and he shifted to settle between her legs. Her body clenched, and her hands trembling as she clutched at his broad shoulders. "We can't do this," she said weakly as his tongue traced the delicate line of her neck.

The tender skin seemed to catch fire, sending a melting sensation throughout her body. Boneless, she sank deeper into the bed as the siren's call of passion began to lull her, loosening her inhibitions and robbing her of her good sense.

Lucien raised his head when she whimpered and shivered. He mistook those signs for fear.

His hand rose to stroke her cheek. "Shh…you have nothing to worry about."

"I *don't?*" Her skepticism was clear despite it being transmitted in a thready whisper.

He cocked his head, and she could see he was smiling at her in the moonlight.

"Well, not too much. I won't lie to you—I *will* have you… But when I do it will be in the ducal bed after a proper ceremony where I can savor you at my leisure, And there will be no interfering Italian siblings within ten miles."

The man was incorrigible, and she suspected his promise as well as what he was doing with his hands were really an elaborate way of making her want him more. "Lucien…"

He stopped her with a finger to her lips, his face sobering. "I didn't come here to rob you of your choices. You will still have those when I leave. I promise you that."

"Er…thank you?" she mumbled against his fingers.

Moving his hand, he replaced it with his lips, taking her mouth for another hot open-mouthed kiss.

This time his tongue flicked out to tease hers.

Helena collapsed back on the mattress, melting as he deepened the caress. He tasted her with restrained hunger she sensed he was barely keeping in check.

Stroking fingers worked their way down to cup her breasts through the fine lawn of her nightgown, while Lucien used his body to open hers up. The way he settled against her—it was like a lock fitting to a key. Helena felt like she was drowning, her breath fast and shallow when he slid down her body.

"*Lucien?*" Her voice shook as he began to pull up the hem of her nightgown.

Helena clenched her legs in embarrassment. She hadn't worn drawers tonight because the air was so warm.

Lucien said something she couldn't understand, but his soothing tone was loud and clear. He ran his hands over her legs, closing his eyes as if savoring the silky smoothness of her skin. But Helena didn't dare close her eyes.

She had felt this touch before during his midnight visits. But this was an experience so completely different, and every sensation felt so intense with him here in the flesh.

The heat built so high and fast she worried she was going to shatter like a crystal goblet filled with *vin brulé*, mulled wine that had been served too hot. Flushing from head to toe, she writhed on the bed as Lucien gently parted her legs, slipping his fingers between the petals of her flesh. And then his lips kissed the hooded bud at the apex, his teeth grazing it before taking it into his mouth. One hard suck and she bowed, almost bucking off the bed, but he released the little nub almost immediately with a satisfied murmur.

He took a long slow lick. "I love how you taste."

Helena could not reply. She wanted to but couldn't speak.

Time slipped away, the silvery moonlight transmuted into liquid mercury that swirled around them, the work of a mad alchemist whose medium was desire and sensation instead of base elements.

She lost all sense of self, as if the limits of her body were blurring. Here in the dark under Lucien's determined ministrations, Helena was *more*.

His tongue lathed, and his mouth sipped, his fingers joined to gently probe and stroke in time to a pulsing heartbeat she could feel at her very core.

The teasing ticklish pleasure tightened until it grew unbearable. "Please, I can't—" she gasped in Italian.

At first, she believed he didn't understand, but of course he did. She'd taught him the tongue herself. So, he sped up, moving in concert with her until she shuddered, breaking apart, the little pieces flying away. With Lucien's help, Helena reached the stars.

LUCIEN LICKED HIS LIPS, easing back from the beautiful woman who'd just shattered in his arms. A sated Helena was impossibly more gorgeous than ever before.

A light sheen of sweat covered her body making the fine lawn gown a little more transparent. It conformed to her body with every panting breath, revealing the perfect outline of her breasts. Her golden skin, inherited from her Italian parent, was a little washed out in the moonlight, but it was porcelain-fine and smoother than silk.

With the salty sea taste of her in his mouth, he pressed a last lingering kiss to her inner thigh. His cock was rigid with unsatisfied desire, but he had meant what he'd told her earlier.

If he stripped and lay with her, Helena would not push him away. She wanted him as much as he wanted her—*almost*. But Lucien would not rob his darling of her choices. When they married, it would be because she wanted to spend her life with him.

But first, he had to fix whatever was broken inside him. His rampant desire waned a bit as he contemplated just how he could end his uncontrolled soul-wandering. His determination to do so was stronger than ever, but his affliction had plagued him his entire life. His previous attempts to curtail the episodes had failed, sometimes spectacularly so.

Lucien closed his eyes, taking a steadying breath. When he opened them, Helena was looking directly at him. She had pulled the hem of her nightgown down and was sitting on the bed with a delicate porcelain arm wrapped around her knees.

He didn't have to ask for her help with his affliction. It was there in her eyes. So was her fierce will and determination to help him end it. Yes, he would miss the unexpected pleasure of seeing her during the visitations, but the wretched loss of control of his daylight wanderings was not worth the cost. Besides, he could see her in person now.

"We will find the answer."

Lucien smiled. Helena had spoken in Italian and was probably unaware of it.

He took her in his arms, squeezing her against him. He expected her to protest over the tightness of his grip, but she just held on, letting herself be crushed until his conscience got the better of him.

"I should go before my luck runs out and your brother rouses," he said, pressing a last kiss to her sweet lips.

Helena smiled at him, but he could see the anxiety behind her eyes. "Tomorrow," she promised. "We'll begin our call early."

"You mean today." He'd waited until after midnight to come here to minimize the risk of being seen.

One corner of that delicious mouth turned down. "Then I take it back. Don't expect us early."

Groaning in as low a volume as possible, Lucien threw on the loose black greatcoat he'd worn to easily blend into the shadows. Then he stole another kiss and silently let himself out of the room.

He managed to escape without running into an irate Italian ready to chop his head off.

Approaching the locked kitchen door, he slipped away into the night, giving the frame a mental nudge to re-lock it once on the other side.

Once he was safely under cover of the trees, his furtive steps grew sure and determined. Even if his soul wandered away, he had nothing to fear in these woods, not with all of his mounts safely stabled for the night.

And no one but Helena knows where you are. Lucien stopped short under a spreading oak. The niggling sense of frustration he'd been feeling kindled into suspicion. Not at Helena of course, but at the nameless force that had wrenched him out of his body yesterday.

Despite what most people believed about those in his station, a duke was not his own person. Growing up in the castle, he'd had a devil of a time getting a bit of privacy. His father had never been inclined to give him any, and after his death even Jocelyn hadn't budged on that respect. So in his youth, Lucien had rebelled, haring off into these very woods and making camp like the tramps and vagabonds who occasionally passed through his lands.

To breathe the night air like this, no one knowing where to find him had been the first taste of real freedom he'd ever felt. And to the best of his recollection, his soul had never wandered while he was out here, anonymous to the world. Maybe in his dreams but at this point that was a reflex, like breathing.

But the violent episodes...

He sat on a fallen log, racking his brain. The worst experiences of his life had taken place when his whereabouts were known. Which begged the question—why had he only been in danger when he was supposed to be safe?

No sooner had the thought crossed his mind than a shooting pain passed through his right eye. Clapping a hand to his head he expected another wrenching out-of-body experience, but his mind stayed firmly where it was.

The pain receded as quickly as it had arrived, leaving him winded and mildly nauseated. Taking a deep breath, he resumed his walk only to catch movement out of the corner of his eye. Spinning on his heel, he saw a light retreating over a nearby hill. Someone was walking with a lantern—one fitted with panes of green glass instead of yellow or frosted white.

He was already halfway up the rise when he questioned the wisdom of the act.

Lucien could be running after poachers. It wouldn't matter that as lord of these lands he was known to be fairly lenient about the villagers setting small snares and even bringing down the occasional buck during a long winter.

But even a pair of friendly locals would not hesitate to shoot him if he ran up straight into their midst in the dead of night.

With that in mind, he slowed his steps, attempting to move with more stealth without sacrificing speed. And then between blinks, the light shifted in an impossible manner—following a path that did not exist. It rose and bobbed where no man could have walked. Which meant there was no man holding the lantern.

Heart beating like a drum, he followed the light for as long as he could. Up until it split into six smaller lights. These formed a circle that spun faster and faster until it was a solid ring of light. It twisted and bent, contorting into different patterns like a child playing with a ribbon, or so he thought until the motion speed up too fast for his eye to follow.

"Bloody hell." He spun on his heel, realizing he'd come full circle. The house Helena and Tomas had rented was just beyond the trees on his left.

Lucien put a hand up to shield his vision as the bobbing light brightened like a blazing flare. When he put them down, the lights were gone. He was alone in the dark…except for the sound of labored breathing.

Very slowly, Lucien turned.

He found the beast a few yards away.

CHAPTER 18

"*A*re you sure you're well enough for this, My Lord?"

Lucien started, shaking out of the stupor he'd slipped into between footsteps—not for the first time that morning. He found himself pleasantly surprised to find Helena leaning toward him, her fingers inches from his face.

"For pity's sake, don't stroke the man in front of me," Tomas scolded as they stopped in front of the large double doors of the main library.

Helena and her brother had appeared at mid-morning, too late for breakfast. Tomas had been so disappointed Lucien had sent for a tray from the kitchens, despite Helena's assurance that they had already broken their fast.

She turned to her brother, addressing him in rapid Italian in tones too low to follow. It must have been a reprimand, because Tomas's lips mulishly clamped shut, and no further snide comments were forthcoming.

"Are you sure you wouldn't prefer to retire? At least for a little while?" Helena ignored her brother's sour expression as Lucien ushered her into the library. She settled into the chair at the table laden with books with a graceful swirl of linen skirts.

"You had so little sleep. And it must have taken hours to dig the grave for that poor animal you found."

"I'm fine," he assured her, tucking in her chair.

But it wasn't quite true. He was in that mildly euphoric state people experienced when they hadn't received sufficient rest but were paradoxically energized.

Lucien found he was jumpy and on edge, like a high-strung horse. Finding the dying deer hadn't helped. It had been a small doe, which appeared to have been caught in an amateurish trap. The poor thing had escaped, but not without catastrophic damage.

He'd searched the supply shed of Hapley House, borrowing a shovel to bury the poor creature. It had taken hours.

Afterward, he'd had a long bath, eschewing sleep altogether. One sleepless night didn't matter. As long as Helena was here in his home, he would be at her side—as long as Tomas wasn't dragging him out to the stables or out on the grounds for a ride.

Lucien sat across from his love, drowsy but content, nudging a stack of journals written by some long-dead relative to the side so he could have an unobstructed view of her graceful form.

Helena had commandeered this part of the library weeks ago, researching his family history with a zeal he doubted anyone else, including his own relatives, had ever matched.

Today, concern for him made her hazel eyes sparkle like topaz jewels.

Lucien had told them both about the lights the moment he met them outside but dismissed the bizarre vision as swamp gas. He did *not* mention that the only marsh remotely conducive to such a vision was on the north side of his property—not the southern bit where their cottage was situated.

Soul wandering was one thing. Seeing lights moving and twisting from one pattern to another was quite another. Lucien didn't want to give them more reason to think he was mad. Not if he was going to convince Helena to marry him.

Lucien considered not mentioning the lights at all. But Helena had known at a glance that he'd barely slept.

Her first guess had been that he'd resisted sleep because he'd been afraid to go soul wandering after the incident in front of the stables. She had been disconcerted to learn he had instead been wandering the woods long after the lights had disappeared, burying the poor animal they had led him to.

"Are you certain you wouldn't like to retire? Even for a short nap?"

"No. I'll stay," he assured her quietly, his smile small but intensely private. Their glance grew heated, and Helena blushed, looking down at the table demurely.

If Tomas had caught the exchange, he would have called Lucien out on the spot. Fortunately for him, her brother was too concerned watching for the maid with his food to take note.

"The only edible part of our meals is the bread," Tomas groused when his sister teased him for his vigilance. His eyes remained fixed on the door as he waited for the tray from the kitchen. "We really need another cook."

"My offer to stay at the castle still stands," Lucien said, a hint of a smile playing at his lips, because he knew how much Tomas disliked the idea. "It would please my chef enormously. I think she grows bored with so little opportunity to demonstrate her culinary talents. We don't entertain enough to suit her, but hopefully that will change in the near future," he added with a meaningful glance at Helena.

This one Tomas did catch. It earned Lucien a glower, but the Italian cut it short when Maggie, one of the sturdier downstairs maids appears at the threshold with a heavily laden tray.

Tomas fell on the food as if he'd been locked in a dungeon for the past month, subsisting only on bread and ale, which was, to some extent, true.

The part of Lucien that wished he could entertain more was pleased with the man's reaction to his chef's cooking. He really *had* chosen her well. As an added bonus, the meal would keep Tomas too occupied to speak.

Taking advantage of the small reprieve, he pulled his chair closer to Helena's.

"Are you certain you've never seen those lights before?" she asked, the naked concern on her face heartwarming.

"No," he began and then paused. An elusive memory danced in the corner of his mind, just out of his reach. He frowned to himself. "At least I don't believe so."

Helena read the doubt he tried to conceal more easily than she'd transcribed his father's almost illegible experiment journal. Her gloved hand rested on the back of his hand, and for a moment he closed his eyes, savoring her warmth.

The intense memories of her the previous night overcame what little discipline he had around her, and he found himself reliving her sounds...her scent...the softness of her skin. Her taste flooded his mouth and he had to forcibly wrench himself back into the present, reminding himself that there was an Italian with a bricklayer's build ready to brain him over the head if he so much breathed wrong on his sister in his presence.

She removed her hand, returning to her work. Reluctantly he sat back, realizing he should help.

It wasn't the first time he'd dived into his family's history in search of answers. But his earlier perusals hadn't been short-lived, half-hearted efforts. Why would he bother to delve into his family's history when the answer to his questions always led to stories of odd behavior or outright madness?

The town's rumors of the eccentricities in his family line weren't unfounded. He had seen firsthand his father's mania and pre-occupation with experimentation. That obsessive behavior had grown in severity with each passing year.

Lucien could remember many disappointments as a child where his father had promised him an outing or a game, only to forget because he'd lost track of time in his laboratory.

The former duke hadn't appreciated being reminded of his faults either.

"I will not be taken to task by my own wife!" he had shouted on one notable occasion when Jocelyn had gently chided him about breaking his promise.

His father had grabbed his arm, marched him outside, and asked him to call his new pup. "If you want to spend time with me, we will do it now in my laboratory. But we will not do it alone."

Certain that his hound would end up tied to the duke's electricity machine, Lucien had grabbed the pup and run off to hide in the woods behind the orchard. Jocelyn had wisely never mentioned any of the duke's little failures ever again.

In the years that followed, his father had withdrawn more and more until Lucien saw his own father perhaps once or twice a month, if that.

Truth be told, he had been relieved when both Jocelyn and the duke gave up all pretense of trying to be a family.

But his father was hardly alone in such behavior. According to the stories passed down in the village, the same proclivity for obsessive behavior had been shared by his grandfather and his great-grandfather. The latter, a disciple of Newton, fancied himself the last "true" alchemist.

So, no, confirming his own inevitable mental decline had never held any temptation. Perhaps he would have tried a little harder had there been even a hint that one of his ancestors shared the peculiar nature of his affliction. As far as he knew it was unique.

Of course, now he was starting to wonder if his family's trademark eccentricity was something quite different. Tomas and Helena's matter-of-fact discussions on magic, sprites—even demon possession, forced him to revise some long-held beliefs about himself and the legacy he'd inherited.

As Helena worked, Lucien acted as her assistant, fetching books, diaries, and maps from different parts of the library, including Debrett's peerage, which included a lengthy section of the St. Germain line. But even that was not extensive enough to suit Helena, so he made lists of his closest relatives, jotting down notes on each, details on their age and overall health and tastes—everything he could remember. Granted that wasn't much.

He appealed to Jocelyn for more details. That was when she

reminded him of the elaborately rendered family tree she had commissioned from a London artist years ago.

"Are you sure it's necessary to remove it?" Jocelyn asked, her hands fluttering in the air as he and Tomas muscled the massive portrait, taking it down from the wall. Jocelyn had displayed it in the red parlor off the portrait gallery, named so for the color of the upholstery.

"We will return it to this room once we are done with it," he promised with a grunt, gesturing for Tomas to take the lead back to the library.

"I still don't understand why it's necessary to have the portrait as well—the family tree is accurately depicted in the St. Germain bible," Jocelyn pointed out as they crossed the main foyer.

"True, but a large visual might be valuable, especially given the number of books we currently have set out."

"Yes, about that, may I ask why a horror novelist needs so much information?" His elfin stepmother wore an uncharacteristic moue of displeasure on her face as she minced along next to them.

It was slow going. The massive painting was almost as tall as he was. The frame alone must have weighed at least four stone.

"All this effort is not for me," Tomas explained with a charming smile that Lucien didn't think him capable of. "I don't pen biographies. But His Grace has conscripted my sister into compiling details for a family history to be written up—by another author. My sister is a zealous and skilled researcher and quite enjoys that sort of thing, so I have no choice but to acquiesce to their wishes."

The lie was told so smoothly and with such skill that Lucien was suddenly grateful the Italian was on his side, even if that was only for the sake of his sister.

"Oh, well that is a lovely idea," Jocelyn enthused, clasping her gloved hands in front of her. Her annoyance had dissipated like morning dew.

"It's so nice that you're finally taking an interest in the St. Germaine legacy," she added coyly, adding a suggestive waggle of the eyebrows.

Lucien was very glad that Tomas could not turn to witness the obvious innuendo about him and Helena without dropping the painting and doing himself bodily harm. But he made a mental note to have a chat with Jocelyn later. It would be nice to have an ally in his suit for Helena's hand.

His stepmother accompanied them into the library, where thanks to his and Tomas's burly strength combined, the family tree arrived without incident.

Jocelyn promptly commandeered Helena, chattering on about the imaginary family chronicle. Fortunately, his quick-witted intended picked up the story of the history, accepting the dozens of suggestions for interesting characters in his family line—including one or two he had never heard of.

Normally, the gaps in his knowledge of his own bloodline would not bother him at all. He knew the highlights, and that had always been enough for him. Now he regretted his disinterest.

The true power lies within the soul, a little voice said. It sounded remarkably like Helena's. Startled, he gave her a second glance.

Was it possible Helena had spoken to him just now, mind to mind? She noticed his intent expression and tilted her head quizzically over his stepmother's bright silver head.

Can you hear me, my love?

But Helena did not so much as bat an eyelash as she continued to speak to his mother.

Perfect, he thought. Now he didn't get to be a little voice in Helena's ear. *I get to hear them now as well...*

His stomach plummeted to the fine Persian carpet. If this wasn't his connection with Helena in action, then it was the other thing—the curse in his blood. Because his true inheritance was madness.

Oh, yes. He made a fine marriage prospect indeed.

CHAPTER 19

$\mathscr{H}$elena was thinking Lucien was being uncharacteristically quiet when she realized she wasn't being particularly garrulous this afternoon herself.

It was the heat.

A layer of damp hot air had settled over Devil's Slide in the last few days, cloying and oppressive without the slightest breeze to break it.

This was why Tomas hadn't objected to her going for a stroll with His Grace. Lucien had promised it would be cooler in the woods. Miraculously, her brother had declined to join them in favor of a much-needed nap. He had been assisting one of Lucien's prize Arabians to deliver a colt early in the predawn hours.

His Grace had assisted as well, but he did not appear to require additional rest. Or at least he pretended not to.

"Tell me the truth. Did you have the head of your stables summon my brother because of his expertise in equine parturition? Or did you call him out before first light so he'd be too tired to chaperone today?"

Lucien drew himself up, giving her a mock-serious glance. "Your brother is my stable master's new favorite person. I think Joseph would cheerfully toss me aside for Tomas any day of the week if his position didn't depend upon my continuing patronage."

She laughed. "I would chastise you for fibbing, but I happen to know that the stables are where my brother shines. All of the landowners for miles around our estate in Viterbo know to consult him before they buy a new mount."

"That I can easily believe. And truth be told I only stayed with Themistoclea until your brother arrived. Then I went to bed like any sensible duke would, leaving the experts to their work."

Helena removed her fan, snapping it open and fanning herself.

Lucien stopped under the shade of a spreading oak, his teasing expression dropping away. "It's not enough—the shade of the trees."

Helena wanted to deny it, but a trickle of perspiration chose that moment to run down the side of her face and down her neck.

Feeling breathless, she leaned against the trunk of the oak. "Forgive me...I just need a moment."

He winced. "My apologies. I should have realized the exertion of a walk would nullify the benefits of the shade."

"I suppose the thick stone walls of the castle offer some protection against the heat."

"Quite a bit," he acknowledged. "In fact, some rooms are cold enough for a fire at night."

She shook her head, fanning herself vigorously. "I can't imagine that at this moment."

He gave her a considering look. "Well, I could go fetch the carriage and give you a tour of the castle's icehouse, but I might have a better suggestion. If you're feeling a little daring..."

Lucien stepped away, holding out his hand. The wicked glint in his eye was concerning.

"What are you planning?"

"To give you relief."

Her face flamed and he laughed, but it was a self-deprecating sound. "I meant from the heat—before it makes you swoon."

"Good, because I don't think that other thing would help at all."

Lucien burst out laughing. "Oh, Helena, I adore you."

She rolled her eyes but couldn't help the twitch of her lips. Unable to resist, Helena took his hand.

Lucien led her off the path, deeper under the trees. After about ten or fifteen minutes, he came to a stop in a sun-dappled clearing next to a small but swiftly running stream no wider than two or three meters across. It sent up a fine mist into the air.

"Oh," Helena exclaimed, crouching and removing her glove so she could dip her hand inside. She looked up at the duke. "It's cool."

"I believe its source is an underground stream, so it stays that way even on the hottest of days." He gave her a delicate nudge. "Go ahead. I won't tell anyone."

Startled, she rose to her feet. "What?"

His smile was sin personified. "If you undress and take a dip. I promise not to tell a soul."

"*Your Grace,*" she gasped.

Sobering quickly, he took both his hands in hers. "Lucien. Always Lucien when we're alone."

Coloring she looked down. "I can't disrobe in the middle of the woods."

His expression transformed, the very picture of innocence. "Do you need help removing your gown? I thought you didn't employ a maid. If you require assistance, I'll be happy to provide it. I will even close my eyes. I might fumble a bit, so you will have to bear with me. Be patient."

"*Lucien,*" she protested when he went for the buttons at the front of her gown.

He stopped, placing his hands on either side of her face. Lucien drew her closer, pressing her against him. "I keep my promises to you. I will always keep them. But I would like to give this to you."

She took a deep breath. "What exactly are you offering?"

A husky murmur brushed her ear. "Pleasure."

Helena shuddered involuntarily. Lucien murmured soothing words, his hands moving to caress her arms over her the sleeves of her gown. When his fingers began to undo the buttons again, she did not protest.

Soon she was standing in the gossamer-thin chemise. It was completely transparent in the dappled light.

Lucien's eyes burned down her body, lingering on her breasts. Her nipples were outlined through the sheer material.

He lifted his hands, taking the shift in his hands. But he didn't pull it up, didn't try to remove it. Instead, he pulled it taut, stretching it across the sensitive tips.

The stimulation of the linen against her straining nipples sent bolts of sensation down her body. She looked down instinctively, down to where she was growing wet. His eyes followed hers.

Lucien made a rough sound in his throat. "You're not wearing drawers again."

"Still too warm," she whispered, shivering despite the heat.

He took a sharp step away from her. Helena blinked, an incipient pang beginning to well in her chest, but it stopped the moment he began to undress.

"A-are you certain that is wise?" she stuttered.

"My love, I am seconds away from combusting. I think I need to jump in the stream more than you. But a word of warning, the water may boil when it touches my body."

Helena's laugh turned into a squeak as large expanses of male flesh were revealed. Lucien stripped off his waistcoat and linen shirt exposing a ridged abdomen and chest so sculpted she had only ever seen its like as statuary.

But when he began to unfasten the falls of his trousers, Helena squeezed her eyes shut, her breath coming faster.

Two thuds, his boots hitting the ground were followed by more rustling and then his arms were wrapping around her.

"This does little to give relief from this heat," she said, biting her lip. A large warm hand stroked down her back, settling on the upper curve of her derriere.

"Take my hand."

Obeying, she let him lead her down the slight incline leading to the stream. Helena hissed as the water swirled around her bare feet. The shock of the cold water made her gasp and cry out, but soon she was sighing in relief as it rushed over her overheated skin.

She didn't open her eyes until the water was lapping just below her breasts. Helena looked down, her hands flying to cover herself. Enough water had splashed on her chest to make her already sheer gown as clear as the water around him.

"If someone comes upon us," she began.

"No one will come here. It's very isolated," he said, and then his head moved from side to side in a disarming gesture. "Also, this part of the woods is rumored to be haunted."

Her lips parted. "Haunted as in possessing real ghosts?"

He held up a hand. "It doesn't, I assure you. My grandmother used to have a cabin nearby. It's where she met with her lover—the spinster daughter of a local gentry family that used to live in this area."

Helena's eyes widened. "*Oh.*"

Pressing closer to her with a hand to her back, he grinned. "Grandmother spread the story of a ghost to discourage anyone from coming to this part of the woods. Not that she cared about her reputation. She enjoyed being a bit scandalous."

"But she cared about her lover, enough to protect her."

"Yes." He pressed his forehead to hers. "Just like I will protect you. No one will ever know about this. I swear it. I did not bring you here because this part of the woods is shunned by the locals—although, that is a side benefit."

"If privacy is not your aim, then we are here because of the stream?"

"In a way." His lips grazed her cheek. His hands stroked all over her body, sending shivers throughout. "My true motive was the stone."

Eyes hazy with sensation, she blinked. "A stone?"

Lucien's mouth came down on hers, his tongue breaching the seal of her lips. Her legs lost cohesion. His arms swept her up, and he waded through the water a few meters.

Helena gasped as he laid her out. Her hands splashed through the surface of the water to rest on a large, flat stone just a few inches below the surface.

The current was faster here in the center of the stream. It rushed over her, making her squeal.

Chuckling, Lucien positioned himself at her back as her legs dangled in the water. Helena sucked in a breath as his hand came around, cupping her breast with conscious gentleness. At least until his fingers pinched her nipple through the wet cloth.

Crying out, her hand flew up to cover his, her legs curling up instinctively. To her surprise, he sank deeper into the water behind her, adjusting her legs and pushing them open wide.

"What are—" she began, and then the water rushed over her most private of places. Crying out, she shifted, inadvertently positioning herself in the perfect spot. Her entire being spasmed as the delicate flesh between her legs was blasted by the force of the water.

Her vision darkened and her body bowed up, bliss twisting and contorting her muscles. "*Lucien,*" she gasped.

Strong arms came around her convulsing body. He stepped between her legs, pulling her to him as the spasms began to fade, and she could see again.

"You are the most beautiful thing I have ever seen." Lucien kissed her again and again.

Helpless against the conflagration, she opened her mouth, stroking her tongue with his. His length pressed against her, a burning brand she felt despite the chill of the water.

His mouth was on her neck when she reached to stroke him over the wet cloth of his drawers. She tried to push them down.

Lucien grabbed her hands, pushing them behind her back and holding them with one of his. "No. Not until we are wed."

Helena's heart ached. She knew he desired her, the proof of it was in her hands. And right now, she'd give him what he wanted, because she wanted it too. Desperately so. But he was still trying to protect her, saving her from herself.

Lucien's hips worked themselves between her legs, his straining length rubbing over her sensitive flesh. His length rubbed against the straining nub at the top of her sex, sending another blast of bone-melting fire through her.

She wasn't the only one feeling this overwhelming hunger, a voracious thing with claws and teeth.

The friction of his cloth-covered member sent her into a second shuddering paroxysm. Then Lucien's hands gripped her waist, his face burrowing into her neck. His muscles shook, a groan escaping from deep within his throat. There was a fleeting warmth between her legs, but it was quickly carried away by the running water.

Being in the stream was a blessing. Holding tight to Lucien, she let the cool kiss of the water soothe her overheated skin. Then Lucien stepped back, his hands positioning her so her legs were open to the storm of the current.

"No," she laughed. "I don't think I can stand it."

But he urged her to try anyway, with hot words spoken in her ear. Then his hand moved working between her legs. All too soon she was writhing, tensing, and clenching around his fingers as she was swept away, twisting and shattering for his delectation.

When sense returned, he was carrying her out of the water. He took them to a grassy part of the bank where the sun had broken through the trees. Then he lowered himself, taking her with his mouth. His tongue ran over her folds, licking and tasting, drawing her taste deep with pleasurable groans. His sounds of satisfaction were so shockingly pleasurable she climaxed on the spot, his tongue thrust into her core, her pearl throbbing between his fingers.

His eyes hot on her skin, Lucien reached out and used his strong arms top pull her into his lap. Muscles lax, she lay quiescent in his arms as the sparks in her sensitized flesh slowly died away.

"I've been thinking of this spot of the stream for days now, how forceful it is and how the stone would be the perfect pedestal for you," he whispered, stroking her cheek. The buttons of her loose chemise were undone now. Hot breath on her breast. Then he was sucking and touching, making her melt like a piece of ice cast into a fire.

She gasped as his fingers penetrated her sheath, stroking in and out. A warm slippery wetness coated his hand, easing his passage. Helena lay back, legs spread for him shamelessly as he worked his index finger against a spot deep inside that made her tighten up all over. The unbearable tension built and built until she was writhing, clasping his fingers with a hungry desperation she only experienced in his arms.

"You were a goddess in the water. A divine deity being claimed by an elemental god. Like Aphrodite with Poseidon." His deep voice thrummed in her ear, the very vibrations sweeping over her, sending her over the edge.

Lucien kept whispering in her ear, telling her how beautiful she was, how brilliant and generous. How much he enjoyed pleasing her. His words carried her through the storm into calmer currents. She opened her eyes with a small shudder, pressing her face into his neck as his fingers relaxed.

When the last throb died away, Lucien pressed his mouth to hers, a long sipping kiss. "The French call the paroxysm the little death," he said, looking very pleased with himself.

"That is a terrible way to describe it," Helena said after a startled laugh. "But...not an inaccurate one."

Lucien pressed his forehead to hers. "When we are married, we'll come out here on these insufferably warm days with a basket from the kitchen, spend the entire afternoon frolicking in the water."

Helena forced a smile despite the constriction in her chest at the mention of marriage. "If I were the sort of woman who made wagers, I would bet that you'd already done a fair amount of frolicking here. Perhaps with a parlor maid?"

"Bite your tongue," Lucien laughed before sobering. "You know the village girls gave me a wide berth. I was waiting for my sweet and brave Helena to come and seduce me."

"I seduced *you*?" Helena burst out laughing. "Heaven help me, you are such a wicked man."

He held her closer, but a glance back at his face told her he was amused...and happy. She had never seen him so content, so carefree.

Could she really leave him now? Was it even possible? Helena closed her eyes, pushing the rising guilt and recriminations to the back of her mind.

"You did raise an excellent question. Why has no enterprising fortune hunter come to seduce you? I would think your face and fortune would have guaranteed one would have come to the Slide to try her luck."

"I think only men are fortune hunters, my love," he said, nuzzling her close. "I think the women you're describing would be termed..."

"Strumpets?" she supplied.

He scowled. "I was going to say enterprising."

Helena sank deeper in his arms. "Society would call me a strumpet for being here with you like this."

His tone sharpened, his arms tightening around her. "They will call you the Duchess of Blackwater. Anyone who slanders you will answer to me."

Her lips parted, but no words came. Sighing, Helena sat up, pulling up her knees so she could watch him. Following her lead, he sat up as well. She could almost see his thoughts, the arguments he was marshaling to convince her to abandon her life and family in Italy to stay with him. But his lips opened and closed as his face creased in concern.

Lucien rose to his feet, an arrested expression on his face.

"What's wrong?"

He sucked in a breath through his teeth. "Helena, we must get dressed."

Alerted by his tone, she scrambled to her feet, turning to see what had alarmed him.

"Is that the kitchen chimney at the cottage?" The direction and distance were roughly in line with the smoke rising in the distance, visible through the break in the trees.

He didn't answer. Lucien ran, leaping into the stream and crossing to the other side. He bent to gather their clothes, holding hers high as he waded back through the water. He hesitated, then dunked his clothes in the rushing water to saturate them.

He dropped his sodden clothes on the ground next to her.

"It's too much smoke for a chimney," he said, throwing her dress over her head and tugging it down. "We need to run."

CHAPTER 20

*H*elena's heart was a drumbeat. Lucien had pulled on his trousers and boots and then taken her hand to guide her to the path. Sprinting the rest of the way, they attempted to put their clothes to rights as they went.

They burst into the clearing, and Helena promptly forgot about her disheveled state.

"*Tomas!*" she screamed. Smoke was pouring out of the cottage. It was coming from every opening—the windows and the open kitchen door.

Lucien was halfway across the clearing when Sally and Judy stumbled out of the back door, coughing.

Judy saw Helena, and she ran toward her but fell to her knees a few feet away. Rushing to her, Helena hauled her up as Lucien went to the aid of the cook.

"Where is Tomas?" Her words came out jagged and shrill.

"I don't know, Miss." Tears were streaking through the soot covering Judy's face. "We were in the kitchen when the smoke poured in. Sally called for him, but we didn't hear a reply—the smoke was too thick."

She punctuated her words with a wracking cough, wrenching and spitting bile on the grass.

"*Lucien*," Helena cried out. "My brother must still be inside!"

She released Judy and began to run to the back door, but Lucien snagged her around the waist, pushing her into Sally's arms. "Don't let her follow me," he ordered.

Then he turned and ran into the burning building.

THE KITCHEN WAS FILLED with smoke so thick he could barely see.

Crouching, Lucien stripped off his shirt, grateful that it still held moisture from the stream. Wrapping the damp cloth around his face, he covered his mouth and nose and went down on all fours. Imitating the loping gait of his hounds, he ran on his palms and feet, trying to stay below the smoke.

"Tomas," he bellowed, praying the man wasn't upstairs.

He went from room to room, clearing the servant's quarters first on accident because he didn't know the layout of this part of the house.

The fire had started in the library. The heat and smoke pouring from behind the closed door were proof. It had not begun in the kitchen as he'd guessed.

And that was how he knew without a doubt Tomas was in the library.

Swearing, he reached up and turned the knob, spinning and sitting on the floor to kick the door open. A blast of burning air and smoke blew past him, the heat enough to scorch his lungs as if it were the literal door to hell itself.

Pressing down to the floor, he sucked in a breath, holding it before crawling inside.

Tomas was lying in front of the fireplace—a poker in his hand. Behind him a fire raged, so large and ferocious it had escaped the confines of the fireplace. The wall, the ceiling, and the bookshelves and their contents were ablaze.

Even the stones of the fireplace appeared to be burning.

Black smoke furled to the ceiling, the noise of the fire like the growl of a beast from the netherworld. Not stopping to ask why Tomas was unburned, he began to drag the heavy man to the window.

His arms were strong, but Tomas was dead weight, the force required to pull him threatening to pull his arms from the socket. But he wouldn't let him go—not only would Helena never recover, but Lucien *liked* the bastard.

Once Tomas was at the window, he doubled back for the poker. But the sash was sealed or swollen shut despite the fact it had opened easily for Helena on his last visit to this room just a week prior. Smashing the window out with the iron poker, he leaned out and shouted for help.

The ceiling was starting to disintegrate. Burning bits of debris rained down on him, sizzling on his rapidly drying shirt or burning the bare skin of his chest.

Teeth clenched, he coughed to clear the smoke, sucking in clean air at the window. But that precious smoke-free air seemed to make the flames worse, feeding the fire until the voracious beast consumed everything around them.

Resolving not to become fuel, he hauled Tomas up with effort. He hadn't knocked out enough of the glass. Jagged slivers remained embedded in the wood frame, which would slice up skin and muscle, but there was no choice.

"Here." A voice outside, a man. Stark wide brown eyes in a ruddy face appeared at the window. Lucien recognized the butcher's boy—a strapping lad of three and twenty. There were others behind him, more men from the village alerted by the smoke. It could be seen for miles around.

Sweating and swearing, he managed to get Tomas high enough up on the sill for the other men to grab him. They pulled him into the blazing sunshine, laying him out on the yellow grass.

Lucien was a quarter of the way out the window when the ceiling gave, and the burning world collapsed on him.

CHAPTER 21

*H*elena took a deep breath as her brother focused his eyes on her, recognition in their depths.

She wanted to weep again but didn't release the tears. Such feminine demonstrations had always frustrated Tomas, though he'd never been unkind about them. If she had hurt herself or was feeling sad, he would wrap his big arms around her, rubbing her back until the little storms passed.

But he was the one who had been hurt now. Her tears would not speed his recovery, so she wouldn't indulge in them, no matter how relieved she was to see him awake and breathing freely.

"Helena."

Sitting on the bed, she took his hand, squeezing it tight. "I am here. Are you in pain?"

"*Cazzo*, my head is aching," he said, switching over to Italian. Tomas reached up to touch the back of his head.

"You were struck by something heavy. The fire was an attempt to burn you up and destroy the evidence. Someone tried to murder you."

His scowl was immediate. "*Murder me? And what fire?*"

"The cottage burned to the foundation. The fire began in the library. Lucien said it was arson. He saved you."

She told him how he had been found with the poker in his hand. "You should know that the entire village believes you to be culpable. They think you started a fire in the library fireplace with the flue closed, and it got out of control, escaping the confines of the hearth."

His nose scrunched up the way it used to when their mother served fennel-laced vegetables for dinner. "Are they stupid? Why in the hell would I start a fire in this heat?"

Her lips parted as she searched for the right words. "I told them you would not, but very few seemed to believe me. No one would be that daft. I think they prefer to think that foreigners are half-mad. More than one has mentioned that Italy is a much warmer clime than England."

"It's not the bloody surface of the sun," Tomas scoffed, rising up. But he fell back on the bed, wincing. His normally tan skin was pale and sweaty, and he swallowed as if his gorge was rising. A blow to the head could result in severe nausea.

"Don't move," Helena ordered, pressing a hand to his chest. "You are not allowed to leave this bed for at least a week—at the very least. Not until I'm satisfied that your skull is healed and sound and everything has mended to my satisfaction."

He must have been in considerable pain, because Tomas didn't argue with her. "Was I struck with the poker?"

There were a few other possible weapons in the library with enough heft to strike him down, but it had been the poker in his hand that was the most likely suspect.

"We believe so, but Lucien didn't have a chance to examine it very thoroughly—the ceiling was a bare minute from collapsing. He got you out, but it was a very close thing," she explained, adding how the village men had helped haul him to safety.

"And your bloody duke?" he asked querulously.

"Some timbers fell on his legs as he was being pulled out, but they were glancing blows. He suffered some damage to his lungs, but it was not deep, because he covered his mouth before entering the cottage. And he was not burned badly, because his clothes…"

A deep line appeared between her brother's eyes. "What? Why didn't they burn?"

His eyes widened. "Did he do something magic to keep them from burning?

"No. They were wet...from the stream." Helena flushed, gripping her hands together. "So were mine."

Her brother's groan could probably be heard in the kitchens. "Please tell me you were wet because you splashed through the water when you smelled the smoke."

The impulse to hang her head was strong, but Helena was no longer a child to be scolded. "I can't."

The shock of the fire had hushed the scandalized whispers for the time being, but they would rise again soon. Too many of the villagers had seen the state of her clothing, its disarray more than could be explained by a mad dash back to the cottage.

Her buttons hadn't been fastened properly.

A heavy sigh. "When is the wedding?"

She took his hand, pressing a kiss to the top before squeezing it. "You know as well as I do that this was inevitable when Lucien proved to be a flesh and blood man. From the moment I first saw him, I knew I would never be able to leave him. Our connection is..."

"I know." Tomas waved to forestall further explanations, an exhausted resignation on his face.

After a long, silent moment, he asked for water. Eager to do whatever she could for him, she poured him a glass from the pitcher waiting on the bedside table, which he drank up with sloppy haste. He was half-done with the second before he spoke again.

"Has the engagement been announced?"

"Not yet," she shrugged. "Truthfully Lucien hasn't even asked again."

"He doesn't have to."

"No," she acknowledged with a laugh before subsiding. Her duke would marry her at the earliest opportunity. He had made no bones about that. But the thought of what she was leaving behind was almost too much to bear.

She swallowed to relieve the tightness of her throat. "Do you think mother will ever forgive me?"

Tomas's face softened. "Of course, she will. In fact, she'll be ecstatic that you've found someone you obviously care deeply for. The only sticking point will be the distance, but even that won't stop her relief."

"Relief?" Helena laughed. "I knew she was concerned about my unmarried state, but I never realized she despaired of me making a match."

Her brother's expression grew thoughtful. "It wasn't that. Isobel just wanted you to meet a man who understood you. And for all his faults, the blasted Duke does seem to. It's father who will take the news of the marriage the hardest."

Helena sucked in a breath and let out a groan of her own. "You're right."

Tomas patted her hand. "You know he will be happy for you too. It will just take him longer to get there. So, where is my irksome future brother-in-law?"

She rubbed her cheeks with her hands. "The minute he rose from bed he went down to the cottage. It was still smoking this morning— it's mid-afternoon now. The fire burned so fiercely the upper story has no structural integrity. Rather than let it collapse on its own, he's going to have his laborers raze it to the ground."

"And this requires supervision?"

"He didn't say so, but I believe he intends to search the debris for clues of your assailant."

Tomas blinked. "Oh yes, there is that."

"Yes, and don't think it's rather telling that you were more concerned with the fact I have been ruined than with the fact you were almost murdered."

A grunt was his only reply.

Helena tapped his hand. "You can't recall anything from before you were struck?"

"No, nothing." His heavy brows pulled down and he stiffened, tensing. "Damn, even thinking hurts."

"Here, I prepared this earlier." Rising, Helena went to the sideboard, opening the wax paper sleeve into a glass. Adding water, she stirred it vigorously. "This is mostly Willow bark extract."

He sat up straighter and took the glass, grimacing at the taste. "Not mother's recipe."

"No—I should have had the kitchens bring some mint at least to ameliorate the bitterness."

"It's all right." Tomas choked down the rest of the mixture, laying back on the pillows with a groan, a sheen of sweat appearing on his forehead. "You have a great many other things to consider."

He scowled. "All of our clothing is gone. My shaving kit, your books…everything."

"It was fortunate that we brought all of the books of value to the castle library to facilitate our search. The duke is already having some of his clothes altered to fit you and has ordered new garments for both of us from the village tailor."

She lifted her arms to show him the sleeves of her gown. Made from serviceable mid-weight linen, it was rather plain but fit well considering it had probably been altered in a mad dash. With an apron borrowed from the housekeeper, it was more than suitable for attending a sickroom.

"The Dowager Duchess lamented being of too small stature to lend me her gowns, but Lucien has already sent for a dressmaker from London. I told him the village seamstress would do, but he was adamant it had to be a Parisian modiste."

Tomas was no longer thinking of their lost belongings. "Wait, I think there is—"

He lapsed into silence, a look of intense concentration on his face. "There was a knock."

"At the cottage?"

"Yes, that was it. I was on the front stairs. I'd gone upstairs to splash water on my face and was headed back to the library to write some letters when I heard it. Judy and Sally weren't about, so I went to answer."

"Who was it?"

A grimace. Her brother was beginning to look green again. "I have no idea. I'm wracking my brain trying to recall, but there is nothing after the knock. No memories at all."

"It may come to you later," she suggested.

But in truth, there was little hope of that. Memory loss of the events preceding a blow to the head was common. Tomas had told her that himself. That he hadn't lost more of his wits was a blessing.

She watched over him long after he fell asleep.

Helena pursed her lips, trying to figure out who would have wanted to harm her brother. She was still turning over possibilities in her mind when Lucien found her in the library. It was the room where she felt most comfortable in the castle, aside from the greenhouse outside. She rose from her seat, holding out her hands.

Lucien ignored them, choosing instead to pull her entire body against him into a tight embrace.

Helena wrapped her arms around his warm, solid body. "You're trembling."

Not only that, but his heart was also racing. Pressing her hand to the rapid thud on his chest, she pulled back to look at him in silent inquiry.

"The cottage was a complete loss. Ash and cinders. Not a single room survived intact." He gritted his teeth. "I could have lost you."

Her finger gripped his arms. "I was with you when the fire was set."

"By chance only." Lucien's hands cupped her face. "Seeing the condition of the house now, how badly it was damaged…"

He broke off to press a kiss to her mouth before burying his face in her hair. "It's a miracle your brother survived. If you had been inside…"

Helena put a hand to his lips. "Hush. I'm fine."

They stayed in that embrace for a long moment, her head on his chest listening to his heartbeat.

"The entire population of the Slide came to see the cottage demolished. Most of the second story is gone now. I sent for laborers across the village to get it done as quickly as possible."

"I thought you were going to look for evidence of an attack."

"I did, but there was nothing." He rubbed her back. "I brought back the poker, but the heat had burned away all traces of blood. It was misshapen as well. That fire burned very hot, unnaturally so."

She bit her lip. "I thought that might have been the case given how quickly the house went up. But I have no experience with such things. I was hoping I was wrong."

"Whereas I am having a difficult time that someone in our small town could be a killer." He scowled. "The scholar was there."

"At the cottage? What was he doing?"

His scowl darkened. "Helping. He was very effective hefting a heavy mallet to take down what was left of the beams. He's a bit on the wiry side, but Mr. Ellison possesses a great deal of muscle for an ecclesiastical student."

She knew that tone. "You believe the scholar would try to kill my brother? What possible motive could he have?"

Lucien leaned against the table with her in his arms. "Aside from you and Tomas, he is the only stranger in the area. You, I trust you with my life—and possibly my eternal soul."

Her mouth quirked up at the corner. "And does this faith extend to my brother?"

"Tomas didn't strike himself over the head. And I do trust him with my horses, some of whom I value nearly as much as my life."

"Stop jesting," she chided, poking him in the chest.

He flattened his hand over her, pressing her fingers over his heart. "We know nothing about Nigel Ellison. He might not even be a scholar."

"But we've both spoken to him about his studies. He certainly speaks as if he has spent years studying his subject matter. Although..."

Her lips parted in sudden recollection.

Lucien gripped her shoulders. "What is it?"

"I remember now where I saw that design—the one on the pin Mr. Ellison wears. It's a rune." She backed away a step. "But where did I see it? I can't recall."

"Then he is a—what do call it? A *stragone*?" Lucien had raised his voice, his temper igniting now that he had cause to lay blame at the scholar's feet. But this was not the strong evidence he thought it was.

She held up a hand. "We cannot say that for certain," she cautioned. "Jewelry etched with a rune is not as uncommon as you might think. Even in my limited social circle, I would see them from time to time in families I knew did not possess a drop of magic. It could simply be an heirloom as Mr. Ellison described. Objects with protection runes, in particular, are often passed down in families because they are thought to bring luck. But the wearer has no idea *why* that is the case."

"Well, I'm not convinced it's a coincidence," he groused. "He's the only stranger in town."

"And what if the culprit is not a stranger?"

He sucked in a breath. "I won't deny that Mr. Ellison may be a convenient scapegoat. This is why I am having the footmen, game-keeper, and stable hands do regular patrols of the castle every night. I'm also thinking of sending for more help from London—from Bow Street."

Her brows puckered as she went over the stories her mother had told her small family over the years. "Do you mean a runner? The thief-takers?"

"A runner does more than capture thieves—at least some of them do. I want a proper investigation done into the cottage fire. I'd also like someone who can direct my men and shape them into proper guards. I don't have a great deal of experience in that arena, and our local magis-trate is a septuagenarian with gout. As far as I know, he's never had to do anything more strenuous than run a highwayman out of the county."

Helena straightened. "Well, that sounds promising."

"It would be if it hadn't happened over thirty years ago," he said, tapping his skull. "In any case, old Sathers is in no condition to run around the castle keep at night. He doesn't even go about in daylight anymore if it's too damp. Rheumatism."

"Is a runner necessary?" What if this brilliant investigator saw too much? Exposure was a constant threat when you were a witch.

But the look Lucien gave her pushed all those considerations away.

She touched her hand to his cheek, concerned at what she saw in his expression. "Darling, what's wrong?"

A muscle in his cheek twitched. "I still think the scholar did it, but I couldn't help but wonder as I rode back…what if *I* somehow caused the fire?"

Helena's head drew back. "No, that's not possible. You were with me."

Lucien licked his lips. "Helena, we already know I don't have to be present to have an effect."

"I assure you setting a fire is entirely different."

He raised a fine dark brow, a corner of his mouth pulling down. "I can touch you without touching you."

"That is not the same thing," she insisted with a fiery blush.

They were two of the *streghe*, connected by a bond both mysterious and unique, she told herself sternly. "As difficult as this may be to hear, you are gifted, but you are not *that* gifted."

She added another gentle poke to the sternum for emphasis.

Lucien blinked. Then he burst out laughing. "Thank you, my love. I needed to hear that. And for what it's worth, these are not the circumstances I envisioned you moving into my home."

His expression turned wry. "And Tomas will be fine. In fact, I predict he will make the speediest recovery imaginable—he won't want to leave you alone with me any longer than he can help."

That made her lips twitch. "Well, in any case, you should pray for his speedy recovery."

"And why is that?" He was staring at her lips now.

"Because I couldn't possibly get married without my brother present."

Lucien jerked back. "What did you say?"

Helena gripped her hands together a little too tightly, but she schooled her tone into a calm casualness. "I'm accepting your suit."

"Are you certain?" There was a stunned expression of patent disbelief on his face.

Helena nodded. "I have considered it very carefully. My family is very important to me, and it will be difficult living so far from them, but I...I cannot leave you. I want to be your wife."

He made a rough sound in his throat. "You said wife, not a duchess."

Her nose wrinkled. "Ah, I had forgotten that part."

A startled bark of laughter escaped him. "I love you."

"I suppose I can learn to be a proper duchess. My mother began as a governess and learned to be a Contessa who is beloved by all of my father's tenants and retainers. If she can accomplish that, then so can I. And..." She took his fingers and kissed them. "I love you, too."

He stared at her for a moment, before doing a slow collapse to his knees.

"Oh!" she exclaimed, startled. "Lucien, are you ill?"

He threw his arms around her waist, pressing his face into her skirts. "You won't regret this—well, you may, but not for long. I promise."

At least, that was what she thought he said. His voice was a touch muffled toward the end.

She ran her fingers through his hair. "*Scioccherello*. What am I going to do with you?"

He looked up, a wicked glint lighting his eyes. "Well, I have a few ideas."

Then he tossed up her skirts, crawling underneath with a deep chuckle she felt everywhere.

CHAPTER 22

"*Y*ou look beautiful."

Helena smoothed her hands over her gold skirt. Her wedding dress was a dream with short, puffed sleeves and an embroidered bodice over a cloud of silk faille gathered in a graceful fall with a small bustle. London's most fashionable modiste and her team had slaved over a week to make it.

By now the local minister was probably waiting downstairs.

Lucien hadn't asked any school friends or relatives to their wedding, saying there none were worth the delay it would require to extend an invitation. But contrary to expectation he had invited over half the village to the wedding breakfast that would follow the ceremony.

She turned to her brother with a grateful smile. Helena knew Tomas still had misgivings about her marriage, but he very generously was keeping them to himself.

"Fine feathers," she said. "Anyone would look beautiful in this gown."

"It is spectacular," he sniffed. "But it's honestly unnecessary. As much as it pains me to admit it, you are lovely regardless of what you're wearing. Which means the duke could have postponed the wedding long enough to let the seamstresses sleep this past week."

"They slept," she protested before her nose wrinkled in acknowledgment. "In shifts. And you look very fine in that suit they altered for you."

His cheek creased, but he joined her at the looking glass, his cane in hand. He didn't need the cane to walk. His legs had been unharmed in the fire, but Helena insisted. Her brother was still experiencing the odd dizzy spell, the aftereffects of the blow to the head. Blessedly, these were growing less frequent. His strength was returning apace.

Tomas preened in front of the mirror. "I do look well," he sniffed, fluffing his hair like a dandy.

Snickering, Helena nodded, adjusting his cravat. "Yes, you do. Your color is back. Any pain?"

"No, I'm fine. Better than the duke. I saw him downstairs, running around like a bee-stung colt." He laughed. "I never thought I'd see any man so eager to marry. He is concerned you will change your mind and ask me to take you home now that I'm able to leave the sick bed." He cast her a sideways glance. "There's no chance of that happening, is there?"

"I'm afraid not, dear," she said, brushing imaginary lint off his shoulders before sighing. "You look so much like papa today. It's almost like having him here."

Tomas bit his lip and grunted, but she could tell he was pleased with the comparison. "Speaking of..." he held up a distinctive cream-colored envelope. It bore her father's seal.

Helena's breath caught. Tears in her eyes, she reached for the letter, but he snatched it back.

"*Stop.* You can be at ease." He held up a finger, anticipating her reaction. "I already read it. Father and mother were caught off guard by the recent turn of events, of course, but they have given you their blessing, along with a demand to bring your new husband home to meet them as soon as possible. Also, the twins are doing well. Both of them are thriving, so there is no need to worry on that score."

He set the letter down on the table. "I suggest we save this for after the marriage ceremony, because it will inevitably make you cry. No one wants to see a bride who has obviously been weeping."

Scowling, he stopped and reached into a pocket, fishing out a handkerchief and pressing it into her hand. "See, you've already begun. Try to think cheerful thoughts, else everyone will whisper that the duke is forcing you into this union."

"No one will think that," she lied. But his logic couldn't be argued with. Two days ago, Helena had received a very poorly spelled missive from Judy the maid. The girl had requested a private meeting.

Assuming Judy wanted to ask for employment at the castle, Helena had gone to meet her. Instead, Judy asked with an appropriately dramatic but heartfelt plea whether or not Helena needed help to escape the demon duke's clutches.

"My cousin Jon is the blacksmith's son. He can take you and your brother to the neighboring village to catch the mail coach. Wait until midnight before you attempt to escape." Judy waved her arms, eyes as round as moons. "You can ride in the back under a tarp so no one will see you."

Taking the maid's hands, Helena had taken gently explained to her that no midnight flights were necessary.

"This is a love match," she told the overwrought girl. "Rest assured I'm very happy, and if you ever need a position, you are more than welcome to apply at the castle."

Naturally, Judy had *not* rushed to accept her offer, but Helena had soothed her fears enough—she hoped—to discourage any further misguided rescue attempts.

Things would improve once she and Lucien had been married for a few months, a year at the most. The inhabitants of the Slide would shed those suspicions after their duke settled into contented domesticity. Perhaps their fears would ease once she and Lucien began their family.

But that would not be for some time. This morning she had brewed a tea against conception. It was one of her mother's recipes, the one the overburdened mothers on their estate came to request from her the most.

Lucien had asked her to prepare it.

"Don't mistake me. I want a family with you—desperately," he'd told her, the earnestness of his expression taking her heart and squeezing it tight. "But until all of this insanity of a mad arsonist and my soul-wandering is under control, I don't want to risk bringing a child into the world. Not until things are calmer."

She had readily agreed. There would be children. Bright, beautiful ones. In a year or so they could revisit the matter. She'd stop drinking the tea. Then there would be a child.

The image of her holding a dark-haired babe nearly took her knees out from under her. It would happen. She would *make* it happen.

Tomas touched her arm, bringing her attention back to the present. "It's time."

Butterflies took flight in her stomach. Pressing a hand to them, Helena looked at the brother and laughed. "I'm about to be married."

He managed not to scowl. "Not if we don't get downstairs."

Summoning a smile, Tomas offered her his arm. Helena took it with both hands, giving him a squeeze. "Thank you for not calling out my husband-to-be."

"As if you would allow me to touch a hair on his head," he groused before covering her hand with his. "You will make him take care of you."

It was an order.

"Never doubt it." Helena patted his arm reassuringly. "Now all we have to do is find your bride. Because you know that mother and father will be turning their attention to you now that I am settled."

Tomas stopped, aghast. He clutched his cane in the other hand. "Oh good lord, you're right. As long as you were unmarried, they were content to leave me to my own devices. But that will be over the minute I come home without you."

Helena patted his arm sympathetically. "There's always Giulia de Colombo."

Her brother grimaced. "That girl has horse teeth."

"This is why she's ideal—you *adore* horses," she teased.

Scowling, her brother led her down the stairs, lecturing her the entire way.

"One can love a horse and still not want their offspring to resemble them."

It was a harsh judgment on Miss de Colombo, but the young lady had been one of those among the local gentry who whispered about Helena and her oddness for years behind her back at all of the local assemblies, so she didn't feel too distressed about it.

In fact, all of the slights and innuendos formative in shaping her personality no longer mattered. She was marrying the man she loved. Not to mention Lucien didn't give a toss about his own blackened reputation. The only thing that mattered was how she felt about him and the life they were going to build together.

Continuing to needle Tomas for no other reason than it made both of them smile, she swept into the ballroom to wed her ghost.

Lucien could hear Helena preparing for bed with Marjorie, the maid he'd assigned to her. He'd selected a likely-looking girl at random out of a group suggested by the housekeeper. However, judging from the girl's giggles and the pleased pitch of his bride's voice he'd made the right choice.

As their duke, Lucien hadn't asked any of his people what they thought of their new mistress. It wouldn't have made a difference if they decided they disliked the idea of serving a foreign-born duchess.

However, their enthusiasm for his new bride couldn't have been clearer. It was obvious in the care they'd taken decorating the ballroom and preparing the wedding breakfast feast. The castle itself had never looked better. The interior rooms were spotless, the gardens and lawns perfectly manicured.

That and every halfway respectable denizen of the Devil's Slide had attended the wedding breakfast. Though some had hung back, intimidated, many had come forward to make a fuss over his new duchess.

There had been a palpable air of excitement, a sense of a new beginning. Even the hot, stifling air of late summer had dissipated, blown away by a cool breeze that enabled them to move the festivities out onto the lawns. The children of the Slide, very few of which he recognized, had run wild.

He could still hear their laughter and screams of delight, all due to his lovely bride.

Unbeknownst to him, Helena and Tomas had organized a series of games and contests for them and then proceeded to wreck his composure and nearly make him swoon like a lovesick youth by joining in.

Now the wedding breakfast had been consumed, and the villagers had finally gone home. More importantly, his large and aggressive brother-in-law had retired to his chamber in another wing of the castle.

And Helena was waiting for him.

After stripping off his shirt and washing up, Lucien resumed his post at the door, listening until the sound of voices died away. It took ages, long enough for his ears to begin thrumming with the over-worked organ in his chest.

Sucking in a sustaining breath, he opened the door to the Duchess's chamber with one hand.

The room was wreathed in flickering shadows, the only source of light the blaze in the fireplace. But despite the lack of light, he could see his bride, Helena's white nightgown glowing like a beacon.

The curtains of the massive four-poster bed were pushed back. She was sitting in the center of the mattress, her knees drawn up. Drawn like a magnet, he drifted to the bed.

"Hello," Helena said in a hushed voice.

"Hello," Lucien whispered back.

They stared at each other before bursting into laughter. Lucien crawled onto the bed.

"I...I'm very happy that you're here."

She giggled. "Thank you."

Lucien wanted to see her expression, but he could barely make out the outline of her face due to the blasted darkness. "We should have come up here this afternoon."

"So you suggested on at least four occasions, but we could not possibly leave our wedding breakfast."

"I strongly disagree but defer to your superior sense of propriety."

It had been a near thing. He'd hovered just behind his bride, fighting the impulse to carry her off so he could be alone with her. But he'd had a difficult time tearing her away from the festivities.

Helena had been a revelation. She had spoken with the minister and his wife with the same ease as she had the butcher and the farrier and his wife and children. Helena charmed them all.

He hadn't even minded that the blasted scholar had been there, squiring his stepmother around and mingling with Harold and the others.

It had felt so good, so right to see how deftly Helena slipped into the role of lady of the castle. More importantly, she'd made him feel like the lord. For perhaps the first time in his life, he felt satisfaction and pleasure in that role.

Lucien had few illusions about himself. Given his affliction, he was a bad bargain as a husband, one destined for madness perhaps sooner than later. There was no way to say when he would begin to devolve. But today, with the help of his people, Helena had experienced something he hadn't realized he could give her—a perfect moment in time.

He would try to give her more of these. As many as he was able.

Lucien reached out for her, intending to pull her into his arms, but he misjudged the distance in the dark. He scooted closer across the mattress. "This blasted castle is too dark."

"That never stopped you before," she laughed. "But I do understand. I want to see you as well. More importantly, I think I can help."

Helena rose up on her knees. Shuffling around, she undid the straps holding the curtains back, tugging them until not even a crack remained.

Plunged into stygian darkness "Err, darling, the point was to see your beautiful face."

Lucien stopped short, gasping when Helena murmured into her hands. A spark unfurled like a seed. It swelled in her hand, growing into a ball bigger than her fisted hands.

"What is this?" he breathed.

"It's what my mother calls the sun spell."

A spell. She had cast a *spell*. Lucien laughed, wiping his face with his hand. "This is magic," he marveled, bending at the waist and leaning closer to inspect the glowing sphere.

"Yes, one manifestation of it. As a child, there was a period of years where I had terrible nightmares. My screams would wake the entire household."

Lucien blinked. Yes, he remembered that. She had confided in him, her secret friend. "You had cause. There was an incident with a hound…"

"Yes, it came to my room after it was attacked. It died in my bed."

Lucien remembered the doe. It had been heading to Hapley House that night, but it hadn't survived long enough to clear the tree line.

The full weight of the reason the beast had been there sunk in. But he didn't share his epiphany. Helena didn't need that image in her mind. Not tonight of all nights.

"I'm so sorry. I forgot that. You must have been terrified." She had been five or six at the most.

"Please forget I mentioned it—it's not something I want to dwell on. Especially not on this night. I'm simply trying to explain the reason my mother taught me this spell. As long as my curtains were drawn and no one could see the light from outside, I was allowed to cast it whenever I wished so I wouldn't be frightened of what might be waiting in the darkness."

Touched by her mother's concern and skill, he reached out to touch the glowing golden ball cupped in his bride's hands. "It's warm," he marveled.

"This spell is designed to mimic daylight, both illuminating and emitting warmth."

"It's beautiful."

Now that he could see her face, Helena's anxiety and concern were clear. "This is the legacy of my family, the one we'll be passing on to our children," she said, eyes grave. "I would have taken greater pains to make that clear had it not been for the fact that magic...magic is also your legacy."

Lucien sucked in a breath. *You knew this.* Tomas and Helena had spoken about it, acknowledging it as a part of reality. And they'd said enough to make him understand it was a part of his as well. But hearing it aloud in this manner was jarring.

Our children will inherit magic. From both of us. What did that mean for them?

No wonder Helena feared his reaction. He could see it in the quiet watchfulness in her expression.

His first impulse was to comfort her, to assure her that all was well. Her words had not been a shock. But he wasn't quite sure how he felt.

"Are you certain I can cast spells?"

Helena nodded. "Someone without our gifts would never be able to do what you do—the ability to leave your body is inherently magical."

His laugh was a touch bitter. "I would not call my soul wandering a gift. More of a curse, really."

"Many of my abilities would not be considered a gift either," she confessed. "But over time I've learned to channel the energy that lives inside me, to use it industriously. And there are compensations. Some very useful and even beautiful ones."

The corner of Helena's mouth turned up and she flicked her hand. The ball of light rose just over their heads and stayed there, a celestial body suspended right over their bed.

A renewed sense of wonder filled his breast. "It really resembles a sun. Why doesn't it burn like a flame?"

"It does not possess that kind of heat, but it could if I fed it more magic." She reached out and took his hand, turning it over so both his palms were up. "Here."

With a gesture, the sphere lowered until it was cradled in his hands. He gasped as the ball of light made contact with his skin. Energy warm and bright coursed through him. Familiar energy.

Then Helena took a deep breath and the sphere pulsed.

His lips parted as a heated rush passed over him. The closest thing to it in his experience were those early experiments with his father's electricity machine. Except it was also nothing like that. This was a million times warmer, more intense, more *right*.

"This is *you*," he whispered in awe after the warm wave dissipated, leaving the tips of his fingers and toes tingling.

Helena nodded. "In a sense. It's my power, my essence. I could have severed the connection, let it live on its own, autonomous. It would eventually dwindle away, burning itself out. But I left the channel open so I could do this…"

Leaning forward, she pressed her hands down on the ball. It flatted, losing integrity until it was running over his hands like water. But the droplets didn't fall to the bed. They coated his hands, running over his skin as if he'd plunged into a pool of liquid sunshine.

Lucien fell back on the bed as the magic coated him, and he began to convulse.

CHAPTER 23

*G*asping, Helena crawled over Lucien as he began to moan, his breath stuttering.

"*Your Grace,*" she cried, slipping back into formality in her alarm. "I'm so sorry. That was not supposed to happen."

The energy was supposed to touch him, to connect them briefly before dissipating on her command. But the golden energy had leapt at him like an eager puppy, covering him like a living blanket before sinking into his skin, leaving it faintly luminous.

Lucien grasped her sleeve, pulling her closer until she was half lying on top of him. "I'm fine. Better than fine."

His words were slurred as if he'd been indulging in fine spirits.

That was when she realized Lucien was not in pain. Quite the contrary. His lips were parted, and his eyes were glazed, shining bright with the light of her magic.

Tentatively, she touched his cheek. Golden light pooled around her fingers, paler than it had been before. Lucien flowed up from the bed, his breath fast. He ripped at the packet of his trousers, pulling off his shirt with clumsy hands. She could hear the sound of fabric tearing, but he didn't seem to care.

He tossed the shirt aside, wriggling out of his trousers, working them off with jerky movements.

Helena was surrounded by a wall of pliable hot steel as Lucien's heat covered her. Then it was Helena's turn to shudder as a bright pulse passed from his body to hers.

"Is it working? Am I sharing it?" he gasped.

But she had no words. Helena couldn't speak. She was glowing too —more dazzling than daylight. And the sensation. Dear God. It was decadent, sinful.

Except it isn't. They were married. This was *allowed.* How was it possible to be on this side of the pearly gates and feel like *this....*

Her breasts were swollen, the sensitive tips abrading the sheer linen of her night rail.

As if he read her mind, Lucien reached down and pulled the hem of her nightgown up, not stopping until she was bare to him.

Another pulse of light coursed between them.

She closed her eyes as Lucien surged over her, the impact of the skin-on-skin contact igniting a blinding flash that forced her to shut her eyes until it faded.

Helena gripped his shoulders in startled surprise. She had put the merest drop of magic in the spell, too little for such a reaction. Except it wasn't just her energy anymore. The gold was threaded through with bright silver, and she knew instinctively that it was Lucien's power with a sense that was neither smell nor taste.

When she lifted her fingers, those starlight bright threads trailed after them, melding together and glowing brighter still. More than should have been possible, as if their energy together was more than the sum of its parts, too great to be contained in either of their bodies.

The fact that her spell had kindled a similar spark from him, like so many things between them, defied rational explanation.

Lucien lifted his head, staring at the connections illuminating the space between them. But though his gaze held a sort of pleased fascination, there was no real surprise or astonishment. He simply accepted that some things *were*, while she knew that such things— even in the realm of magic—should not *be.*

But Helena forgot her misgivings almost immediately. She was in bed with her unclothed, virile husband. Even the rules of magic paled in comparison.

Helena was glowing, and not just with magic. It was the way Lucien was looking at her. "This will be another perfect moment," he rasped, gathering her into his arms.

His words had the intensity of a vow.

"Lucien," she breathed as he settled on her, a delicious weight that made her skin spark and sing.

"Every moment with you is perfect." Helena pulled him closer until his hair roughened chest was abrading the soft and sensitive skin of her breasts.

He took her mouth, his tongue stroking her until she saw golden sparks. She saw them when she opened her eyes as well.

A hot brand rested against her thigh, thick and hot. Helena moaned as Lucien began to piston his hips, rubbing his heat against her slippery folds. He was velvet smooth and iron-hard at the same time. She gasped as his cock stimulated the pearl at the top of her sex.

His lips worked down her neck, tasting and licking down her body until his mouth fastened on her breast. Lucien groaned, drawing hard on her nipple and lathing it with his tongue. The act sent a shot of electricity to her core. Helena gasped, writhing underneath him as he continued to suckle one rosy tip while pinching the other neglected bud with his free hand.

Her sheath clenched, aching and empty. Her hips jerked, and she opened her legs, wrapping them around his hips and drawing him flush against her.

His hands moved up to cup her face.

"Thank you," Lucien breathed. "Thank you for wanting me as much as I want you."

Her breath grew ragged, stuttering as his cock probed her entrance. It should have hurt. It probably did. He was large and thick, and she was much smaller, so much so she felt overwhelmed, so small and delicate in his arms.

Then he was entering her, pushing past the constricting ring of her entrance. He pinned her down to the mattress as he forged a path inside her. Her mouth gaped as Lucien pressed deeper, opening her. The sensitized muscles of her sheath going wild, fluttering as if they were fighting to keep him out when the opposite was true.

"You feel so sweet, so right," Lucien whispered, his breath hot against her forehead as he pulled her hips closer so it felt as if she were participating in his possession, every inch by hungry inch.

It felt as if he were so close he'd become melded to her when he began to pull away.

Helena panicked and attempted to keep him close, but he held her hips, pinning them to the bed as he pulled his hips back

"Trust me," Lucien whispered, retreating until he was nearly free before driving back in.

"Oh God, *Lucien.*" Her lips parted on a silent scream as he continued pressing his hard length through her slick heat until he was buried, this time to the hilt.

Stunned, she wrapped her arms around his wide upper back, her hands spreading over the muscled expanse, his strength highlighted by the flex of steel under her fingertips.

There was someone else in her body. But the sensation was not foreign. It should have been, and yet it was more as if something was clicking into place, a piece of her soul she hadn't know was missing.

Then Lucien began to rock, his hips surging, plunging in and out until it was a regular rhythm. It was gloriously unfamiliar but easy for her to follow. Despite being pinned down by his delicious weight, she found she could participate, rocking with him, her body growing slippery wet to accommodate his relentless strokes that were marking her, claiming her in the most primitive and elemental way.

"I've dreamed of us like this—so many times," he panted in her ear, stopping to lick and suck on the lobe as if he couldn't resist tasting her. "But the dreams don't compare. Not even close."

Shifting, he pressed a long wet kiss to her neck. "My god you feel incredible—so slick and tight around my cock. I really, *really* love this."

Helena muffled a giggle against his shoulder. She sometimes

forgot that in this each was as inexperienced as the other, but neither were they untried and ignorant. They had touched before, shared intimacies on another plane of existence few were aware of. So perhaps it was not so surprising that in this they did not *feel* like novices.

But that did not change the fact that this was the first time she'd felt this—being stretched by a man, with an organ both hard and inexplicably smooth.

"I love loving you too," she said in a halting voice, her breath short as her body began to quicken inexplicably. It was as if with each stroke of his shaft some secret spot was enflamed. "I love—*oh, Lucien.*"

Helena dug her nails into his back as the strange twisting sensation grew in intensity, vaguely aware of Lucien's continued speech. He was praising her, but she was too overwhelmed to respond.

She was burning up, her breasts rocking with each of Lucien's thrusts.

The waves of illicit pleasure were building. She thought the tension would drive her mad until the waves finally crested and that hungry, desperate need broke, bursting over her like a star exploding in the sky.

Helena cried out, whimpering and clutching at him, meeting his surges and thrusts even though it hurt a little, because the pain was inconsequential to the ecstasy.

"I told you," Lucien panted, grinding his hips against her with a broken rhythm, his control in cinders. *"You are mine."*

Those voracious, wet pulses pushed her over the edge, and she fell, clenching and rocking and crying all at once. The climax felt like being turned over and over by a stormy sea. It was accompanied by a glowing flash, as if a sun was going supernova just overhead.

Her sweat-sheened body was still trembling with violent aftershocks when Lucien finally spoke.

"I'm going to crush you," he mumbled into her neck.

Helena gathered him to her, not allowing him to leave her body. "I don't care."

There was a sluggish chuckle, his breath tickling her nape. He rolled over, taking her with him until she was lying next to him, still intimately connected.

Lucien gave her a sheepish grin. "Well, I uh, I think that went rather well."

She snickered weakly, her spent body still recovering. "Agreed."

Her fingers trailed down the bare expanse of his muscular chest. They stopped at the top of his abdominal ridges where their hips were fused together. "The luminescence has faded."

He held up his hand, studying his skin. "So it has. I gather making us incandesce like a will-o'-the-wisp wasn't your intention?"

"No. It was meant to be a transient bond, a way for us to commune, if only for a moment. But my magic, it wanted to be with yours. Instead of being rebuffed as it normally would have been, I believe your magic welcomed mine."

Lucien let his head fall back on the pillow. "Yes, I wouldn't have known that was happening until you explained, but that sensation—it was as if *you* were pouring into me, and then I was able to push something of myself back. Yet it didn't leave me weak. Instead, I felt stronger...and passionately aroused. A most singular sensation."

"Was tonight the first time you were aware of your own magic?"

He squeezed her to him, a thoughtful expression on his handsome face. "As in a force separate from myself?" He stopped to think, stroking the skin of her shoulders reverently. "I do believe it was."

He grinned. "Will we ignite like embers every time we are together?"

"I certainly hope not. I've no desire to restrict our marital relations to the actual marriage bed itself," she laughed, gesturing to the closed curtains around them. "However, as long as we don't begin with that particular spell, we should be safe conducting our, ahem, our business anywhere."

By the time she finished speaking, her face was flaming hot.

Chuckling, Lucien shifted closer, wrapping his arm around her until their bodies were entwined. "Your blush covers your entire body."

She pinched his side in light reprimand. "We've stopped glowing, and it's pitch dark in here. There is no way you could know that."

His sigh was knowing and satisfied. "Oh, I know my love. I know."

He pressed his mouth to her neck, finding her pulse and running his tongue over it before he made it race once more.

CHAPTER 24

*L*ucien had never slept so soundly in his life, but waking up
next to Helena was better than even the best slumber.
Everything was better. Despite his misgivings about his own
mental state, he felt optimistic. Renewed.

Making love to the woman who completed him would do that. It
didn't hurt that he had done what he had set out to do—he gave
Helena another perfect moment. Or judging from her sweet cries,
several of them.

And by giving her that, he'd gotten to experience them himself.

It was tempting to wake her and try to create a few more perfect
moments, but Helena deserved her sleep. So, he lay next to her,
reliving the memories in his mind.

Helena must have parted the curtains in the night, because the
bright morning light was pouring through the beveled glass windows,
illuminating his new bride in all her glory.

She was nestled next to him. The sheets and heavy brocade coun-
terpane were pushed down to her waist. Helena had donned her
nightgown as well while he slept, but the lightweight cloth was sheer
enough that he did not need his imagination to fill in the blanks.

Besides, he planned to divest her of that nightgown the moment her lashes fluttered open. But for the moment he was content to watch her sleep. It was enough to trace the lines of her face and shoulders with his eyes, biding his time until he could do it with his hands.

He was therefore rather irritated when a knock on the door interrupted his reverie. He scowled when Helena's brother opened it, poking his head inside.

Tomas scowled right back.

"Go away," he hissed.

But the stubborn Italian ignored him, jerking his thumb behind him. "Get over here."

Realizing his bothersome brother-in-law wouldn't leave him alone to enjoy his newly wedded state, he climbed out of bed, jerking on his discarded shirt and trousers. "*Fine.*"

"This better be good," he growled, closing the door behind him, grateful Helena had slept through the rude awakening.

Tomas ignored his dark expression. "We have a major problem in the kitchen."

Swallowing his instinctive retort that Tomas had no idea what a problem was—yet—Lucien followed the irascible Italian down to the kitchens.

To his dismay, he discovered his brother-in-law had a gift for understatement.

HELENA DID NOT KNOW who was more surprised to find herself alone in bed—herself or the maid. Assuring the girl that she did not require a breakfast tray, she dismissed the servant with a gentle smile. She dressed without aid in one of her lightweight muslin gowns.

When her husband had not returned by the time she was done, Helena took matters into her own hands. It was too humiliating to go around asking the servants if they knew the location of their master, but Helena was a witch by birth. With the right materials, she did not need to ask the staff for help in determining his whereabouts.

After searching the pillows to find what she needed, Helena made quick work bespelling one of her stone pendants into a rough tracking charm. The polished amethyst stone was bewitched to warm as she drew nearer to her quarry.

In an edifice the size of Blackwater castle, that might not be sufficient help, but a more precise spell would have required an additional half-hour of preparation as well as a map—and perhaps more of the duke's hair.

Since Helena did not want to go hunting for her beloved's hairbrush, she made do with logic, beginning with the most likely places he might be, the breakfast and formal dining room. Those were empty, but the stone warmed enough to let her know that he was nearby.

She tried the adjoining rooms before backtracking and heading into the kitchens.

Helena hadn't had occasion to tour the kitchens, but she was not prepared for the size of the expansive set of rooms or the number of staff. Nor did she expect them to freeze and generally behave as if they'd been caught stealing biscuits from the larder when she walked in the door.

"*Mon Dieu.*" The cook, Madame Boche, who Helena had been introduced to the day swore under her breath before hurrying over to her. She proceeded to offer her a feast for breakfast.

"If you could just wait in the breakfast salon, one of my girls will bring you tea and coffee while you wait," she promised in her broken English.

But Helena was not about to be distracted. It was obvious from their guilty manner and the tension in the air that something was wrong.

She switched to her schoolroom French. "*Merci.* I would love all that and more—especially those eggs coddled in cream that I sampled yesterday. But first I must have a quick word with my husband."

She stepped around the anxious woman before she could stop her. Using the rapidly heating charm as a guide, she made her way to the back of the kitchens, nodding benevolently at the shell-shocked scullery maids.

Like a real duchess, she thought, trying to make herself believe it. It was a bluff, of course.

But she walked with too much confidence for any of them to interfere. With no one to gainsay her, she made her way to the back of the kitchens and through a wide arch leading to a series of store-rooms, several of which had been converted to kitchen pantries.

A disheveled Lucien was standing in deep conversation with her brother, the butler, and the estate manager. The group of men clustered around the narrow open door of one of the pantries, blocking the view of the interior.

Tomas saw her first. He spread his arms out and began to walk toward her. Hands out to block his embrace, she pushed past him.

"It's *Sally*."

Their former cook was sprawled on the stone-flagged floor, her white-filmed eyes unnervingly opaque as they stared unseeingly at the ceiling.

That wasn't the only change. Sally had always been a substantial woman, but now her body appeared swollen, her pale dirty blonde hair liberally streaked with white that had not been there before. But the most alarming difference was the color of her face. The cook's ruddy skin had darkened to purple, her protruding tongue black.

Helena recoiled. "What happened? What is she doing here?"

Lucien grimaced, gesturing to the butler and estate manager to leave them. He wrapped an arm around her as Tomas huddled closer. "She applied for a position under Mrs. Boche. Her only stipulation was that she not be required to serve Tomas directly."

He shot her brother an apologetic glance. "Apologies, but she's part of the small but vocal minority of villagers who hold you responsible for the fire. Or, rather, she was."

"And yet still you hired her." Tomas rolled his eyes but stopped when Helena gave him a hard nudge with her elbow.

"We are in the presence of the dead," she reminded him in Italian.

"Of course," he replied, chastised. He turned to the duke, who merely shrugged.

"We didn't need the help, but I thought taking her on would foster goodwill among the locals."

Helena pressed her hands over her eyes. "And how long has she been lying here?"

It was clear the woman had been dead for some time. But had it been long enough to explain such a dramatic change in her coloration?

She exchanged a loaded glance with her husband, who knelt to take one of the woman's arms. It barely moved. The cooler temperature of these rooms, protected by the thick walls, had ensured the rigor stiffening the body hadn't dissipated.

"She was found toward the end of the wedding breakfast," Tomas confessed. "I told the staff not to inform either of you. I only told Blackwater this morning."

"Tomas," she scolded in exasperation. She adored her interfering brother to bits, but he should have told her about this immediately.

He grimaced and held up his hands. "I'm sorry. But I didn't want to ruin your wedding day."

Lucien sighed, tightening his embrace. "Has the body been moved?"

"No." Her brother shook his head. "She was found here. Her position is unchanged. I had Huggins lock the door and post a footman to guard it until morning. I waited as long as I could before waking Blackwater to give him the news. If we delay any longer before summoning the local magistrate, it might look suspicious."

He turned to her. "And as I was trying to explain to your stubborn mule of a husband here, I wanted you to have a chance to examine the body before it was taken away."

He did not need to explain why.

Helena took a fortifying breath. "Tomas, can you run up to my room and fetch my blue satchel?"

He was gone before she finished the question.

Lucien drew her to his side. "I take it you will need complete privacy for what happens next?"

"Yes." She studied the body. "Poor Sally. It's obvious from the

168

contortion of her features that she was in pain. What a terrible way to die."

～

LUCIEN MADE A COMMISERATING noise in the back of his throat, studying his wife's pensive face. This was not how he wanted to spend his first day as a married man.

At least we had the wedding night before all hell broke loose. And to think, he owed that to Tomas.

"I'll call the men back in," he said, trying to sound more decisive than he felt. "We'll move her to the icehouse and summon the magistrate. He lives a short drive away, but I believe I mentioned that he is old and infirm. Even if we send for him now, you should have enough time to conduct whatever rite or ritual you are planning."

"Good," Helena murmured as they exited the pantry. "We should begin as soon as possible."

Nodding, Lucien summoned the butler and his estate manager with a gesture. A few minutes later the coachman was dispatched, driving the ducal equipage to bring the magistrate.

Tomas met them in the icehouse, where his men had laid out Sally's body on a long, flat table that had been transferred from the greenhouse.

After making sure there was no way for the castle staff to peer through any gaps between the wooden slats of the icehouse walls, Helena began to lay out her materials.

"I thought it best," Tomas told Helena as he added a small bag of salt in addition to the satchel she'd requested.

"Yes, I agree," she acknowledged, tucking an escaped lock of hair behind her ears.

"What is the salt for?" Lucien asked.

Helena decided to demonstrate as she explained, opening the sack and letting the salt stream out in a thin line. She laid a neat circle around the table, leaving enough room for the three of them to walk around the body inside the interior.

"The salt creates an impermeable barrier that magic can't pass. Water would work as well, but we don't have time to create a moat." She set the bag of salt aside and glanced around them. "Also, I have no desire to shift these blocks of ice to create a wall around us."

"There's not enough ice for that."

At this time of year, the ice stores were close to depleted. It would have lasted longer in the castle basement, but the dukes of ages past had never stored their ice there, presumably because the cellars were only accessible via a single set of narrow stairs.

That and the remaining cellar space had once been dungeons. Haunted ice was the last thing this Drury Lane melodrama required.

Helena bustled around the body, examining it from every angle. Her expression was restrained, evincing only a restrained sympathy over her determined professionalism.

It struck him then how grossly inappropriate this was. Last night Helena had been a virginal bride on her wedding night, innocent despite their recent encounters. And this morning she was examining a dead body...

His eyes ran down her back, downcast as he wished this hadn't happened. The two of them should have been in bed, just waking. It should have been a moment of sweetness and discovery.

Frustrated and guilty about the kind of life he was offering her, he made a move as if to stop her. She looked up at him from across the body, correctly reading his intent to gather her up in his arms to carry her out of there.

"There's no need," she told him softly. "I've been my mother's help-mate since I was a girl. Death is no stranger."

"In his defense, the deathbeds you attended with mother were natural—occasionally tragic but ultimately due to any number of prosaic causes." Tomas shot Lucien a dour look. "These instances were always accompanied by a lecture on the natural order of things, the cycle of life."

"You're convinced this is not a natural death?" Lucien asked.

"The streaks of white in her hair and the color of her tongue should be enough evidence to the contrary." Tomas crossed his arms and sat on a crate one of his gardeners or footmen must have left behind. "Helena already knows the cause of death. She dallies to spare your feelings for as long as possible."

There was a beat of silence as she glared at her brother.

Lucien turned to his wife. "What is he talking about? Why would my feelings require special consideration?"

Helena sucked in a draught air sharply between her teeth. She shot her brother a blistering glance. "It is *not* the same."

"What is different?" Tomas put his arms down and craned his neck, to get a better view of the body.

"There is no evidence of crushing damage to the exterior of the throat." Her tone was detached, precise, the way he imagined an instructor at a medical college would sound. "All traces of strangulation are internal, as if the throat were being crushed from the inside."

Tomas flicked his eyes from one to the other. "He could have refined his technique."

"What?" Lucien scoffed.

Then he looked at Helena and felt his soul shrivel, retracting from the borders of his body and leaving empty space behind.

Staggering back, he leaned on a wooden post, needing the support as the world spun away. He shut his eyes. "You...you think it was me."

CHAPTER 25

"*N*o." Helena's voice was sharper than she intended. She hurried around the table, narrowly avoiding tripping on her skirts.

Forgetting herself and the fact she had been handing a dead body, she clasped her husband's too-pale face between her hands.

But judging from the shattered expression on his face, Lucien was beyond caring about such morbid details.

"I don't," she assured him, removing her hands to wipe them on her skirts before pulling him into her embrace.

"This is similar enough to what the men attacking you suffered to ask the question." Tomas sounded almost apologetic, but his words brooked no compromise. "We must evaluate the evidence honestly."

"I am, Tomas. And the fact remains that we know exactly what he was doing at the time of the murder. There are nearly a hundred witnesses."

Taking his chin in her hands, she forced Lucien to look at her. "Listen to me, my love. There is no way for you to have been responsible for Sally's murder."

"I didn't say it was murder," Tomas protested. "Perhaps he accidentally lashed out with his magic, and it struck down a random innocent."

Helena began shaking her head before he finished the sentence. "It simply is not possible. *Trust me.*"

"But— "

"No. You don't understand because you don't have magic," she interrupted her brother. "I was no more than ten feet from him the entire time. I would have *felt* it."

Stung, Tomas flinched. Immediately chastised, Helena rushed to apologize, but her brother waved her awkward efforts away.

"You are right," he said in a formal clipped tone. "You are the expert here. I am insensible to occult forces, and if you say you would have felt it then, of course, he didn't do it."

"*Tomas,*" she breathed, genuinely sorry for the hurt so clearly visible in his eyes.

"I understand," he said more softly, unbending his stiff posture. "Really, I do. Which means we have a rather large problem—someone is out there murdering people with magic."

He rubbed his forehead with the flat of his palm. "It has to be the scholar, right? He was wearing a charm with a well-known rune."

"Not that well known," Helena corrected. "Truth be told, it's rather esoteric. Which would suggest he's very learned in the craft, or it could be a trinket that turned up in his family as he claimed."

"I agree with Tomas," Lucien added. "No one else seems likely. But I also don't want you to think I'm eager to point the finger at someone else."

"We know you wouldn't do that." Tomas was being uncharacteristically generous. "But perhaps we should leave this discussion for another time. Helena needs to do whatever it is she's planning to do. The castle staff isn't a patient lot, and the magistrate is on his way. Not to mention poor Sally's family. They must have heard by now."

"He's right," Lucien said, his voice sounding surprisingly raspy. His throat had swelled, growing tight. "Sally didn't have many friends among the staff yet—she was too new, but she grew up in the Devil's Slide. It won't just be her family asking questions."

He cleared his throat. "We need to construct a plausible fabrication to explain Sally's death. We cannot afford rumors of magic or murder to get around. People will panic. They'll start accusing one another or us of this dark deed. Magic is not a rumor that is ever taken lightly in these parts. And hysteria can be more damaging than murder in a small village. This person knows that. Else they would have hidden the body."

Helena nodded, considering. Then she straightened her shoulders determinedly. "I believe I have an idea that may work, but it depends on the composition of your greenhouse."

"What are you thinking?"

Helena worried at her lip with her teeth. "I'm afraid we have to make it appear as if Sally was a victim of her own ignorance."

She stepped closer to the body, waving her hands over the unfortunate woman's face. "Given the coloration of her tongue and skin, we might be able to pass this off as a case of accidental poisoning. One administered by Sally herself."

Tomas gestured to their former cook's discolored features. "You're going to make it appear as if she poisoned herself with something from the greenhouse? Because I don't recall anything dangerous in there. Nothing that could explain this."

Helena nodded. "I know. But I have a plan. I require a plant from foreign climes—the most exotic specimen you can find. Bring it here, but let no one see it. No one can know what we are doing in here."

Tomas nodded and hurried out to fulfill her request. Lucien brushed his trousers off and came to stand with her. The dizzying, unmoored feeling was dissipating quickly.

His wife had faith in him. That was all that mattered.

"The idea I have is not foolproof. It depends on whether or not the locals, Sally in particular, forage in the woods very much."

"I assure you they avoid the woods like the plague. Even the most determined poachers skirt the exterior. I doubt they go more than half a mile in from the tree line."

He lapsed into silence, chewing on his lip for a moment. He must have looked bereft, because Helena was there, leaning against

174

him. "This is what you looked like as a child," she said, tears in her eyes.

The fact that she was likely right made his heart hurt. "You're certain you would have felt my power lashing out?"

"*Yes.*" Helena was adamant. She took his shoulders and gripped them tightly. "And so would you, because now you know what that feels like. You *know.*"

He gave her a skeptical glance. "My soul wandering can happen without my knowledge."

She shook her head so vigorously a pin fell out of her hair.

"Only in your sleep. However, you were wide awake when this death occurred. Believe me when I say you would have been aware of this—the amount of power leaving your body would have enervated you, especially an uncontrolled release like that."

Her cheeks burned. "And not to conflate two entirely different acts, but you were, er, quite fit last night. Some might say downright vigorous..."

His lips quirked. "That is true. No uncontrolled releases there."

Helena pressed the back of her wrist to her mouth to stifle the sudden and inappropriate case of the giggles.

Lucien stood and leaned closer, pressing his lips to her forehead for a brief kiss. "I'm sorry we aren't there now, enjoying our first morning as a married couple."

"I know. But this only makes me more determined to wrest control of this situation. I'm tired of being caught unawares by every new disaster."

"Agreed." Lucien crossed his arms. "And from your expression, I take it you've thought of a way to do so."

"I have. The way I see it, we have two choices. One is that I begin to train you in the fundamentals of magic. You have too much raw power to continue as you are. You must learn how to use it. Otherwise..."

"What?"

Helena sucked in a deep breath. "I can bind you. No magic would touch you—but you also couldn't wield it."

Understanding lit his eyes. "You can do that?"

"Yes. You would still possess the magic of course, but it wouldn't be able to leave your body. Which is why it must be a last resort."

"Why?" He grimaced. "I would happily consign the soul wandering to Hades. As far as I am concerned, it has served its purpose by bringing us together. Now that you are here at my side as my duchess, I have no use for it."

"Except I'm not certain it would stop your soul wandering," she began cautiously. "That has been happening for so long that I can't be certain it's not an innate manifestation specific to you. I know you can expend energy in that form, as we saw when you rescued me. But the act of traveling itself may require little to no magic on your part."

"I was exceptionally fatigued when I woke that morning," he acknowledged, his expression darkening as if he was recalling the events by the lake.

Determined that he not fall into a pit of self-recrimination for defending her, or worse, begin to suspect himself of Sally's death, she gave his hands another squeeze. "The true reason is that Sally's death is clearly magical malfeasance. Some unknown party is responsible—a practitioner of considerable strength or skill."

"Are they not one and the same?"

"Well, no. That is the whole purpose of spell craft, you see. A spell concentrates and directs your magic. Properly constructed, a spell can compensate for a lack of innate power. A weak but learned practitioner can accomplish a great deal."

Lucien was beginning to understand. "Or a witch of middling power can conserve her strength to wreak even more mischief." He glanced askance at the body. "Although mischief is too weak a word for whatever the hell is going on here."

"Agreed," Helena said softly. "In light of the gravity of the situation, I would hate to bind your magic. It would leave you defenseless."

"I am many things, but defenseless is not one of them. I may not have had the opportunity to train to shoot at Manton's or honed my skills at one of the pugilism clubs, but I still learned how to defend myself."

"Did your father teach you?" she asked hesitantly. He recalled some of the things he'd said about the former duke that must have made her skeptical of the idea.

"Good God, no. I hired men to come up from London to instruct me."

You did?" Helena was startled despite the morbid circumstances.

He shrugged. "A girl preparing for her season hires a dancing master. I hired a highly decorated rifleman who has settled in the next county as well as a fencing master and a pugilist who made a living doing exhibitions. The latter made a tidy sum losing to the dandies of London."

"*Losing to the dandies?* How skilled could the man have been if he regularly lost his matches?"

"I assure you he was a very skilled and shrewd man."

"I see," she said, although the pucker between her eyes suggested she did not. "However, while I have every faith in your formidable skills on the earthly plane, I'm afraid we must prepare for another kind of assault altogether."

"Yes." Lucien's sigh was heavy as he studied the cook's corpse. He'd woken feeling so light and happy, but now it was as if leaden weights were tied to each of his limbs. "I do understand. But it's frustrating—the knowledge that I cannot defend myself."

Helena stepped closer until her skirts were brushing his trousers. "Which is why we must do more than construct a protection charm."

His mouth pulled down. "I thought you didn't want to bind my powers."

"I don't. I have something else in mind, but we'll speak more of it after," she said as Tomas came in holding a small potted tree with bright pink petals, which he'd concealed under his discarded coat.

"Will this do?" Tomas set down the plant on the table.

"Plum blossoms?" Helena stroked the pink petals.

"Chinese plum blossoms," her brother corrected.

"This plant is from Asia?" Lucien stared down at the plant. "How can you be sure?"

"When you grow up with Isobel as a mother, you learn how to

identify every weed, shrub, and flower that grows under the sun, along with the proper Latin name for each. Believe me, Helena and I are experts."

Tomas wiped his brow with his sleeve and raised his brow. "But I fail to see how this will help explain how the cook died."

"This will do nicely," Helena said. "Leave it to me."

Her brother's brow rose. "You're certain you want something this innocuous? There is some nightshade and Valerian root in that green-house that might serve better."

Helena shook her head. "We have no way of knowing how well-versed Sally was in plant lore. We could blame those plants and then learn Sally knew how to administer them. No, we must cast the blame farther afield."

HELENA REACHED for the deceptively capacious blue bag, withdrawing a wax paper envelope. Touching the contents with the tip of an index finger, she withdrew a digit covered in a sooty brown powder. She proceeded to spread it around the roots of the plum tree.

Lucien's brows rose. "I take it that is not dirt?"

"No." Helena wiped her hands on her apron. She cracked her knuckles, shooting the men a brief glance of apology. "It's about time this cursed talent was of some use," she added in a mutter.

Heat began to gather in her palms. It wasn't the bright burn of a flame, more a gentle warming, as if she were immersing her hands in a warm bath. The center of her palms began to itch but quickly subsided as the spores she had spread at the roots began to grow.

The fat white blobs of spherical buds swelled quickly, separating into a cluster of mushrooms.

Directing her energy with determined intent, she altered the form as it grew. She made the bulbous stem thinner, flattening the normally red-brown rounded cap as she changed the color to a brilliant pink several shades brighter than the plum petals. The gills took on a moss-green cast.

"Were those porcini spores?" Tomas asked. He sniffed when she nodded. "Pity."

Helena turned to her husband, who was watching with open-mouthed fascination. "I always carry a few useful spores in case we are waylaid somewhere without the hope of a decent meal."

Lucien blinked. "I realize some mushrooms can grow overnight, but that was startling."

"Making plants and fungi grow in an accelerated manner is a minor talent of mine, one that has been more a hindrance than a help."

"You grew a mushroom and changed its color." Lucien blinked at her several times.

"And the shape," she said, explaining how many alterations she had forced upon the prized edible. "My ability has always altered the natural form of growing things. In fact, this is probably the first time it has been remotely useful. You see, it frequently renders medicinal plants useless. Mushrooms are far more stable, but in this case we should grateful it worked to alter the form so dramatically."

"Has it been rendered poisonous?" Lucien leaned over the gaudy cluster.

"Unfortunately, that is beyond my skill. I figured our best course would be to make the specimen as flamboyant and attractive as possible. Nothing like it grows in these woods. As your new foreign-born Duchess, I'll identify it as a venomous toadstool and hope they don't decide to test the theory by taking a bite."

"That's brilliant." He turned to the body. "Except for the fact we have to make it appear as if she ate it. I don't suppose you can magic her jaw loose?"

The rigor stiffening the corpse would not dissipate for several more hours—far too late to suit them. Even the elderly magistrate wouldn't tarry that long.

"Er...well," she hedged. "No, I was going to attempt something else."

She exchanged a significant glance with her brother as she twisted off a fat pink mushroom and began to crumble to pieces in her hand. Her brother knew what was coming.

"There is no reason it can't work in reverse," she told him.

Tomas grimaced. "At least it won't be as messy."

Lucien's head followed the exchange. "Wha—"

He reared back when Helena walked up to the body, her hands slamming down over the woman's distended belly.

She rubbed until her palms lay flat on the serviceable broadcloth of Sally's dress. When she lifted her hands, the bits of mushroom were gone.

Lucien flinched when she repeated the process—making an audible slapping noise—over Sally's cheeks with a smaller fragment.

"Any way we can introduce a filament or two between her teeth?" Tomas asked.

Helena shrugged and was reaching to try and pry the cook's lips apart when Lucien held up his hands. "I think your work is finished, my love," he said hastily.

He turned to Tomas. "I take it she's done this before?"

"Our mother actually," her brother replied. "One of our father's hounds died unexpectedly. It showed signs of being poisoned. Rather than cutting the poor beast apart in front of us, Isobel pulled out certain remains from the stomach. Personally, I found that more disturbing. She should have just cut the beast."

"You say that now, but he was your favorite hound," Helena said. "Although I admit I wasn't so sanguine at the time either."

Lucien looked from one to the other. "Was the animal poisoned intentionally?"

"No, it ate a poisonous toadstool."

"Ah," he said. "Your inspiration, no doubt."

She nodded.

Lucien threw Tomas's coat over the plant. "Come, we've done our best to make this death unremarkable. Let's take this tree into the castle and leave it someplace we can conveniently discover it—I suggest a shadowed corner of the kitchen gardens. I'll point it out to the magistrate as soon as he arrives."

With that, he hustled both of them out of the icehouse.

CHAPTER 26

*L*ucien was not the least surprised when Sather, the local magistrate ruled Sally's death as an unfortunate case of accidental self-administered poisoning.

"That went surprisingly smoothly."

"I believe I told you Sather wouldn't be an issue," he told Helena as they waved off the magistrate's coach.

"Yes, you did," she said, allowing the strain of the past few hours to bleed into her expression. "However, I expected he would have more questions, especially considering the state of the body."

"Well, as to that, I imagine at his age he's seen worse. He mentioned the various drowning victims he has been called upon to deal with more than once. But thanks to your extensive preparation he was more than willing to accept the explanation we presented him with. Especially once we pointed out the conveniently situated evidence in the kitchen gardens."

Her pensive expression did not soften. "Still, I am surprised he swallowed the story."

Lucien shrugged. "I believe I warned you that he was not the type to bestir himself when presented with a mysterious death. Especially when the mystery has been solved for him. It does not hurt that you have a decided air of authority when discussing medical matters. Indeed, I think you established a reputation today. I would not be surprised if the curious castle staff were to start approaching you for help when they fall sick after this."

"Oh." Helena paused, her face lighting up. "I would be happy to take charge of those duties, provided Jocelyn has no objections. I haven't had the opportunity to speak to her about taking the reins of her charitable endeavors."

"To be honest, my stepmother has always been a rather absent-minded Lady Bountiful. She makes an effort to take small gifts to the tenants during the weeks of Christmas and Easter—if she happens to be in residence. But otherwise, Jocelyn doesn't bestir herself. She's too busy with her scholarly pursuits. The tenants and village locals are accustomed to her ways. If they require aid for more serious issues, they make their inquiries to my estate manager as they did during my father's time."

"Well, in that case, I'll give thought to establishing a more robust tradition," she said with growing enthusiasm.

Taking her arm, Lucien pulled her closer, pressing a kiss on her forehead before guiding her toward the stables. "My tenants will be fortunate to have you, as am I. But for the moment I must leave you in the care of your brother. I need to call at the bakery to extend my condolences to Sally's family. I expect we'll adjourn to the Bucket for a time."

He noted her puzzled look. "Everyone leans on Harry at times like this," he explained. "His presence will make this easier."

"What if the scholar is there?" She reached out to take his arm. "I haven't had time to make you a protection charm."

"Even if Nigel Ellison is responsible for Sally, as your brother believes, he won't risk calling attention to himself with another great act of mischief. Not in front of an audience. I expect the Bucket will have more than its share of visitors today. Events such as these always make the crowds gather to gossip over a pint."

She hummed, nodding absently. "Are you planning on giving Sally's father money? A small bereavement gift?"

"Should I? Don't you think he might find it suspicious?" He paused, looking around to make sure there was no one close enough to overhear them. "I would not want him to feel as if we were trying to bribe him into accepting her cause of death."

"I don't think he would take it as such. My father always made such a gift when a tenant or laborer died in unforeseen circumstances. As long as you make it clear you consider Sally's death a terrible accident, he's unlikely to question it."

"I suppose that's true." He pursed his lips. "I can say you gave me the idea, because of your father."

Her eyes narrowed in question.

Lucien lifted a shoulder. "We have no such tradition at the castle. My father was notoriously tightfisted—except when it came to his scientific apparatus. He begrudged every book Jocelyn purchased and was constantly complaining about the high fees he paid for my tutors. But when it came to his burning lenses and every new and improved electricity machine, no expenditure was too great."

She put her hand on his arm. "Our marriage is going to be very different from the one your father and Jocelyn shared."

Heedless of the eyes in the courtyard he pulled her into his arms, kissing and embracing her tightly before leaving her and Tomas to their preparations.

Lucien needn't have worried about the baker blaming them for the death of his daughter. The grief-stricken man said little, but what he did manage to convey was a concern that as the duke he would blame Sally's family for blemishing his wedding day. But Lucien's reassurances, and the promise of the bereavement gift, went a long way to assuage his concerns.

"Tis a fine tradition, this gift," Harry said once the man had left. He wiped the counter down with his ubiquitous towel. "You say her grace's father makes these gifts after these unfortunate accidents? Very generous, aren't they, these Italians? And very kind of you to adopt the practice."

"It's the least I can do," Lucien said, finishing his pint before making his excuses. Harry didn't mind. Everyone understood he was eager to get back to his new duchess.

But when he returned, Helena was busy clearing out the long-abandoned stillroom next to the greenhouse. She was determined to ready it for her spell craft and healing work as soon as possible, her priority to create a protection charm for him. After leaving a footman stationed discreetly outside the stillroom, he went to talk to his mother, only to find Jocelyn packing.

"There you are, my dear," she said, rising and taking both his hands in hers. Her usual air of distraction had been replaced with a decisive, urgent determination. "I pray you don't see this as an abandonment. I meant to speak to you in a few days about taking another trip abroad in a few weeks—to give you and your new bride privacy after the wedding. But I confess the death of that poor kitchen girl has me unsettled. I've decided to depart at once. I hope you don't mind."

"Of course not." He returned her embrace with affection.

"Are you sure? I wouldn't want your Helena to think it's because of her—some imagined slight. I do genuinely like her and approve of your choice of bride."

"Thank you, and I assure you she will not think that," he said, warming to the idea of Jocelyn's departure.

I should have thought of sending her away myself. For her safety.

"You've been nothing but welcoming, and I appreciate it," he added aloud. "And while I know better than to try and dissuade you from one of your collecting trips abroad, rest assured you'll be welcomed back with open arms."

Jocelyn gave him a sheepish shrug. "I also might spend more time in London now that I know you won't be here knocking about the castle on your own alone. It's been an age since I spent any length of time in town."

Lucien nodded, wondering why he felt a little guilty. It wasn't as if he'd restricted her travel to London. Jocelyn had chosen to spend her time away on the continent. She could have easily chosen town. Unless she felt obligated to keep him company when in England.

Did that mean she only felt free in Italy or Spain?

"Of course." He cleared his throat. "The season is still some weeks away, but there is no reason why you shouldn't partake. You can open Blackwater House, go to the theaters, and attend a few balls. Who knows, now that I am a married man, I may join you at some point. Helena has never experienced a London season. She may find it amusing."

"Are you sure that is wise?" Jocelyn's clear brown eyes widened. "With your affliction, isn't it better to stay close to home where it's quiet and calm?"

His stepmother had always theorized his problem grew worse when he was agitated and excited.

He gave her a reassuring pat on the shoulder. "It goes without saying that I would be extremely cautious, but I am no longer as concerned about my little problem as I once was."

"No?" Her pale brown brows disappeared under the frizzed and messy coils of her coiffure.

"I detested the need for a keeper in my youth, but a wife is a different thing entirely, isn't she? I doubt anyone will question why a newly married man is living in his wife's pocket."

Jocelyn beamed. "No, they wouldn't. Not when that wife is as lovely as your Helena."

She put her hands together and squealed like a child. "Oh, this is exciting. Everything is changing. You're married. Soon you'll be filling the nursery. Oh, I do so want a babe to hold and cosset."

He laughed despite himself. "You'll have them soon enough."

Just not as quickly as she hoped.

He bid her goodbye, deciding he'd had enough.

Whatever his talented bride wanted to do to him, he would consent. It was time to wrest control over his magic and his life. Because he wanted to have a child with Helena. Eventually.

First, he wanted to travel. They would visit Helena's family and see the wonders of the world.

Helena would help him stop soul-wandering. Once that was dealt with, the only thing standing between him and the life Lucien dreamed of was the scholar.

And he was not about to let Nigel Ellison get in his way.

CHAPTER 27

*H*elena leaned over her crucible, peering at the herbs as she slowly reduced them to powder.

There. The invisible vapor was finally emanating the correct scent, a pungent clay smell at odds with the normal odor of the living plants. She was almost done adapting the spell required to create a protection spell for Lucien. All that was left was reducing...

Helena swore under her breath as the dry herbs morphed from a dry grey-green to black ash. Turning away, she rested her forehead against the wall, resisting the urge to bang it against the plaster surface.

Several weeks had passed since the excitement of the wedding, and she was no closer to adapting the ritual to create a protection charm for Lucien.

It wasn't her recollection of the intricacies. With her excellent memory and the journals she had brought with her, the actual steps to the procedure were not in question. The problem was her ingredients.

The ritual called for a certain combination of minerals and herbs, each precisely calibrated to meld into a unique potent vapor she could pass an object through, a stone or a necklace. Once the desired charm had been covered in the steam, it would absorb the entirety of the vapor, imbuing the object with an ability to deflect or bind magic.

None of the ingredients were particularly rare. Between her and Tomas, it had been a relatively simple matter to gather them. But the problem was that these ingredients, specifically the herbs, were different here.

Helena was prepared for this to some extent. There could be a great deal of variation within a single species of plant, sometimes almost as much as between them. She was aware of this and could compensate, usually by altering the amounts of the starting material. At least she could under normal circumstances. But it appeared that the differences between the English and Italian versions of the requisite plants were too great.

It wasn't an insurmountable problem. But overcoming it would take time and patience, commodities Helena didn't have a great deal of. She *had* to protect Lucien.

There was a great deal of irony in her situation. Her grandmother Helena had created this spell using Scottish herbs. Her mother had spent months adapting it to work with Italian plants in order to craft a protection spell for Matteo, her father. And here she was trying to reverse all of that hard work.

The original Scottish recipe would have been far easier to adapt.

At least there was no immediate need for the charm. There had been no sign of Nigel Ellison in the weeks following the wedding.

According to her brother and Lucien, Mr. Ellison had sent a note to Jocelyn a few days after the wedding, wishing her a good voyage with a charming hand that had greatly pleased the older woman. Then Jocelyn herself had departed for London with a flurry of bustling maids, trunk-carrying footmen, and a great deal of hand waving.

Lucien had joked that she'd taken half the contents of her study in her trunks. But Helena could tell that he was affected by his stepmother's departure.

"I've been holding her back," he confessed one night as they lay holding each other, sated from their lovemaking. "It's good that she's taking advantage of your presence to go off and enjoy the pleasures of town. I know she always felt guilty leaving me alone here. But as soon as we solve my soul wandering problem, we can join her."

"Or perhaps we can set our sights a bit higher," Helena suggested. "I know my parents will be eager to meet you."

Lucien sat up, the sheets pooling around his waist. "You know, I was thinking the same thing."

Her lips parted. "You were?" Helena had been concerned her new husband might not be ready to venture so far abroad, not for a long time.

But she needn't have worried. Lucien was thrilled by the idea of traveling to the continent. He began to pore over maps in the library, planning routes to tour the entire continent, including a stop of several months in Santa Fiora.

In the meantime, she, Lucien, and Tomas had the castle to themselves. Though Jocelyn's company had been more than pleasant, Helena was relieved that she was gone. There was no longer a need to be circumspect in their speech, no requirement to hide their research or their many failed attempts to create the protection charm.

Speaking of which…

"Damn," she muttered as she accidentally knocked over the bowl, spreading powder ash in the air that made her cough. "Damn and blast," she repeated for good measure after she cleared her throat.

"Thank you for swearing in English that time darling, but it is no longer necessary to translate your frustrations. Your dear brother has been teaching me all manner of colorful Italian phrases."

Helena turned to face her brother and husband as they came in the stillroom door. "Hello," she said, accepting Lucien's kiss as she wiped her hands on the apron that protected her new day dress.

Lucien insisted on sending for an exclusive London modiste to create a new wardrobe. "Your lovely Italian gowns will soon be inadequate for winters in the Devil's Slide," he'd argued.

She had relented on the condition he also refresh his wardrobe. As fond as she was of the castle, there was no way Helena would be content to stay there without the promise of traveling again. And as fine as her husband looked in his snug breeches, trousers were steadily eclipsing them in popularity.

But she would miss those breeches…

"No luck with the reduction?" Tomas asked, setting down a mid-sized chest onto a nearby table.

"Not yet. But it's only a matter of time," Helena said with more confidence than she felt. It would not do to let them know how poorly things were going. She didn't want either of them to worry.

Fixing a smile on her face, she waved at the chest crowding her supplies to one side. "What is this?"

"It was just delivered…It's from home, from mother."

Helena's breath caught, hesitating halfway to the table. "*Oh.*"

Neither Tomas nor Lucien spoke as she closed the distance to the trunk. She reached out, caressing the wood between the metal bindings. There was a moment of connection, a double-layered streak of warmth that went straight to the center of her chest.

Her mother had packed this trunk, but her father had locked it, no doubt securing the straps tight in preparation for the sea voyage.

With a shaky smile, she undid the bindings and lifted the lid. The top layer contained four letters, one from each of her parents for her and Tomas.

Handing him the missives addressed to him, she tore open the one addressed to her in her mother's hand. But the words wavered and danced because of her tears. She put her hand on the top of one of the cloth bundles at the top of the trunk, then frowned as a familiar scent wafted up to tease her nose.

She caught the bundle in her hands. It was a satchel made up of clean unbleached cotton, one of her mother's favored methods of storing dried herbs. Turning to her brother, Helena brought it up to her nose for a deep sniff.

"She knew—somehow she knew what we'd be doing."

"That doesn't surprise me," Tomas said dryly.

"What is it?" Lucien glanced from one to the other. "What is going on?"

"This is a type of Calendula from our garden." Helena quickly scanned beyond the first few lines of her mother's missive, putting down the satchel and digging through the first layer. The trunk was full of similar parcels and glass jars.

"My mother had a dream. It didn't tell her what we needed these ingredients for. All she knows is that we do."

She looked up at Lucien and her brother, unable to hide the relief she was feeling. "In time I would have been able to modify the rite enough to use the local plants, but we no longer have to wait. My mother has sent everything we require and more, including things she uses in her healing practice."

"No doubt mother sent a bit of everything she had on hand," Tomas said with a grin. "I also got a trunk. Mostly sweets, but my favorite saddle arrived as well. I suspect that was father's addition, however. He wouldn't have needed a prophetic dream to tell them I would want it."

Laughing ruefully, she began to unpack her treasures, enlisting Lucien's help so she could begin to instruct him in the various uses of each plant and mineral.

Her husband didn't have an overwhelming urge to learn the craft, but he acknowledged his lack of knowledge in the area had left him vulnerable. Consequently, he was a willing, though not over-eager, pupil.

Once the trunk was unpacked, the preparations for the protection spell were a mere formality.

They gathered in the stillroom she claimed for her use the next day.

"Are you going to use bespell ink?" Tomas asked, picking up the preparation she was going to burn to create the vapor.

"Not yet." Helena turned to her husband, who was holding fingering the medallion he'd chosen to be made into a protection charm. "As you can see, he's chosen something less permanent. It's safer."

"Are you certain?" Tomas was skeptical. "To me, it seems the opposite is true. Trinkets can be lost."

"At this moment, flexibility is paramount," she explained. "In time

Lucien will learn to use his magic. But having a fixed protection charm inked onto his skin from the outset will hamper that development, perhaps stifle it altogether."

"Wait." Lucien lifted a dark brow. He turned to Tomas, startled. "You have a tattoo?"

Tomas responded by stripping off his waistcoat and undoing the buttons of his linen shirt. He parted the sides to reveal an intricate design inked over his heart around the size of a man's fist.

The design was deceptively simple—a series of interlocking circles were connected by small triangles. It was only on closer inspections that one realized the heavy lines of the design were elaborate sigiled phrases, words of protection.

Lucien bent closer, studying the fine details. "The only tattoo I've ever seen is on old man Kelso in the village. He was a sailor in his youth. By comparison, his is quite crude. This must have taken a great deal of time and patience on the part of the artist."

"It did," she confirmed with a grin. "The artist was my mother. She designed this protection sigil, originally for my father. His is older and a touch rougher but no less intricate. Mother has added to it over the years. She never wants him to be vulnerable to magical attack again."

He rounded on her. "*Again?*"

She gave him a small smile as her brother closed his shirt and began to redress. "That is a story for another time. Now that I have everything in readiness, I am eager to proceed."

He nodded in acknowledgment, stepping out to allow her to focus on her task.

It took a few hours. By the time all was ready, Helena was in a steam-filled room. It was so thick she could barely see her own hand in front of her face.

"Helena! Are you still in here?" The sound of Lucien's voice was quickly followed by a crash.

"I told you she's fine." Tomas's voice was a touch more distant as if he had prudently waited by the door. Her husband on the other hand…

Another crash, closer this time.

"Darling, please do stop moving lest you tip over the table. This will only take a moment."

Helena held up the medallion over her head. *"Colligentes ut."*

The mist swirled, gathering into thick strands with a swirling sucking noise. They coalesced on the hard surface of the medallion. The pearls of liquid were opaque but quickly dissipated as it was absorbed into the metal itself.

"That was remarkable." Lucien's eyes were as round as the medallion when she slipped the chain over his head. "Truly wondrous."

His approbation warmed Helena's heart.

"Keep this on at all times, but never forget this protects you only from magical peril. If you fall off your horse, it cannot stop you from breaking your neck, so ride with care this afternoon."

It was the one activity that brought pleasure to both Lucien and Tomas, so she encouraged it, but she didn't pretend not to have any qualms about how fast they rode.

"We always take care," her brother said, bussing her cheek on his way out the door.

"I mean it," she admonished as Lucien lingered for a longer, more private parting. "I've seen the way the two of you race and jump your mounts. He brings out your competitive side."

He gave her a broad grin. "Tomas is the one you should be lecturing. The man could goad Santa Christina into a race or a bet."

"In that you are well-matched, I think." Helena sent him off with a kiss, the tight little spring of anxiety loosening.

Her men were as protected as she could make them. There would be no more incidents of soul wandering as long as Lucien wore the medallion.

But Helena couldn't afford to rest on her laurels. She knew her job was only half done. The rest would be complete, her family protected, when they found and dealt with Nigel Ellison.

Sooner or later, the scholar would return. Too much death had meted out for it to be otherwise.

When he showed his face, they needed to be ready. She had more spells to prepare.

CHAPTER 28

*H*elena and Lucien retired early for the evening. They left Tomas in the library, composing a letter to their parents. He was informing them that they would soon be traveling home for a visit.

The protection charm had worked reliably to prevent Lucien's soul from wandering for the past month. Helena was confident it would continue to do so. Lucien was eager to leave the Slide and Blackwater Castle for a leisurely tour of the continent, including an extended stay with her family.

First, they would deal with a few outstanding matters, including the one they all considered critical. But tomorrow was soon enough for more discussion of the scholar.

She had far more pleasant plans for the evening.

"Have you noticed that my brother always makes it a point to excuse himself before we do every evening?" Helena's lips couldn't repress a broadening grin.

They were walking up the stairs at a sedate pace, but only because she was hampered by her tight skirts.

"He does not want to picture what we do when we leave him at

195

night, so it's more expedient for him to leave us," her husband replied with a salacious wink.

She laughed, realizing it was very likely true. Helena was about to make a quip about her brother's delicate sensibilities when they were interrupted by the sound of running footsteps.

Tomas skidded to a stop at the foot of the stairs, visibly panting. He took a moment to recover. "He's here. Ellison is back in the Slide."

Lucien turned, giving her his arm so she wouldn't trip as they rushed back down the stairs. "When?"

By mutual silent agreement, they retired to the library. Once safely ensconced where the servants had no chance of overhearing, Tomas resumed his report.

"Mr. Ellison returned to the village this afternoon."

Tomas went over to the sideboard to pour two brandies and a sherry. Helena accepted the glass he handed her, a small fortification for the discussion ahead.

"He's taken his old rooms at the Bucket, told Harry that it would be for a few weeks."

"How do we know this?" Helena frowned, sipping her drink. The sherry was cloyingly sweet, but her brother wasn't about to pour her a whiskey.

Lucien would if she but hinted at it.

Tomas took a large swallow, making one of those male noises of satisfaction as the liquid burned down his throat. "I asked Harry to send word should he return. I implied that I missed his company."

Lucien considered that. "Did Ellison say where he went?"

Tomas shrugged. "He told Harry he was touring Roman ruins in nearby towns for a time. He took the rooms for a few weeks but suggested it might be for the entire autumn."

"That's a long stay." Lucien rubbed his chin. "I wonder what he has planned."

He and Tomas exchanged knowing looks.

"No doubt he will call on us shortly to renew his acquaintance with the castle inhabitants." Helena pursed her lips. "Perhaps he will ask to use the library, as Jocelyn invited him to do."

Tomas leaned forward, resting his forearms on his knees. "What is our next step?"

Helena bit her lip, considering the question. "I think as the duchess in residence I should extend an invitation to call. After all, Mr. Ellison is a valued acquaintance. He was at our wedding. We would merely be observing the proprieties to have him over to tea."

"And what will be in this tea?" Her brother raised his eyebrows suggestively.

This answer was considerably easier. "Just a few herbs that would make him a bit talkative. Perhaps a little burdock and a touch of the poppy to make it a pleasant experience."

Tomas reclined in his seat. "Well, that would definitely make him speak."

"Isn't opium more likely to put him to sleep? It is the primary ingredient in laudanum, after all."

"Not the way Helena would use it."

Lucien frowned. "What happens if he doesn't take tea? He turned Jocelyn's offer of refreshment down several times in my hearing."

"He did?" Helena frowned. She had not known that.

Tomas scoffed. "What self-respecting Englishman turns down tea?"

Lucien shrugged. "Perhaps he prefers coffee. I'm not certain Jocelyn offered him any. But we shouldn't count on adulterating his drink, just in case."

Judging from his expression, Tomas shared Helena's displeasure at this news. "We'll need a second snare."

Lucien set aside his empty glass on a nearby table. "I don't suppose we can just tie him up and throw him in the dungeons until he talks?"

The corner of Helena's lip curled. "No, but the idea has merit."

He perked up. "It does?"

"I think the library will serve better than the dungeons should Mr. Ellison return and eschew tea."

Helena stood. "Can we move this table over the carpet?"

Lucien rose. "Of course." He gestured to Tomas, bidding him to rise. "Between the two of us, I think we can manage."

She stopped him with a hand on his arm. "First, we need to roll back the carpet. I'll need some chalk as well."

Tomas fished a piece out of his pocket. Helena took it with a questioning look. "I thought it best to be prepared, since you never are."

Helena rolled her eyes. "This dress does not have pockets. I'd like to see how well you fare wearing a gown this constricting."

Lucien threw back the last of his whiskey. "Clearly we need to have a word with your modiste. Did I mention that my grandmother favored masculine attire?"

"Did she?" She was really starting to really like this ancestor of his.

He hummed. "It's in her diary. Apparently, she and her lover were quite fond of setting the stage, as it were."

She chuckled as Tomas's brow puckered in confusion, but he did not ask for clarification.

Helena spent the next few hours drawing a circle, one unlike any other she had ever drawn. Lucien and Tomas helped as best they could, by bringing her books and refreshments. It was well past midnight by the time she was done.

"Be sure to avoid smearing the design," she said, hovering as Tomas and Lucien lowered the heavy Aubusson carpet over the circle.

She had drawn the lines as thick as she could without making the runes illegible to prevent exactly that. But it was a very heavy carpet, and the two men were struggling with it.

In the end, it took all three of them to position it over the circle without damaging it.

When they were done, they moved the table, positioning it so that the occupant of the chair would be seated in the center of the circle.

"Will it drain his magic?" Lucien asked.

"No." Helena paled. "I can't do that."

"Why not? Draining Ellison of his magic sounds like an excellent plan to me."

"I know. But…"

"It would nullify the threat he presents."

"You don't understand." She cast a pleading look in her brother's direction when Lucien persisted.

"She's right. It would make us no better than him," Tomas murmured.

Sensing the undercurrents, Lucien relented, waiting for an explanation.

"It's what black witches do, you see," she explained in a halting voice.

Helena wiped the chalk dust off with a spare handkerchief. Her eyes were on the bookshelves, but she wasn't seeing them.

"It's a very violent act. Black witches drain the magic of others with circles. They feed on it. If they take too much—and a black witch always aims to take it all—then the person inside the circle dies. They gain the magic, but a person can only hold so much. Eventually, the magic is spent, or it dissipates. Draining is a parasitic act."

Helena broke off, shuddering. Had it not been for her mother, that would have been her fate. She put her hands over her throat. It hurt. And her heartbeat had picked up merely from discussing such dark matter. "They can do it to beings without magic as well, taking their life-force. Many spells call for the death of small creatures. The release of energy is harnessed to catalyze the reaction."

"Have you ever done that?" Lucien frowned. "With insects, I mean?"

"No, but my great-grandmother Helen did on occasion. Only very small things, like birds or insects. She wrote that a competent and trained witch did not require more. There's a skill to it. With practice, one can become very efficient, enough that larger sacrifices are not required. My own mother found that harvesting a plant was enough. But then she is highly proficient."

Lucien's expression was of curiosity mingled with relief. "I see. Well, I hadn't considered the requirements of your craft in great detail, but it's good that we won't need to capture the castle vermin or local fowl for experimentation or your lessons."

Tomas chuckled and refilled their brandy, a reward after their exertions moving the furnishings.

"The rumors of my family's proclivity for the occult never truly die down, as you are well aware. But I would hate to see what sorts of things they would fabricate if the castle's livestock were to start disappearing."

Lucien pivoted, considering the drawing hidden under the carpet. "If it doesn't drain Ellison, then what does the circle do?"

"It forms a barrier, one fed by the magic of the person."

"What if they have protection?" He tugged on the chain that held his medallion by way of explanation. "You said Ellison had some."

"The circle works regardless of whether or not the stragone has a protection charm, as we suspect Mr. Ellison does. Though he could deflect a magic strike, he cannot stop the circle from reflecting his own."

Tomas broke out into a grin. "A self-sustaining prison. Brilliant."

"So only someone who possesses magic would be trapped?" Lucien shifted uncomfortably. "Because I'd hate for one of the maids to stumble inside. Not that that's a great danger—I've requested that the staff not enter this room, not even to clean. But one cannot depend on absolute obedience."

"They'll be quite safe," she assured him. "Only a person with our sort of gift can be trapped."

"Good." He sighed, lifting a hand to rub his face. He missed and slapped his own ear.

Tomas laughed as he began to back out of the room. "I believe that's a sign we should all retire. Tomorrow will be here before we know it, and we can't be sure Ellison will wait for an invitation. He may call at his earliest convenience. Which means Helena must prepare his special blend first thing in the morning."

"He's right." Lucien reached for her, taking her hand. "Let's get some rest while we can."

Helena hesitated. She wanted to blend the herbs for the special tea now, but the hour was late, and this was not the London season. Blackwater Castle kept country hours. She was accustomed to rising early. If she continued tonight, her fatigue might lead to mistakes in mixing up the brew. And as much as she wanted to confront Nigel Ellison, she did not want to accidentally poison the man.

"Very well. The tea can wait till morning." They retired, too exhausted to do anything but bathe and fall into bed.

But despite the luxuriousness of said bed and Lucien's solid comforting presence, Helena could not sleep. She was afraid of what might happen tomorrow.

What if Ellison attacked straight off as that stragone did all those years ago, evading their carefully laid plans?

She would defend her family, of course. But what if she had to take more extreme measures? Could she...kill?

There may not be another path.

She of all people knew that the hunger of a black witch could never be satisfied. And as strong and capable as Lucien was, his lack of training in the craft made him vulnerable. Tomas too was a possible target. A stragone would not hesitate to go through him to get to the prize Lucien presented, that of a powerful but unskilled witch.

When she put it in those terms, her course was clear. Helena would do whatever was necessary to protect her family.

Her grim decision made, she fell into a fitful sleep. But it was still dark when a cold breeze roused Helena. She opened her eyes to find herself alone in the bed, the curtains of the huge four-poster drawn back.

The huge casement window that led to the ramparts was open. It lay discarded on the floor. Illuminated by a shaft of moonlight was the St. Christopher medallion, the chain links broken.

Lucien was gone.

CHAPTER 29

$\mathcal{T}$he wind drowned out Helena's panicked cry. She scrambled out of the bed, her heart beating so hard and fast it was threatening to burst out of her chest.

Stopping only to scoop up the medallion, she ran to the open window. She leaned over the edge, terrified that she would see Lucien's broken body lying on the paving stones of the courtyard below.

To her great relief, the stones were empty, but she did not have a chance to take a breath before she caught sight of movement straight ahead.

Lucien was walking on the ramparts. She began to call out to him before thinking better of it. His movements were jerky and uncoordinated. If he wasn't soul wandering, he might be sleepwalking. Attracting his attention now could send him over the edge.

"Is that *me?*"

Startled, Helena jumped. Lucien's voice was right next to her. What's more, she could *see* him—at least a transparent and slightly amorphous version of him.

It was as if she was viewing a reflection of him through a haze of smoke. His image was sharper and almost clear in the center but hazy at the edges in a way that made her eyes water.

She jerked her head back to the parapet. Lucien's body was still moving, shambling to the end of the ramparts.

"Stop," she screamed nonsensically. Lucien was next to her, not in control of his body.

And yet for a moment the empty shell of her husband hesitated. But it only lasted a moment. Then his body lurched forward like an automaton, a puppet being led on strings.

She sucked in a sharp breath. That was it. Of course, she should have known. Someone else *was* in control of Lucien's body.

And they always had been.

Lucien's transparent image flickered again. "What happens if I fall?"

Helena shuddered, grabbing the window sash and pushing it wide. "The soul cannot live without the body," she said, climbing out onto the narrow ledge.

"*No.*" Lucien's image began to flicker. "You can't go out there. The ramparts are crumbling. Get Tomas."

"There's no time."

Helena didn't hesitate. She began to make her way across the parapet.

The wind whipped across her face, lifting her long, loose hair and slapping it across her face, obscuring her vision. She cursed the fact that she'd been too tired to braid it. Using one hand, she tucked the mass of it into the neckline of her nightgown at her back.

"Helena, go back."

She didn't turn her head to know Lucien's spirit had followed her out onto the ramparts. He was practically shouting in her ear. "Please stop distracting me."

She was having enough difficulty keeping her balance, and the unnaturally high winds were very strong. She was in danger of being knocked clear off the ramparts.

Hunching her back, she tried to make herself smaller but was forced to get down on her knees when the wind continued to buffet her nearly to the edge.

"Turn around and get Tomas." Lucien's voice had taken on a preternatural resonance.

Rain began to spatter all around them. A drop hit her square in the eye, temporarily blinding her.

"*You* get him," she snapped. Lucien was visible to the naked eye. He must have tapped into his own magic to do so. That probably meant Tomas could see him too.

She was about to insist when the rampart suddenly gave way beneath her.

HELENA WAS right to ignore him. Her situation and her balance were unstable enough. Lucien was about to jump off the rampart when the stone under Helena crumbled under her feet.

His wordless shout vibrated the very air around them.

Lucien threw himself forward, making a desperate grab, but his hands passed through Helena's.

And yet she didn't fall.

Helena had managed to catch one of the jagged lips of stone and decaying mortar that used to be the rampart.

He looked down to see Tomas stumbling into the courtyard, pulling on a shirt as he went. The Italian took in everything at a glance. He started to run, heading for the stone steps across the courtyard, but there was no way he would reach Helena in time. Her position was too precarious.

There was no choice. He had to get back into his body. But the chasm in the ramparts separating him from it was at least six feet in length.

His wife, his reason for living—she had no time.

Wait. If he didn't have a body, he couldn't break it, could he?

Not thinking about it, Lucien took a running start, jumping over Helena and the gap. He didn't think of the physics or mechanics as he landed with a jolt that would have rattled his teeth if he had any. He sprinted down what was left of the rampart. Too afraid to look back, him he slammed into his own body...and bounced off.

"No, no, no." Spinning around, he shouted for Tomas. "I can't get back in. Get Helena."

But it wasn't Tomas who answered him.

"Bloody hell," a new voice said.

He whipped around to see a man's figure on the rampart just behind Helena, his white-blonde hair gleaming like silver in the moonlight.

In one electric glance, their eyes met, and Lucien realized Nigel Ellison could see him.

Then Ellison began to run straight for Helena.

HELENA'S ARMS WERE SCREAMING. She was sure every muscle in them was torn, and her fingers were bleeding, but she lacked the strength to pull herself up. The only reason she hadn't fallen yet was that she had managed to wedge the tip of her toes into a crack in the mortar of the wall below the hole in the rampart.

Though she could not see him, she knew from Lucien's shout that he'd failed to reclaim his body.

Mio Dio. I'm going to fall.

She wouldn't survive the fall to the courtyard below. Or if she did, she'd wished she hadn't. Her body would be too broken. She'd be an invalid for the rest of her life.

The cramped muscles in her left hand lost their grip. For a second, she flailed as her body swung backward over the yawing void, her right hand and that precarious toehold the only thing preventing her from plunging to the stones below.

A hand like a steel manacle grabbed her left. Helena jerked her head up, expecting to see her brother, but it wasn't him.

"Give me your other hand," Nigel Ellison yelled. He was crouched at the jagged lip of the broken rampart. Bits and pieces fell away from the bit under with ominous thuds. "Now! Give it to me *now*."

Helena had no choice. With her heart in her mouth, she let go of the rampart. She was suspended in the open air, Nigel's hold the only thing between her and disaster. And then she flew up as the scholar yanked her.

Flight should not have been painful, but her entire body shrieked in protest as she sailed over the jagged rampart lip. She ended up sprawled over Nigel Ellison, hitting his tall, lean frame with the impact of a boulder striking a wall.

They ended up flat on the ramparts, a tangle of limbs.

"*Oomph.*" Nigel's complexion was tomato red, and he was sucking in the air with loud gaps. She'd knocked the breath out of him.

But he must have kept up a regular exercise regimen, because the next moment he was giving her a weak, slightly green smile. "No offense, cousin, but you are heavier than you look."

Helena stared at him, her mouth open. "*Cousin?*"

"I'll explain later." Without ceremony, Nigel pushed her to the side, off of him. He stood up and retreated several feet. Then he took a flying leap, clearing the broken part of the rampart with a physicality and grace she would never have guessed her possessed.

Her hands flew to her mouth. "Oh my god, Lucien."

In her ordeal, she had not seen Lucien's body wandering to the edge of the ramparts on the far side. His spirit was there, less distinct but still visible to the naked eye. He could do nothing but watch help-lessly as his body took a jerky step, putting one leg over the open air. He was seconds away from plummeting to his death.

The shrill screams from the servants below were drowned out by her heartbeat. The organ was seconds away from shattering. Helena knew she would not survive if Lucien did not.

Tomas had cleared the rampart stairs. He and Nigel reached Lucien at the same time, hauling him back from the brink before he tumbled off over the edge.

CHAPTER 30

*T*omas sprawled into one of the library's armchairs, keeping a finger on the rim of his cut crystal tumbler to keep the brandy from spilling out. "This is very awkward," he said in Italian.

"Which part?" Helena asked from the couch as Nigel Ellison pressed his index and middle finger to Lucien's neck.

Her husband's body was sprawled next to her. His spirit however was pacing a worn track in the carpet, or it would have had it possessed some substance.

"His pulse is strong," she assured their unexpected savior. "His Grace's body is in perfect health. This affliction is magical."

"Yes, I can see that," Nigel murmured, casting an incredulous glance behind him at Lucien's irritated spirit.

"Can you not go back into your body?" Nigel tilted his head toward the duke's prone form. "This is rather unsettling."

"Is it?" Lucien snapped sarcastically. "How unfortunate. Please accept my deepest apologies for disturbing *your* peace."

"Lucien, my love..." she began in a placating tone.

"Does this dunderhead not understand I cannot re-enter my body?"

Nigel's pale brow creased. "You genuinely can't? Not even if you settle over it...gently?"

"I already said no," Lucien snapped, rubbing his glowing visage with hands that could not feel. "It's as if there's a bloody door that I can't see, one that is barred against me."

The edges of Lucien's once-defined image wavered as if his temper was directly tied to his ability to maintain cohesion.

Well, of course it is, Helena thought. He was focusing his magic to appear solid.

Fortunately for them, from the courtyard, he had appeared a great deal less distinct. According to Tomas, Lucien had been a blurred, vaguely man-shaped form from the ground. The sight would fuel rumors of castle ghosts for decades to come.

Lucien stopped pacing directly in front of Nigel Ellison. "I want a bloody explanation for your presence, and I want it now."

"I told you," Helena said softly, resting her aching hands in her lap. "He claims to be a relative."

Tomas had done his best to clean the scrapes on her hands, binding them with clean cotton bandages. But there was little he could do for the torn and strained muscles under the skin.

She had eschewed a drink of her own to avoid showing her husband and brother just how badly she was damaged.

Tomas sniffed. "If you're about to tell me that you're another one of Aldo Garibaldi's bastards, I won't believe you. You look nothing like me or my brother Matteo."

Nigel frowned. "I thought the Conte was your father."

Tomas gave him a dark look. "Answer the question."

Nigel drifted to the sideboard, pouring his own drink. "Technically, that wasn't a question. But no, that is not the side of the family I am related to."

He looked back at Helena.

"You called me cousin," she replied, studying his finely formed but pale features. She could find nothing familiar there. "But I have no aunts or uncles."

"That you know of." Nigel passed a hand over his face. He leaned against the mantle, passing a hand over his face in the first sign of weariness he'd displayed. "Although to be precise I am your first cousin, once removed."

His intonation stressed that last part. But Helena merely frowned, exchanging a puzzled glance with her brother.

Nigel sighed. "I told mother this would be more difficult than she believed."

"Your mother claims to be my aunt?" Helena's lashes fluttered.

"Actually, she is your mother's aunt, your great-aunt. Her given name is Moira, but she began using Mary before I was born. It's rather odd to refer to her as Moira now."

He came round to the spare armchair, sitting in front of Helena and leaning forward. "Has Isobel never mentioned her?"

"Moira Sterling is dead," Tomas said repressively before she could answer. "She died before we were born."

Nigel looked both relieved and resigned. "Except she didn't. But she came very close to dying. My father saved her."

Lucien's spirit came round to join her on the couch. He sat down in between his body and Helena. The picture they made, the spirit and the shell side by side, was startling, to say the least.

"I don't know this story," Lucien said, his irritation a minor complaint in the face of his curiosity.

"Neither do I—not in its entirety," Helena began. "But I know a bit. You see, Moira's story was a cautionary tale."

She inclined her head at Nigel, indicating that he should start.

Even though it was painful, she slipped her hand into the pocket sewn into her wrapper, closing around a small spell bag. If his facts did not align with those her mother had told her, she had to be ready.

From the wry twist of his mouth, Nigel appeared to understand this. His glance at her hand in the pocket was both knowing and concerned. But he knew they would go no further without this explanation, so he turned to Lucien, settling more comfortably into the chair in preparation for a long story.

"My mother Moira was four or five years older than Isobel's mother. Though by her own account her modest dowry wasn't enough to entice a gentleman, she also wasn't truly surprised when she caught the eye of a gentleman staying with friends in her village one summer. She was the most beautiful girl in town, and Duncan McNally was instantly taken with her. He proposed within the week. But my grandmother Helen, who I presume was Helena's namesake, did not approve. Mother did not want to wed without her consent, but Helen wouldn't give it—not unless Duncan married her from the village church. But Duncan told my mother that he had to be married in his family's ancestral chapel. He said it was tradition, one that ensured happiness for the couple in question. He convinced her to make a runaway marriage."

"Let me guess," Lucien drawled. "He never intended on marrying her."

Nigel lifted a shoulder. "That part is a bit unclear. My father says he believes Duncan did intend to marry her."

Helena tilted her head to one side. "And how would your father know that?"

"Because he was invited to officiate the wedding. The letter specified the bride's name."

Even Tomas sat up at that declaration.

Nigel smiled wryly. "My father, Nigel Smythe, is a poor relation of the McNally clan—a second cousin happened to be close in age to Duncan. They were born weeks apart."

He broke off to take a fortifying sip of brandy.

"When Duncan was sent to Eton, his father decided to sponsor my father's tenure there as well," he continued. "Angus believed my scholarly sober father might be a good influence on his feckless son. My father was well aware that his own future depended on Duncan's, so he applied himself to the thankless task of managing his cousin, pushing and prodding him until Duncan managed to get passing marks in school. This forced custodial role continued until Oxford when Duncan ended his studies somewhere near the halfway mark. Fortunately, my father had applied himself, working himself to the bone to finish the divinity program early."

"Your father is a clergyman?" That explained his son's scholarly mien.

Nigel nodded. "At the time he was a vicar in search of a flock—he had not secured a living. But despite his dislike of his cousin, he recognized that it was in his best interests to go and officiate Duncan's wedding to the Scottish lass he'd mentioned in his letter. Because the McNally's were a very wealthy clan. Duncan was also connected to the influential Vass family on his mother's side. My father hoped the wedding would lead to him securing a living some-where. However, by the time he arrived in Stonehaven, where Duncan's family resided, a very critical detail of the party had changed."

"But the wedding never happened," Tomas observed.

"Oh, but it did. Except the bride wasn't Scottish. Duncan called off the wedding following my father's arrival—*after* he was introduced to my mother as the intended bride. But less than a week later, the McNallys announced Duncan's engagement to an English-born heiress with Scottish ties."

Nigel broke off, his sharp clean features hardening like stone. "My father realized Moira had been cast off. And though he never gave me the details, he implied that his cousin had done so after abusing my mother."

"I know this part," Helena said. "Moira was angry. She chose revenge. Her hex maimed her former fiancée."

Nigel's eyes were cold and hard. "It was her right."

Helena raised her brows. "I don't disagree, but she exposed herself..."

Belatedly withdrawing her hand from her pocket, she let it rest in her lap. "My mother told me that Duncan's family hunted her down and killed her."

Nigel's mouth and eyes softened a fraction. He nodded. "They certainly attempted to. My maternal great-uncle Boyd was a nasty brute. He made it his life's mission to hunt my mother down. She evaded him for some weeks, but he was closing in on her."

"Except your father found her first," Tomas said when Nigel lapsed into silence. Their cousin nodded.

"Father went to Stonehaven village," he said, visibly collecting himself. "He spoke with a local family sympathetic to Moira's plight—Duncan and Boyd did not have a good reputation locally. But father was a clergyman who'd come to his calling honestly. His earnestness convinced them of his good intentions. They told him where they had last seen Moira. He took a rather hasty leave from his relations and intercepted my mother before they could find her. He obscured her tracks as best he could, and even tried to make it appear as if she had cast herself off some nearby cliffs outside a neighboring town."

"Did it work?" Lucien asked, caught up in the tale.

He shrugged. "Partly. Most of the McNallys believed Moira dead. Father took her as far from them as he was able—clear across to the other side of England where he was offered a living from Viscount Anders. They reside in Eastbourne."

She and Tomas exchanged a speaking glance. "Then why the continued secrecy?" he demanded. "Why did she never get in touch with Isobel?"

Nigel grunted. "Because my father underestimated Boyd."

He downed the rest of his glass. "Boyd was never convinced that Moira took her own life. It became a mission to him, not unlike a religious calling—one fueled by hatred and prejudice. He chased rumors of witches for years afterward, passing on his zealotry to his sons."

Nigel paused, giving Helena a somber look. "They never found my mother, but they found a few other innocent practitioners over the years."

Helena shuddered, understanding his meaning.

"But your father protected Moira," Tomas supplied after a somber silence. "And they eventually married."

Nigel's expression lightened almost comically. "There was no eventually about it. Father convinced mother to marry him before they arrived in Eastbourne." He smiled. "I did mention that mother was quite a beauty in her day. I imagine Helena looks a great deal like her."

Helena smiled weakly and bit her lip, imagining what Isobel would say. Moira's supposed death had marked her mother. Indeed, it had haunted the entire family.

Her great-grandmother Helen had died mourning her child. How that must have hurt Moira. But unless Nigel was exaggerating the McNally's and Vass families' ire, and she didn't think he was, then it would have been too dangerous for Moira to contact her family. Boyd's clan would have been watching.

She jerked, sucking in a sharp breath. "My mother's marriage to a foreign count protected her."

Nigel inclined his head. "I see you comprehend the matter perfectly."

He turned to Lucien and Tomas. "Helena is right. Boyd watched Moira's entire family, to the point we suspect he had an informant in Carrbridge village, her birthplace. Had Isobel tipped her hand while she still lived there, he would have descended with his zealots. But she lost her home after her parents died and went to work as a governess. My father learned she had married the Conte de Santa Fiora from one of Boyd's letters to another one of our relations. The latter kept him informed of the man's doings."

Helena's stomach swirled unpleasantly, and her hands turned to ice in her lap. "Boyd knew of my mother, didn't he?"

"Oh yes, he did. He was never sure that she had inherited the taint, as he called it. Given the influential families your mother worked for as a governess, he knew he could not risk pursuing his vengeance further. Not without risking the reputation of the McNally clan."

Helena scoffed in bitter amusement. "I'm surprised he chose such a cautious path. Most gentlemen wouldn't bestir themselves to protect a mere governess." Clarence Montgomery hadn't lifted a finger to protect her mother Isobel when danger came calling. Quite the contrary.

"I'm sure that's true," he acknowledged. "Fortunately for your mother, Boyd could not be certain of that. Once Isobel married such an influential nobleman, she passed out of his reach." He sighed. "He resigned himself to the fact, or at least appeared so. He said if the taint persisted it would be Italy's problem."

Tomas lifted a dark brow. "I take it Boyd was not overly fond of foreigners."

A cringe overtook his mouth. "He could scarcely abide the English side of the family."

That brought to mind another question.

"How did you know we had returned to England?" Helena asked with great trepidation. "Please don't say the McNally family spy network continues to function."

Tomas leaned forward. "Even if it was—we left Italy suddenly, after...an incident. I doubt you heard the news through such a pedestrian channel."

"You would be right," Nigel said reassuringly. "It was nothing like that. Nor do I know what this inciting incident you mentioned was."

His tone made it clear this last was a question.

Lucien's eyes flicked to hers and quickly passed away as if trying to convey a warning. Clearly, he was not prepared to take Nigel into his confidence regarding what his bodiless spirit could do just yet.

"We told no one we were leaving. And we traveled under assumed names," Tomas continued. He cocked his head at his newest cousin. "So how is it you knew we were coming? You met us on the bloody train platform for pity's sake."

"*Ah.* That is simple—in a way. My mother dreamed of this, you see. Or to be more precise she dreamed of Helena and this castle along with several vague but unmistakable portents of danger." He smacked his palms on his lap. "Mother wanted to help. And though she and father are hale and hearty for their age, they are too advanced in years for this sort of thing."

"And they sent you in their stead," Tomas said.

He nodded, a trace of modesty bleeding into his expression. "Mother has been training me in the craft my entire life. She made certain I knew how to defend myself. And my father, who is rather brilliant in his own right, has taught me something of equal importance—how to hide this knowledge."

His grin was both mischievous and self-deprecating. "It's rather helpful when everyone believes you to be a man of the church. Most people don't question the movements of a future vicar. At least they did not until I came here, and Helena spotted my protection charm. No one has ever questioned it. Not even the few genuine practitioners I've run into."

Helena closed her eyes. "And now I know why I recognized it. The design featured prominently in my grandmother's writings. She must have designed it herself. It's something your mother would have been taught when she was young."

He nodded. She jerked with sudden realization.

"That was you in my bedroom that night!" she exclaimed, the knowledge sudden and startling. "What were you doing?"

The tension from the other two men leaped. Tomas sat forward, and Lucien whirled, spectral fist raised.

Nigel held up both his hands. "My intentions were honorable!" he rushed to assure them. "I was placing a protection charm under the bed."

Helena put her hands on her hips. "I looked under the bed. There was nothing there."

"That's because I put it in the mattress—I cut a small slit and hid it in the flocking. I'd tell you to go look for it had the cottage not burned down."

He turned to her skeptical brother. "I put one in yours as well."

Tomas harrumphed and shook his head. "Not bloody likely. I would have heard you."

Nigel smirked. "I doubt it. You snore louder than the train that brought you here."

She turned to Lucien, unsurprised to find his expression was still dark. "You really don't know why Helena and Tomas came here to the Slide?"

Nigel blinked. "Truth be told, I was very confused at first. It's not exactly a well-known or fashionable destination. Then I realized it had to do with you, Your Grace. It's obvious you and Helena have a... deep metaphysical connection," he finished delicately.

Tomas snorted but thankfully remained silent.

"But your mother's vision didn't go into greater detail?"

Nigel twisted to face Lucien, both of him. "Well, mother dreamed of parts of it but by no means all." He lifted his shoulder. "I can't help thinking it would have been useful if I'd sent her back to bed to dream some more. Greater details on the threat that would have been very useful…"

Helena couldn't help being amused. "I too find it most unfortunate that you cannot summon prophetic dreams at will. It would save a great deal of time."

Lucien grunted in agreement. "Wha—" he began before abruptly disappearing.

CHAPTER 31

*T*heir impromptu meeting with their cousin was cut short when Lucien unexpectedly returned to his body.

One moment he was sitting there beside himself. Then the transparency of his form suddenly increased, and he was slamming into his body as if a giant had grabbed both versions of him and slapped them together.

This time Lucien's spirit slipped effortlessly into his body—as if whatever barrier had been preventing it had been removed.

Helena rushed to his side as he sat up, checking his heartbeat and the dilation of his eyes.

"I'm fine." But Lucien's voice slurred. He shook his head as if to clear it and promptly collapsed back on the cushions, overcome with fatigue so extreme he was having difficulty remaining upright.

"We must get him to bed," Helena said, getting to her feet after determining he wasn't in immediate danger.

"What is...wrong...with me?" Lucien asked as Nigel and Tomas each took an arm, slinging it over their shoulder to help him up. He was a very large man, so it took both of them to hoist him to his feet and keep him there.

"I suspect you expended too much magic to manifest visually,"

Helena diagnosed in a low voice, picking up her skirts and leading the way. "The fuel required comes from your body regardless of whether or not your spirit is currently inhabiting it or whether it is wandering."

"I sound drink...I mean drunk," he mumbled as they negotiated the main staircase.

"No doubt the servants think you are," Nigel observed, his tone downright sardonic now that he'd dropped his scholarly disguise. Helena suspected this acerbic version of him was more reflective of his natural temperament. "They probably think the castle ghost drove you out the ramparts."

"S'more palatable than the truth," he muttered, his eyes closing.

"Damn, Blackwater. You are a heavy bastard," Tomas grunted. "You need to lay off cook's excellent tarts."

The goading helped rouse him a touch. "You are just trying to hoard them for yourself. Besides, I carried you out of a burning building as dead weight. At least I am helping here."

And he was, assiduously putting one foot in front of the other in an attempt to help the men bear his weight.

"If the servants inquire as to why you're having difficulties,` just tell them you felt the need to fortify yourself with spirits after your ghostly encounter," her always practical brother chimed in between labored breaths. "I certainly did."

Lucien was asleep before they arrived at the bedroom. Nigel and Tomas deposited him in the bed while Helena made sure the casement window was locked.

Tomas dragged a heavy armchair to block the latch in an over-abundance of caution. She also looped the chain of the medallion around his wrist, tying it in such a way that it could not be slipped off so easily. Not without help.

Lucien slept on as she escorted the men out into the hall.

"Will it take him long to recover?" Tomas asked, frowning.

"I don't believe so. But Lucien has only started training to use his magic. Manifesting visibly was an instinctive act. I doubt he realized how much energy he was expending. I expect he will wake up ravenous."

She turned to Nigel. "Why were you up there on the ramparts?"

He leaned against the doorjamb. "I've been watching the castle for a few nights. I cast spells to detect a great release of energy all over the Devil's Slide and Blackwater castle. That's how I knew about Sally and the animals being sacrificed in the woods and— "

Helena grabbed his arm. "Wait did you say animals? As in more than one?"

"Yes." Nigel's muscle's tensed, his disgust apparent. "I found a few small carcasses. Now I don't believe magic was expended to kill them in all but one or two cases. I never found the first one, but the second might have been— "

"The doe," Helena interrupted. "The one that Lucien chased in the woods that night. There was a light. Was that you?"

"Err. Yes. A tracking spell." Nigel closed his eyes briefly. "I realize I should have shown a tad more discretion. But in my defense, I did not think the poor creature would escape its killer, nor did I know there would be anyone wandering the woods at that hour."

Tomas scowled. "He has a point. What was Lucien doing in the woods that late?"

Helena ignored him. "The killer must have had a problem dealing with the larger animals. Perhaps they didn't restrain them properly and resorted to magic to kill them."

"It's as good an explanation as any," Nigel conceded. "Although I still can't fathom why the poor creature tore clear across the woods that way. It must have been scared out of its mind."

Helena was about to explain that bit, but Nigel was already speaking. "Earlier tonight my spell triggered. I ran here and saw His Grace climbing out of his bedroom window. He...did not appear to be in control of his body."

He watched Helena steadily as he shared this last. She realized he'd felt the other consciousness pulling the strings on the ramparts too.

"You didn't return to the village earlier today?" Tomas bristled.

"No," he said slowly. "I merely made it appear that way."

Her brother scowled. "Then how do we know you aren't behind this farce?"

Nigel held up his hands in a placating gesture at odds with the frustration bleeding into his expression. "If my story hasn't convinced you to trust me, then perhaps this will."

He reached into his coat pocket and withdrew a sealed letter.

"What is that?" Tomas demanded, grabbing Helena's hand before she could take it.

Nigel rolled his eyes at her brother. "Mother dashed off a quick letter before I left. It's addressed to you, Helena."

Tomas smacked her hand when she reached for the wrinkled missive. "Why hasn't she contacted my family before now? Our mother would have visited her."

"No doubt she would have, but it would have had to have been in secret." Nigel scratched his chin. "I told you Boyd resigned himself to the fact Isobel was out of his reach, but he still watched your family. Had the wealthy Italian count of Santa Fiora traveled to Eastbourne, he would have known. He had built a rather extensive information network by the time he passed on to his great reward."

The sarcasm in those final words implied exactly where Nigel believed his relation had gone after death.

"When did Boyd die?" Helena asked.

"Almost a decade ago, but I told you earlier he passed on his mission to his sons." His eyes grew coldly distant. "Those two did a great deal of damage in their day, especially in the years following their father's death."

His shoulders eased. "However, I'm pleased to say the current generation, my cousins, look askance at this morbid family tradition of witch-hunting."

For a moment he preened, brushing imaginary lint off his sleeve. "It helped that their worldly older cousin Nigel taught them that such things were irredeemably archaic and outmoded. They pride themselves on being men of the modern age."

Giving Tomas a gentle shove, Helena took Moira's letter, holding it tight. "That is some comfort. But you still haven't explained who or what you are looking for and why you left the Devil's Slide only to steal back in secret. Because I know these vague portents your mother warned you of had more substance than you shared with us."

Nigel paused, appearing to choose his words carefully. "I left, and returned, in the hopes of confirming my theory on the hand behind these machinations."

"I see." Helena worried her lip, considering his words. "You should know…until tonight I believed Lucien's soul-wandering to be a natural manifestation of his talent."

Nigel frowned. "Then this separation of body and soul is a frequent occurrence?"

"A long-standing one," she admitted in a low voice. "This condition has been plaguing Lucien since he was a very young boy."

"*Ah.*" They both looked at each other in a moment of mutual grim understanding.

Tomas crossed his arms, his head going from one to the other. "I don't understand why you're looking at each other as if you realized someone sold you a lame horse."

Helena took a deep breath before slowly letting it out. "If the soul wandering is a longstanding affliction…"

"It is," Tomas interrupted. "Mother says he started hovering over Helena when she was still in the womb. We thought it was a ghost."

Nigel's head jerked to her. "Is this true?"

She cleared her throat delicately, pushing aside memories inappropriate to the discussion. "There was a great deal of confusion as to Lucien's nature at first. Matters were, erm, clarified after our arrival here."

She ignored Nigel's lifted brows.

Helena crossed her arms and sighed. "We were unaware it was a sort of attack until today."

Tomas scrubbed his hair with his hand. "Wait. Let me see if I understand. Someone has been pushing the man out of his body?"

"Yes." Helena felt an unpleasant fluttering in her belly. It was the flip side of what she felt when she looked at her husband.

"The soul wandering, the bodies in the woods, and Sally—all of this is the work of one person. Someone close enough to Lucien to have had access to him since his youth."

An expression of dawning enlightenment overtook Tomas's face. He twisted to Nigel. "Surely you don't suspect Jocelyn? She's a harmless old woman!"

"She has certainly cultivated an air of benign frivolity," Helena observed. "However, the fact she is away on yet another collecting trip would strongly suggest the blame lies elsewhere."

"I've come to that conclusion as well," Nigel said with a sniff. "Unfortunately, I have no other suspects. You'll recall the reason I quit the village. I had hoped whoever was responsible for the animals and the scullery maid's death would grow comfortable, thinking themselves safe and return or show their hand in some way."

"But Jocelyn did not return, and we've had a new assault by persons unknown."

Nigel's lips compressed as if he were going to say something. "I don't suppose Lucien has spoken of a servant or family friend who could be our culprit? Someone who spent a significant amount of time with him as a child?"

"No, but I imagine any number of the castle staff would fit that description. I haven't been here long enough to know for certain."

"The witch doesn't have to be a retainer," Tomas pointed out. "It could be any number of people. The castle is open to the entire village. Hell, it could be Harry at the Bucket for all we know."

Nigel looked down at his shoes. "I admit I've focused my investigative efforts on Jocelyn to the point where I was excluding all others."

"It matters not," Helena announced. "We've been working at cross purposes long enough. Now that we are aware of each other and our common goal, I suggest we join forces. Together, you and Tomas will make a detailed study of the locals. Try to come up with a list of likely candidates for our witch."

"And what will you be doing?"

"I'm going to begin preparing the protection charm for Lucien anew, this time in ink."

"But that is effectively a lock that will make his magic inaccessible."
Tomas frowned. "I thought you didn't want to leave him defenseless."

Helena wiped her hand on her skirts. "We no longer have a choice.
The medallion is not secure enough. But with luck, Lucien will master
his gifts well enough to manipulate the ink, opening the lock as
needed."

Her brother did not bother to hide his skepticism. "Then he has to
do a damn sight better using his magic than he's been doing."

"He will," she said with greater confidence than she felt before
adding in a whisper. "He has to."

Helena had not traveled all this way to find Lucien and lose him to
this unknown threat. That she would not allow.

CHAPTER 32

*L*ucien wiped the sweat off his bare chest with a towel, momentarily forgetting the inflamed and broken skin of the new tattoo that now adorned the center of his abdomen, over what Helena called his solar plexus.

"The location of the marking was important. This spot on the body is a convergence point," she had explained as she had driven the needle into him again and again, forming an intricately embellished spiral pattern. "Learning to manipulate your gift to unlock this pattern will go far easier if you can actually see it."

The past few days, Lucien had done little else but attempt to open the interlocking circle tattoo, with little success. How the bloody hell was he supposed to "open" a tattoo?

The only thing he had to show for hours of squinting down at his chest was a sweat-covered body and the start of what promised to be a very bad headache.

How did Helena open the damn thing? She had demonstrated how several times, putting her hand on his chest. The circles had spun at her touch, whirling and rearranging with a little flash of heat.

She made it look so easy. The same way she could translate the absurdly esoteric phrases in the many spell books she was making him read into clear and intelligible English.

Well, perhaps he was starting to affect the tattoo. One of the lines appeared smudged to his eyes. But that could be because he'd gone cross-eyed from his efforts.

The sting caused by the cloth on his partially healed skin penetrated his fatigued brain. Suppressing a flinch, he tossed the towel aside, scowling across the library's length at Nigel's bright head. It was too close to Helena's.

The pair had been in close conference for a good hour, examining and reexamining their absurdly long suspect list.

"Are you certain he's your cousin?" he asked Tomas, who had been assigned to "help" him by his sister.

Helped how exactly was still open to question. Tomas had spent the morning snacking from a tea tray and squinting at his chest to see if any of the lines of the tattoo had changed.

"He looks nothing like you."

"I will remind you that he's Helena's cousin by blood, not mine."

"Well, he doesn't look anything like her either," Lucien said, sounding petty and jealous, but Tomas was too wrapped up in his tea tray to notice.

Tomas was also a disloyal bastard. "I disagree," he said after choking down an absurd number of jam tarts. "I think there is a trace of Isobel in his face, around the mouth. And Helena looks a great deal like her. Although she has Matteo's ears, poor thing."

Lucien rounded on him, indignant. "Her ears are perfect, damn you. Also, to point out the obvious, they are the same as yours."

"Yes, these long lobes run through the male line. On a woman they are ungainly..." He broke off with a mock shudder.

"Stop trying to distract me." He gestured to the pair. "Do you seriously believe this method of identifying the witch? They have every Tom, Dick, and Francis on that parchment."

And Lucien would know. They'd spend hours quizzing him on the inhabitants of the Slide, writing down every name he could recall.

225

Tomas scratched his head. "Not all. They've eliminated the children and villagers too young to have known you as a youth."

The scoff escaped him before he could help himself.

Tomas nudged him when Helena cast a distracted glance their way. But *cousin* Nigel called her attention back to the parchment the next moment, and she turned away.

"Incidentally, I agree with you on the methodology. I'm not convinced it's the correct approach." Tomas crossed his arms. "I think they should add the youths of the village."

His head drew back. *"What?"*

Tomas waved at the other end of the library. "Helena is living proof that magic is heritable. It's entirely possible we are looking at the actions of a family of witches. The original assault could have been carried out by an elder, the current ones by their heir. Your soul-wandering self might have been a project passed down the same way you inherited your estate. For all you know, you might be a family heirloom—one in a state of total disrepair."

Lucien shot Tomas a look that could have curdled milk. Tomas, who had chosen that moment to freshen his coffee, ended up spilling it.

"It moved."

"What?"

"The line." Tomas pointed at the tattoo. "The outer ring, er, squirmed for lack of a better word. Then it snapped back into place."

Lucien glanced at his wife, but she was still engrossed in conversation with her cousin. A mere wiggle?

"Well, until it waltzes out of the way, let's not disturb those two." Not until he'd made more progress. A wiggle was not progress.

And try as he might, he couldn't replicate that small success. Tomas probably imagined it.

"Perhaps if I annoy you again?" Tomas offered. "Or we can ask Nigel to lean close to Helena once more."

"Kindly shut up," he growled. Then he picked up his towel and sat down in front of the window to try again.

~

"You see this," Lucien crowed.

The outer ring of his tattoo had shifted a hundred and eighty degrees, aligning the sigils of the outermost ring with the second in a new configuration.

Tomas put down his copy of the Times, narrowing his eyes from across the dining table.

"All three rings of the tattoo have to realign," he said flatly before returning his attention to his dish.

"I know that." Lucien scowled.

"That's brilliant progress," Helena said, smiling at him across the breakfast table.

"Thank you, my love," he said, but the tips of his ears were red. To facilitate his efforts at unlocking the tattoo, Lucien had come down to dinner half undressed.

Well, he *was* dressed, but his shirt was open, which was essentially the same thing. The only time he closed it was when the servants came by with a new platter—something he suspected they would do frequently with both Tomas and Nigel in residence.

The pair may not have been related by blood but judging from their shared prodigious appetites they were obviously connected somewhere in their respective family trees.

On the tail of that thought, Tomas shoveled a trowel's worth of flummery into his mouth. "No, it's not."

"It is too. Especially considering it's only been one day," Helena insisted. She leaned over and covered her hand with his. "How is the area itself? Does your skin still sting?"

He shook his head. "No, the balm you gave me has almost completely healed it."

Her miraculous cream had worked wonders. There was a lingering itchiness, but he wasn't about to complain about a minor annoyance in front of his in-laws.

Lucien was starting to get used to having company. True, it was a little irritating that Nigel had inserted himself into the investigation. But he had his hands full attempting to master his magic.

It also helped that Lucien could keep an eye on the newcomer from the other side of the library. So far Nigel had not stepped out of line. He didn't look at Helena inappropriately or try to be alone with her. As long as those things remained true, Lucien was willing to tolerate his presence at the dinner table and in his home.

As for Tomas, well the blighter was probably his closest friend now. A sarcastic one who possessed the profoundly wrongheaded opinion that he was a better rider, but a friend nonetheless.

Lucien would miss him when he went back to Italy. But as long as he had Helena, he would cope. Better than that. He would thrive.

Just as soon as he learned to open this damn tattoo. Reaching for the wine, he laughed at something Helena had said. Determination and optimism colored the conversation at the dinner table.

No one at the table noticed the fact the servants did not meet their eyes. Nor did they meet each other's.

CHAPTER 33

"Wake up, *idiota assonnato testardo*."

Lucien roused slowly, his body responding sluggishly. "What is it?" he mumbled.

"I said get up, you bloody idiot."

Lucien blinked up at the dark drapery of his bed.

Was that Tomas in his room again? *Damn* it. The man seriously had to stop coming in without so much as a "by your leave."

"What?" Lucien struggled to sit up. It was much more difficult than it should have been.

"There's something wrong with me." At least that's what he tried to say. The words ran together and slurred as if he was inebriated.

"Of course, something is wrong with you. You've been drugged."

"What?" he repeated, trying to focus his vision.

"You and half the castle are insensible," Tomas said, giving him another hard shake. "And Helena is gone."

That roused him more effectively than a pitcher of water to the face. Lucien staggered to his feet, surprised he was still dressed. He hadn't even taken off his boots.

Turning around, he swept his hands over the bed as if he expected to find an invisible Helena there. But there was no one.

"We retired to bed." His attempts to move the tattoo had fatigued him more than he'd thought. He'd started yawning at the dinner table. Laughing, Helena had escorted him upstairs.

"But she was fatigued as well." By the time they go to their chamber, they were both dead on their feet. Helena had fallen into bed next to him, still in her gown.

But her side of the bed was cold now. She had not been laying there for some time.

"Where is she?"

"That is what I want to know."

Tomas ran both hands through his hair, pulling on it till it was standing on end. "I went to the kitchen to see if there was leftover venison pie and found half the kitchen staff lying all over the floor—the kitchen maids that stay behind to clean and scrub the pots and pans."

He broke off with a shudder. "I thought they were dead, but each possessed a pulse. Then I went to confront the cook. Her room is just off the kitchens. I thought she had poisoned us all, but she was asleep too. I suspect the rest of the castle is as well."

He opened his shirt to show Lucien his tattoo. There was a faint iridescence in the lines. "I think the castle staff was spelled asleep."

"But I have the tattoo as well. And Helena…"

"Would have been able to ward off the sleeping curse on her own. But she's not here, and you were unconscious, which means the witch didn't rely on the curse alone."

Lucien's stomach swirled unpleasantly. "The wine. Helena and I both drank it. You drank ale."

"Nigel did as well. We have to go and find him. He can help us search for Helena."

Lucien staggered to the door. "Unless dear cousin is a fraud—for all we know he could be the one behind this."

Tomas didn't answer him. He just motioned to the door and began to run.

CHAPTER 34

*H*elena awoke on the floor of a small cabin, her cheek scraping on the rough, uneven wooden floor.

She couldn't see much of her surroundings and could scarcely open her eyes, but she could feel the pulse of the trees pressing in on her from beyond the walls.

Their energy...it was wrong. It felt malevolent and twisted in a way she had never experienced. That more than the drugs in her body was making her sick to her stomach.

Helena needed to shield herself from the unnatural and unwholesome energy of the plants surrounding the cabin. Whatever had been done to them had tainted them. Connecting with them wouldn't help her recover from whatever sedative was pressing her limbs to the ground as if heavy weights had been attached to them.

Think. She had to figure out where she was and how far away help could be found.

The trees were a clue. Not enough time had passed for her to be far from the castle. But where in the woods was she? The only cabin she knew of was the one Lucien's grandmother had built to meet her lover—the one secreted in the deepest part of the woods.

Of course. She suppressed a groan. It was a perfect hiding place. It was close to the castle but still a world away, because no one ever came here.

This part of the woods is rumored to be haunted, Lucien had said, assuring her that it wasn't. He thought haunting was his ancestor's fabrication. Except she knew better now.

There was a very good reason the locals shunned these woods.

Her vision still hadn't cleared when she heard the distinctive sound of fabric abrading against fabric behind her. With a herculean effort, Helena managed to turn her head.

That was when she saw the chalked lines of the circle surrounding her.

However, that was not the most alarming thing her eyes beheld.

"*Harry,*" she mouthed.

A tremor ran through her as she tried to inch away from the giant towering over her.

Taller than Lucien, Harold's red hair was liberally sprinkled with grey. But that didn't soften the brutal edge to him. Though slack, his massive hands were anvil-sized. He could so easily choke the life out of her.

The only thing keeping her safe from them was the circle. He could not cross the border without damaging it.

Should she try and goad him across? *Oh God.* Was being strangled preferable to whatever this circle was meant to accomplish?

How could this be? Yes, Tomas had thrown his name out as a suspect, but it had been in jest. Helena had dismissed the possibility almost straight away. It just wasn't possible. Where would he have learned—

A scraping noise and the distinctive swish of skirts made her eyes dart to the left.

Dainty feet clad in light kid slippers picked their way through the circle. Helena stared bleary-eyed at the woman kneeling to touch her cheek.

"Hello, my dear," Jocelyn cooed.

"Can't." Helena's tongue was thick. Her mouth felt slack, the muscles loose and uncooperative. She could feel a trickle of moisture and knew she was drooling.

Jocelyn's elfin nose wrinkled. "Can't what dear?"

"It...can't be you. You...aren't...witch."

The girlish giggle Helena had found both charming now sounded grotesque to her ears. "Well, that's very sweet of you to say. I too am impressed with my acting abilities." She waved a delicate hand in front of her face, then grabbed her skirts and struck a pose. "Really, I should have trod the boards. Imagine the career I could have had."

BY THE TIME he and Tomas ran out into the courtyard, Lucien was wide awake and on the edge of panic.

Nigel's rooms had been empty, his bed unmade as if he'd been lying in it but was roused unexpectedly. The broken water pitcher lying next to the bed suggested this had been a sudden and urgent reason to rise—enough for the scholar not to stop and clean the broken pieces.

Lucien didn't know if that disarray was a ruse or not. The only thing he could focus on was Helena. There was no sign of her anywhere. Every single other person in the castle was asleep, down to the most junior tweeny.

"I'll check the stables," Tomas shouted, already halfway there. "We need to see if there are any missing horses."

But every mount was accounted for. If Helena had been taken from the castle, it had been on foot.

What if she's still in the castle? Without servants to help search every room, closet, and pantry, they couldn't be certain she wasn't still inside, being held against her will by the witch.

"What the hell was that?" Tomas asked as they exited the stables.

Lucien spun around in time to catch movement out of the corner of his eye—a tiny flash of white disappearing around the main gate of the castle courtyard.

"Run." He and Tomas sprinted toward the swiftly disappearing figure.

"It's Nigel," he shouted as they cleared the keep walls.

They saw him at the same time. Tomas stumbled in confusion.

Nigel was wearing his night clothes and was walking away from the castle—backward.

Damn it, where was Helena?

Tomas's steps hitched, and he shook his head.

"Why is he walking that way?" Lucien wondered.

"I don't know!" the Italian yelled.

They closed the distance. Lucien grabbed the man's shoulder. Nigel shifted backward, pulling out of his grip.

"Why are you walking like this?" Tomas demanded. "What is wrong?"

Nigel's eyes widened as he saw them. "Tlas," he said, his urgency at odds with his meandering pace.

Lucien threw up his hands. "What in the bloody hell is a *tlas?*"

"I have no idea," Tomas said, spinning to check behind him as if expecting the mysterious *tlas* to magically appear. "But he needs it. He can't stop himself."

"Believe it or not, I figured that part out," he snapped.

Nigel had been hexed. And whatever compulsion he'd been spelled to follow, he wasn't able to fight it off.

"Damn it, you're supposed to be trained against this sort of thing," he yelled, getting in front of him. He wrapped his arms around him, trying to hold him back. It was like trying to stop a runaway horse.

Nigel may have been shorter than Lucien and narrower in the shoulders, but he was strong. And whatever compulsion was fueling him might have enhanced his strength. Enough that Lucien's boots were skidding in the dirt, his muscles straining as he and Tomas tried to force him down to the ground.

Nigel should not have been able to keep his footing with two grown men pushing and pulling at him, trying to force him off his feet. But somehow he did...and he was heading directly to the lake.

If they didn't find a way to stop him, Nigel was going to drown.

"Tlas!" Nigel yelled, louder this time. His face was beet red, and he was gasping for air. He was fighting the hex with everything he had, but it wasn't going to be enough.

"Damn it, Tomas, what do we do?"

"I don't know."

"Tlas, tlas, tlas!"

"*Merda*," Tomas skidded, back, one knee scraping against the ground. The other splashed into the water. They had reached the lake's shoreline. "Of course. He's not just walking backward; *he's speaking backward too.*"

Lucien caught Nigel's eye. "Then it's...salt? You need salt?"

"Of course." Tomas spat with a brief string of obscenities. One booted foot splashed into the water as he strained against his cousin. "As long as it's a spell and not poison, salt should break the enchantment."

"Then what are you waiting for? Go get some before we end up swimming."

"It's your bloody castle! You go get the salt."

Lucien grimaced. Tomas had a point. He knew the kitchens better. "Can you handle him on your own?"

"*Tlas.*" Nigel was in the water now too, his entire body trembling as he fought Tomas's vicelike hold.

"No." Tomas was shaking with exertion, his brow and hair damp with sweat. "But what choice do we have? *Go.*"

Lucien didn't waste any more time. He let go with a shout and ran back up the dirt road to the courtyard gates.

CHAPTER 35

*J*ocelyn was humming under her breath as she bustled back and forth across the back of the cabin. There was a long worktable there, identical to the kind used in the castle greenhouse. It was large and heavy and would have taken at least three or four people to lift.

Or one Harry?

Helena turned her attention to the barkeep. He was probably strong enough to carry her out of her bedroom, down the stairs, and out of the castle by himself. But could he have managed that table on his own?

Because Helena seriously doubted Jocelyn would demean herself with manual labor. Which meant Harry was not likely to be her only helper.

Her body grew colder, chilling from the inside out.

If that was true—*Mio Dio.* Lucien and Tomas were in danger. So was Nigel for that matter.

"Harry," she began desperately. "You need to consider this—hasn't Lucien been good to you? Can you really hurt him? Because hurting me hurts him."

No reaction. None. Harry didn't so much as bat an eyelash.

Jocelyn didn't bother to turn. "Don't worry about him, my dear," she snickered, waving dismissively at the giant man.

Her tone was so derisive and insulting. But Harry had not reacted at all. It was beyond odd. He'd never struck her as spineless. Every man had his pride. Didn't they?

"Why are you standing so still?" she wondered aloud.

Helena tried to turn her head, but it was still too heavy. Whatever she had drunk had been potent, and she was still feeling the effects.

Giving up the effort to turn her body, she let herself collapse, only then becoming aware of her bound hands tied behind her back. Her feet were tied as well.

Focus on your breathing. She had to take stock of her body and try to burn away the drug sedating her senses.

"I'm fortunate…you appear to have some skill."

The sounds at the table stopped. Jocelyn turned, stepping to the right to enter Helena's line of sight. "What an odd thing to say."

"It's true." Helena licked her dry lips. Her mouth tasted like metal. "Had you miscalculated the dosage or had the proportion of ingredients in your sleeping potion been even slightly off, I would have lost all muscle control. I wouldn't be able to speak, let alone breathe."

She paused, her eyes finally focusing on Jocelyn's carefully blank expression. "Unless it's a brew you picked up in London. There are a great many skilled apothecaries there. None in the Slide of course. But in London I expect you can find exactly what you needed."

Jocelyn smiled, wiping her hands on her skirts. "As if I would trust such important work to a mere chemist." She sounded amused.

"No." Helena pretended to think about it. "You couldn't risk them making a mistake. In the end, a witch with no family and no coven can only trust herself. All of your potions are handmade. And despite the fact Harry is here, he's not your ally or your confidante."

Jocelyn's lips parted in indignation. Like quicksilver, the expression morphed into outright amusement. She giggled again. "Oh, that's very good. You're far more conniving than I gave you credit for."

It sounded like a compliment. Her head tilted as she considered

Helena's prone form. "It almost makes me wish I'd had a daughter instead of a son."

Helena wanted to blister her ears. Lucien was not Jocelyn's in any way. The woman had no blood tie to him. And the love and affection that would have made her a mother despite the lack—it was a sham.

"Harry is mesmerized, isn't he?"

It was the only explanation for the slack muscles in the face of the Bucket's proprietor and the vacant expression in his eyes.

This time Jocelyn's mouth tightened in annoyance. Her eyes narrowed into icy little slits.

"Is that your gift?" Helena wondered aloud.

The witch didn't answer. "Yes, of course, it must be. It explains so much."

Including why Lucien's first protection charm hadn't worked. He had taken it off himself because his stepmother had *told* him to do so. Then she'd made him forget she asked.

Jocelyn turned her back and resumed her potion mixing. But Helena wasn't done. "Does your compulsion require a potion, or is it a natural aspect of your talent? I'm guessing both.... after all, not everyone is susceptible to mesmerism. Not like Harry here. Or the housemaid and footman from the castle who helped serve dinner tonight. Some people require a stronger push."

Like Lucien. She had felt his will firsthand. No, his magical constitution would have fought it off.

Except she had unfettered access to him since he was a child. And no child, even one as innately powerful as Lucien, would have stood a chance against a fully grown and trained witch.

Was the soul wandering a side-effect of an attempt to overcome Lucien's natural resistance to mesmerism? Or was that too simple an explanation? What had Jocelyn been trying to accomplish?

The need to boast overtook Jocelyn again. "You would be surprised at how simple it is for someone of my gifts."

"I imagine it gets easier with time," Helena observed in a carefully neutral tone. "The more you put the same person under, the easier it is for the compulsion to take hold. Once the groundwork is laid, the force of your commands follows the well-worn path until your subject is nothing but a slack-jawed automaton, ready and willing to follow your commands. But simple tools are not enough, are they? Not when your goal is power. And a black witch always needs so much."

They fed on it, consuming it until it became a void that could never be filled.

"It's why you killed Lucien's father," she continued in a thoughtful murmur when Jocelyn stood there, stone-faced. "The former duke was ripe for picking—a witch by blood who had no knowledge of his gift. Did you kill the former duchess as well?"

Jocelyn hummed. "She was already in the ground by the time I tracked down the power source my spell identified."

Helena shook her head, surprised to find she could. The effects of the sleep potion were wearing off. "Yet, you married your quarry. That requires...dedication."

And why not? The man had been wealthy and titled. The respectability and position would have been as irresistible a lure as access to the St. Germaine bloodline.

"Oh, that part was a pleasure," Jocelyn assured her with a droll wink Helena found grotesque. "My dear departed husband was handsome and well-formed in every respect. As you've no doubt guessed, Lucien looks a great deal like him. The resemblance is quite clear in his portrait. You would have noted it, but I keep the likeness in my chambers—a remembrance of old times."

She tilted her head to the side coquettishly. "Funnily enough, Lucien did not complain when I removed it from the portrait gallery."

"He does not remember his father with fondness."

"No, but then fathers and sons often have difficult relationships. Not like wives and their virile husbands."

Helena's head pulled back a fraction. "If you and the former duke got on so well together, why did you kill him? Was it only to harvest the magic lying dormant inside him?"

Jocelyn lifted a shoulder. "I had secured the title. The advantages and novelty of having a husband were soon outweighed by the inconveniences."

She smacked her lips. "Do you know the fool tried to curtail my allowance? He also tried to dictate who I socialized with and where I went—as if he had that right."

"A decision he did not live to regret."

Helena glanced at Harry, trying to picture how he must have appeared two decades ago when Lucien's father had died.

"Plus, you had all the male companionship you required when you wanted it. Tell me, were all of your…companions…mesmerized when you took them into your bed?"

Jocelyn snatched a flask from the table. Helena braced herself, expecting the ominously clear liquid to splash over her face, but Jocelyn restrained herself at the last second.

The witch raised one finely shaped eyebrow. "It would have been very satisfying to watch the acid eat away at that beautiful face."

"I'm sure it would have been. But then you would have ruined your circle, releasing me." It would have been difficult to limit the liquid to Helena's body. Even a single drop on the flawless chalk curves and letters would have wrecked its power.

Helena was able to move her head now, so she turned it a little to take in more of the chalked lines. "These runes are drawn to hold me. Not drain me of my magic. Which means you have something more elaborate planned. Something more than a meal. Am I to become another grand experiment?"

"Experiment?" Jocelyn echoed, a little crease appearing between her brows. It disappeared. "Oh, you mean like Lucien. I suppose you can look at what I've accomplished with him as such. I prefer to think of him as my masterpiece. I am, after all, a great artist."

Helena raised her brows. Or at least she attempted to. The muscles in her face were still a bit numb, so it was difficult to tell if she succeeded. "At best, Lucien is a work in progress. At worst, he's a failure."

A mixing bowl clattered to the floor as Jocelyn swept out her hand.

"I control one of the wealthiest men in England. How is that a failure?"

Helena noted the telling choice of words. "Perhaps because your control is only partial. Or was ripping his soul from his body the end goal? Does the act release energy you can feed upon?"

No answer. But Helena didn't need one. "If you cannot harvest the energy Lucien releases whenever he begins to soul-wander, then what purpose does it serve?"

"Because once I perfect my spell, I can take over his body completely," Jocelyn said, raising her voice until she was shouting. "What good is the power, when you cannot wield it?"

She waved a hand over her petite form. "As long as I inhabit this body, I have no rights. I cannot vote or own property. I couldn't even control funds allocated to me in the wedding settlement while my husband lived. I had to rid myself of him in order to do that, and even now I don't have control of my funds because they went to Lucien upon his father's death."

Except the money had never been hers to begin with. Jocelyn had bewitched the old duke for her fortune and place in society. But Helena knew better than to point that out to the apoplectic witch.

With a visible effort, Jocelyn bit back her next words, swallowing her rage. "But it matters not. You see, I have learned a great deal in the few decades. I know where my original spell went wrong. And you, my dear, get to be a part of making it right."

Helena hid her frown. That made no sense to her at all. Did Jocelyn want to take over her body? To what purpose? She was female too.

No. The witch had another plan. But she could not begin to guess what it was.

CHAPTER 36

"*Lucien, asino lento, get over here.*"

Panting, Lucien skidded to a stop on the lake's dirt shore. He hefted the sack of salt higher. It weighed at least two stone, but right now his heart was heavier. It was also racing out of control because he couldn't see Tomas. In the time it had taken him to sprint to the castle kitchens and back, thick clouds had covered the moon, making the landscape pitch black.

"Where are you?" he cried.

"Over here." Splashing followed. Using the sounds to pinpoint Tomas's location, Lucien splashed into the water after him, swearing under his breath when he got close enough to see the men's two forms.

Tomas had Nigel in a headlock. He was using his superior strength and all those continental muscles to keep the other man's head above the water.

"Can't you take him off his feet? Try and make him float." Lucien urged as he fought the water to get to them, holding the bag above the water as best he could.

"Why didn't I think of that?" Tomas sneered in between splashes. Nigel was struggling to break free of his grip. "The man is spelled to head to the middle of the lake and drown himself, you idiot. Making him float only makes that happen faster because he thrashes like a madman."

"Right," he grunted. Lucien splashed through chest-deep water until he was a few yards from the men.

He reached them and grabbed for Nigel's flailing arm.

"*Tlas.*"

"I have it." He shoved the bag into Tomas's arms.

"Why are you giving this to me?" the Italian shouted, pushing it back. "You're the gifted one."

"Tlas! Tlas! Tlas!"

"But I don't know what to do with it. How do I use it to break the enchantment?"

"Dump it over him. You don't need words. Saltwater breaks the enchantment."

"Really? Lucien was already pulling at the bag. "It's still sewn shut." He pulled at the seams with all his might, but it wouldn't open.

"*Idiota.* Don't you have a blade?"

"Why would I carry a blade?" Lucien asked incredulously. He was a bloody duke, for pity's sake. Dukes did not arm themselves to go down to dinner.

Nigel's head was submerged now, and he was dragging Lucien's brother-in-law with him. Bubbles rose to the surface in an ominous fashion.

"Do something!" Tomas screamed as Nigel pulled him under.

Desperate now Lucien began to bite at the sack. Using his teeth he tore a hole in the fine burlap, getting a mouthful of salt.

Spitting it out, he leaped up, splashing to the spot where Nigel's head had disappeared. He turned the sack over, upending the bag over the agitated surface of the water.

Tomas popped out of the lake in front of him. He sucked in a huge lungful of air. "I lost him," he panted.

"*Damn it.*" Lucien tore at the bag. "Help me make this hole bigger."

Tomas reached over, digging his fingers into one end of the perforation.

243

The burlap sack was no match for both men pulling on it. The weave gave, sending an explosion of salt over them.

Tomas plunged his arms into the water. "Swirl it, make as much of it saltwater as you can."

Lucien complied, thrashing and mixing the water as best he could. He kept it up so long his arms were aching. He scanned the surface of the lake. "It's not enough. One bag of kitchen salt is not enough to make this entire bloody lake into saltwater."

Tomas stopped flailing. He too watched the spot where Nigel disappeared. "We lost him."

A shudder wracked him. He told himself it was the cold water. "I guess we did."

There was a long silence.

A third voice called out after a hand broke the plane of the water. "Than... "

Lucien spun around, moving so fast he knocked Nigel back into the water with a loud splash. He came back up sputtering and spitting out water.

"I'm slightly less grateful now...but thanks," he said in a grudging tone.

"My apologies," Lucien panted, his relief making him weak-kneed. "I thought you had drowned."

"Yes, that was their plan."

"Whose plan? What happened to you?" Tomas demanded.

Nigel sighed, deep lines of weariness etched on his face. Lucien realized the man was older than him, both in years and in experience. His instincts told him some of the latter had been dark and difficult indeed.

He waved to the shore, and the three of them began to wade. "I got too bloody comfortable is what happened. There was a spell bag under the damn pillow—I checked under the bed and saw nothing, but I didn't go through the bedding. When my head hit the pillow, the bag's ingredients filled the air around me. I won't know how the compulsion to drown myself in the lake was built into the spell until I examine the remains of the bag in the bedroom in greater detail."

"We don't have time for that," Tomas broke in. "Helena is missing."

Nigel spun to face him. *"What?"*

"Did you—" Lucien broke off with a strangled sob. "Did you see her heading to the lake ahead of you?"

Nigel's lips parted. He shook his head. "No, I was alone until I saw you."

"Are you certain?" Tomas looked over now still water with heartrending desperation. "We need to know."

"No." Nigel's face creased with worry. "I'm telling you I didn't see her. But I don't think she's in there. Helena is too powerful to waste."

"What the hell does that mean?" Lucien demanded.

Nigel looked at him as if the answer should be obvious. "It means that if a black witch is after power, he'll want to take it from her."

Lucien looked from one to the other. "Then why didn't this mysterious villain take you?"

Nigel wiped the water off his face. "Probably because I have been making a nuisance of myself, casting my own spells and lures. They must be aware that I have some skill in fighting off magical attacks, which is why they chose a stealthy way of cursing me." He pushed back his dripping hair. "I scour my rooms for traps every night, but I admit I may not have done a thorough enough search tonight—too much ale. But Helena hasn't tipped her hand in a similar manner, at least not overtly."

"Then how would they know she has magic at all?"

"They can probably feel it," Nigel explained, shaking his hands out to remove more drops from his waterlogged clothes. "Some of the gifted can detect another witch's power without spells or charms. All that is required is proximity. I could sense Helena's power the moment I met her—this and her accent are how I knew I had the right witch when we met."

He leaned forward, grabbing his arm. "Helena has a great deal of magic. More than you and more than myself."

"He's right," Tomas said. "Helena's magic would prove too much temptation. Black witches are like opium addicts. They wouldn't want to waste the opportunity to try and siphon off that strength for themselves."

"Where would the witch take her?" Lucien threw his hand out gesturing around him to encompass the castle and surrounding woods. "She could be secreted in any room of the castle or hidden somewhere in the thick of the trees."

Tomas yanked his shoulder, spinning him around. "These are your lands and your castle. Can't you narrow it down?"

"*No.*" He of all people knew the sheer number of possibilities. "Just like the witch," he said with sickening realization. "They know these lands as well as I do."

"Then it's still up to you," Tomas added in a hard voice.

Lucien wanted to tear his hair out. "*How?*"

Tomas threw up his hands. "The same damn way you always find Helena," he shouted. "Soul wander."

"But I can't." He tore open the placket of his shirt. "I've only ever moved a single ring. It needs all three to be realigned to open the lock on my magic."

Tomas whirled to Nigel. "Can you open it?"

Nigel looked at him in dismay. "I don't know how. It's unique. I told Helena when I was doing it that I hadn't seen magic like that. She said her mother crafted it for her father out of necessity to protect him."

He shook his head. "I meant to have her show me how it was done. But we were busy trying to unearth the witch."

"You don't need to bloody duplicate it. Just move the ink to unlock it."

"Fine..." Nigel pressed his hand over the tattoo and closed his eyes. Nothing happened.

"Focus," Lucien barked.

"*I am,*" Nigel snapped back. "It's not working."

"Well try harder," Tomas urged.

"That's not something I've ever done before!" Nigel was red, his face swelling visibly from his efforts. "But manipulation of particles this fine is beyond me. I can't even move the needle Helena drew the tattoo with. My mother's training focused on larger threats."

Tomas thrust his hands into his hair and screamed.

Nigel and Lucien flinched as the sound of pure rage vibrated the air around them. Lucien straightened as Tomas pointed at him. *"You will do it."*

"Yes." He put both hands over the ink circles on his chest. There was no choice.

He had to solve this *now*.

CHAPTER 37

*J*ocelyn was ignoring Helena. She was too intent on completing the preparations of her spell.

The ropes were cutting into her wrists, but Helena couldn't stop pulling her hands apart, trying to introduce some slack into her bonds.

Where the hell had Jocelyn learned to tie knots? Had she been a sailor in a past life?

The small attempt at humor had the opposite effect. She should have been prepared for this. She *was* prepared. Her mother had taught her.

True, Isobel had been focused on healing, but her experience with the dark forces of the world meant she hadn't left her daughter defenseless. One of the first tricks her mother had taught her was to burn a hole in the fibers of a rope without burning herself.

But as long as she was in this circle, she couldn't summon the energy she needed. She couldn't do anything…except talk.

"What were you trying to accomplish with the maddened horse? Lucien was in mortal danger. There was no benefit to you at all."

Jocelyn sniffed. "I suppose there wasn't. But then you didn't attempt to save him with your magic. It was almost as if you were too panicked to think properly." She waved an admonishing finger. "Tut, tut, my dear. Never let a man make you lose all sense and reason like that. You must always keep your head about you in such matters."

Helena saw red. Of all the foolhardy, selfish reasons to risk another's life! Had testing her skill been that important?

"Nothing has changed since you first cast your spell," she said, clipping the words in a way that sounded more like Lucien than herself. "This attempt will fare no better than the last one."

Jocelyn snorted but did not turn around. She continued her preparations, occasionally humming to drown Helena's voice out.

"You won't succeed. Your circle constrains me, but I'm not a defenseless child. My soul will retake my body no matter what you do to keep it out."

This time Jocelyn turned around...to mock her. "As amusing as the idea of your soul—as if there is such a thing—flitting about without your body is, I told you foolish girl that women have no real power. It's not *your* body I want."

Helena's head was spinning. She blinked to clear it. "Then who?"

Jocelyn reached into the cage under the table. She pulled out a bedraggled-looking animal. Was it a small hound or a large cat? A stoat? It was so filthy with fur so matted it was impossible to tell. Nor could Helena understand why she hadn't been able to smell the animal. Judging from its appearance, its stench should overwhelm the cabin.

"Your unborn babe of course," Jocelyn announced, dragging the listless animal toward her. Then she slit the poor beast's throat.

CHAPTER 38

*H*elena was stunned. "My unborn child?"

"Don't try to deny it, dear." Jocelyn nudged the bleeding beast with her foot. "I know you are increasing."

Her dainty boot pushed the animal over and over until it was positioned just so, and the blood began to fill a narrow channel around the circle Helena hadn't noticed before. A single spoke in the channel connected it to the chalk circle.

Helena did not have to ask what would happen when the blood connected to the circle.

"And to think I was worried when your brother and you first appeared in the village. The way Lucien simply leaped on you, claiming you for his own with such haste—it was almost indecent. But I suppose I couldn't blame him. It was my fault he'd seen so little of the world. One could hardly be surprised when he snapped up the first comely young witch to happen along."

Is that what she believed? If so, then Jocelyn had never learned the true nature of their connection. *Good.* "You could sense my magic?"

Jocelyn didn't answer her question, not directly. "I was worried, of course. I knew you would interfere with my hold over Lucien. But all my attempts to perfect and refine my control over the years had failed for one important reason—I started too late. Lucien was already five years old when I married his father. Still malleable, but only to a point."

The cold knot in her stomach tightened. "But an unborn babe is nothing but untapped potential."

Her mother-in-law grinned at her. "Exactly."

She put a hand on her hip. "You know, this is rather refreshing. I've had to conduct my great work in secret for so many years, it's a pleasure to speak to someone who understands me so well."

Except Jocelyn's premise was wrong. There was no way she was pregnant. "But I still don't understand. How can you be certain that I'm with child? The wedding was only a few months ago. It is far too soon in my marriage for such certainty."

Jocelyn set down her knife, her girlish face twisting with blistering rage. But even then her delicate features failed to capture the evil there. She was more of a caricature—an evil elf from a Grimm children's tale. One didn't fear it. Not until the last page when it had snared you in the woods and was picking your flesh from its teeth.

"I take your point. I certainly didn't intend to do this now," she said, her frustration bleeding into her voice, making it grate like powdered glass.

Jocelyn went on. "I had thought to wait until you were in your confinement to conduct this ritual. You can thank the blasted witch hunter Nigel Ellison for rushing matters so. Had I not had to contend with his constant interference, I could have proceeded at my leisure. But it matters not. Thanks to that surly sow of a kitchen maid, he's gotten his comeuppance. And apparently you had sufficient time to do your part. Lucien was certainly eager to do his."

With that, she turned her back to her to resume her work at the table, revealing the poor animal that had been shielded by her skirts. It was still breathing in shallow, labored pants. Not dead yet, but soon.

Helena's shoulders tightened as she met its pain-clouded eyes.

"It will be a great boon having a child with a magical lineage on both sides. Once my spell imprints on the growing babe, I will be able to control it," Jocelyn continued paying no heed to the animal dying at her feet. "Then I'll wipe your mind and send you back to the castle. I'll pretend to return in a few weeks once the fervor of the scholar's death has died down."

She sounded so confident Helena almost began to doubt the efficacy of her contraceptive potion. Dear God, had Jocelyn detected a pregnancy through magical means?

And what had she done to her cousin Nigel? Something pernicious enough to warrant the sacrifice of her former cook.

Then enlightenment dawned. "You mesmerized the housemaids. They told you that my courses had stopped because they did not find blood in the sheets. That's why you are doing this."

Neither Jocelyn nor the maids had any way of knowing her restorative cordial to promote fertility did the exact opposite. Or that it was so efficacious it stopped her courses.

"I mesmerize all of the castle staff on a rotating basis," Jocelyn said, waving an airy hand as she worked. "It makes things so much easier. I can interrogate them at any time, and they will immediately forget they ever saw me."

"Brilliant," Helena murmured. "I dismissed you as the witch because I did not think you'd hang about the neighborhood in a place like this, eschewing the comforts of the castle. But then you didn't have to. Because you have the entire castle staff, indeed the entire village under your thumb."

Except there was one variable Jocelyn hadn't accounted for.

Helena wasn't just gifted. She was also cursed.

CHAPTER 39

*L*ucien despaired of ever opening the bloody lock. He fell to his knees, closing his eyes because he could not stand to see the condemnation in Tomas's eyes. An image bloomed in his mind. In it, Helena was lying on the floor of a cabin, her hands and feet bound.

Something shifted, and there was a click he somehow knew was only audible in his mind. His despair and desperation had opened the lock.

Then he was flying free, hurtling through the air. The trip was short.

He jerked to a stop, dizzy despite the fact his body couldn't possibly be experiencing the topsy turvy head-wrecking sensation of flight. He pushed through the moment of disorientation.

Lucien was standing in the woods outside of a small one-room cabin. There were no windows, but light shone in the crack under the door. He went for the doorknob, but his hand passed right through.

Bloody idiot. He was not in his body. Therefore his hands did not work. But he could walk through the wall.

He was about to do just that when he heard the voice inside.

I knew you would interfere with my hold over Lucien.

The rest of the words sank into the pit that had opened in the middle of his chest. He heard them all but comprehended few. But these few were enough.

Child. Spell. Mesmerized. The words fell like stones raining from the sky, sharp ones that tore and ripped everything on the way down.

Lucien did not have his body, but he didn't need it to bleed.

CHAPTER 40

"*P*lease," Helena mouthed. But she wasn't begging for mercy. Jocelyn had none.

Come to me, she willed, silently this time.

"*Dying animals seek me out. It's as if they seek comfort from me in their last moments.*"

That's what she had told Lucien. But the animal didn't move. The sad quirk of her talent wouldn't apply if the beast was already dead.

Despair filled her. It felt like drowning, as if something was sucking the air from her lungs. Helena would never get to see Lucien again. Or Tomas. Or her parents. Because Jocelyn would kill her when she realized Helena wasn't pregnant.

A shudder wracked her. No, this was worse. Jocelyn was going to wipe her memories and send her back. Which meant she'd simply attempt this again later when there was a male babe inside her.

And Helena and Lucien wouldn't just lose that child. It would become an abomination. Jocelyn would never be content with having the body for a time. She wanted it for all time, a new life with the power and privilege this country afforded its wealthiest nobles.

The pain that welled inside her was like an ocean wave. Helena ached, was drowning in it.

Across the cabin floor, the dying beast that was the witch's sacri-fice moved its head. Glazed pain-filled eyes looked at her without comprehension.

Helena's heart stuttered. She looked the animal in the eyes.

Please come to me. You don't have to be alone. Be with me in your last moments.

Seconds as long as years ticked past. Until finally—*dear God finally*—it obeyed.

The dying animal dragged its body toward her, smearing the chalked lines of the circle trapping her in the process. Its progress was slow. Every moment it paused, Helena was convinced it was dead. But it kept going, its will as fierce as her own.

The beast died just as it reached her. Tears streamed down her face as Helena pressed her forehead to the bedraggled animal.

"Thank you," she whispered.

The energy of the circle evaporated with a crackle she felt more than heard. But she wasn't the only one who felt the power stutter and flicker out.

Jocelyn whirled around, shock twisting her elfin features into something feral and ugly, no longer a sprite but a hideous goblin.

"How did you..." Jocelyn didn't bother to finish the question. She threw herself at the table, grabbing a vial of something before discarding it in favor of a silver dagger resting near the edge.

Helena rolled, but her bound feet prevented her from standing. She touched the ropes. *"Ignis."*

Heat and the smell of burning hemp filled her nose as she pulled her legs apart. Hampered by her skirts, she couldn't get to her feet, but she could roll. Jocelyn chased after her, knife in hand.

Raising her bound hands, she yelled, and the witch fell back, knocked by a blast of raw power.

Jocelyn crashed against the table, striking her head on the edge.

But not hard enough. She turned, clear-eyed with blood trickling down her hairline. "You *bitch*," she spat, clutching the knife.

Her teeth bared, and Helena blinked as the witch's teeth sharp-ened, the gums around it blackening before her eyes.

This. This was the price of what Jocelyn had become, the putrefaction and decay carefully concealed under her genteel mask.

"I'll kill you," Jocelyn hissed. "I will do it and laugh and laugh. Then I'll suck the power from your bones."

Helena somehow managed to get to her feet, and then she spun, ready to run away when she pressed up against something, a hot wind given shape.

Lucien. Helena's lips parted, but no sound came out. She couldn't breathe. It was as if a bolt of lightning had struck her, freezing.

Looking down her mind stuttered. Lucien's arm was *in her.* It was buried in her chest past the elbow.

Sparks of lightning jolted her mind as dread sucked all warmth from her. One thought coalesced in her mind. Jocelyn had succeeded. She'd taken over Lucien, and she was using him to kill her.

"Don't worry my love," he whispered.

The words released Helena from her stunned immobility. Gasping, she stumbled to the side and turned.

Jocelyn was frozen with her hand upraised. But Lucien's hand, which had reached through her, was buried in his stepmother's chest.

The dagger she held clattered to the floor.

The witch's face was red, every muscle in her face and neck tense and straining. Then something crunched like pheasant bones snapping.

Jocelyn fell to the floor. *"W-what?"* she stuttered, shaking and sweating.

Lucien watched her impassively, his eyes frighteningly blank. "What you are feeling is yourself dying."

He crouched down so he was eye-to-eye with Jocelyn.

"N...n..."

Lucien looked down at his hands. "I'm afraid it's true. You see, death is the inevitable consequence of a crushed heart."

Eyes wide and glazed, Jocelyn's mouth gaped, trying to form the words. *"How?"*

"It's simple," he said in a low voice. "You focused on trying to control my body..."

"But the true power lies within the soul," Helena finished as the witch convulsed one last time, her eyes going glassy and still.

CHAPTER 41

*H*elena closed her eyes, letting the warmth of the water seep into her body. She opened them to find Lucien crouched next to the bathtub, a sponge in his hand.

He wasn't wearing a shirt. He'd also shed his pants, leaving only his underclothes, but despite his partial nudity there was nothing amorous about this moment or his manner. He was washing her arms absently, his mind millions of miles away.

And still, he tries to care for you. He simply couldn't stop himself.

Lucien hadn't returned to his body after Jocelyn died. He wouldn't leave her to make her way back to the castle alone. Despite the energy it cost him, Lucien had stayed with her, guiding her out of that poisoned corner of the woods to the lake where Tomas and Nigel were waiting.

Helena had been shocked to learn of Nigel's close escape. It could have easily been Tomas. It would have been too, if not for her mother's tattoo.

"She was a skilled mesmerist," Helena said, avoiding the use of his stepmother's name. It had made Lucien twitch twice now. "That's why you remained vulnerable when the protection charm was a medallion. The triggers she buried in your mind were decades old, implanted when you were a defenseless child. You took it off because she asked you to."

Lucien blinked, refocusing on her. "Can someone else command me that way?"

Helena shook her head. "Not with your tattoo in the closed position."

"And if it's open?"

She stroked his arm, taking comfort in touching him as she thought it through. "Magical mesmerists aren't thick on the ground, thank the Lord. But now that she's gone those pathways will close. She won't be here to reopen them. I think your magic will speed that along."

"Does that apply to the staff as well? They're not gifted. They are normal people."

She considered that. "I don't believe you have to worry about them. As long as they're left alone given time all of it should heal on their own."

He nodded. "That is a relief." Except he didn't look relieved. His face remained sober, grief carving the lines around his mouth a little deeper.

Helena grabbed his wrist. "We have much to discuss, but I think for now you need to get in this bath with me."

Lucien's smile was barely there. But there was a glint in her eye that told her it would return. "No offense darling, but this is not the best time to seduce me."

"Actually, I was thinking that you need to wash the lake off."

"Oh." Lucien blinked and snorted lightly. "That's a very good point."

Stripping off his drawers, he handed her the sponge and climbed into the tub with her. He folded his long muscular limbs as best he could and attempted another smile.

Helena flowed over the water, over him until she was lying on top of him, their legs outstretched, her head resting over his heart.

Both kept silent for a long while, letting the water and the feel of each other's skin soothe what words could not.

"Nothing will be served by exposing her," she said after a long silence. "I think Nigel was right when he suggested she should suffer an accident in London. Perhaps a runaway carriage. Or she can be thrown from her horse."

His hand came up to rub her back. The other came up to stroke the back of her head. "A fatal case of apoplexy is simpler."

"True. Apoplexy it is."

"She killed my father, didn't she?"

Helena lifted her head to look at him. "You overheard?"

"No. But it's a reasonable guess." He took a deep breath, girding himself. "What about my mother?"

"No. She said she met your father after she was gone."

Something in him eased, a small loosening of his muscles. "I think it's time to leave."

"What?" She tipped her head back to meet his eyes.

"That tour of the continent we spoke of," he said. "We will stay long enough to deal with the repercussions of what Jocelyn did and make sure my people are well. Not scarred or vulnerable. But then we are going to pack our trunks and we will leave."

She could feel the weight of his words as a palpable force. They raised the tiny hair on the back of her neck.

I'm going to have to teach him not to channel his power into his speech. It made his promises vows.

"I never want to dissuade you from what you need—I only want you to be well. You know I only want you to be well. You and Tomas are my highest priority. But this revelation was a shock. I am not certain we should leave without confronting what she did here in your home."

"Technically, I have many other estates." His tone was light.

"You know what I meant."

"My love, listen to me," he said, cupping her cheek. "I have more memories of Jocelyn being gone than of her being here."

He snorted. "According to her, she was traveling the world, searching for her rare manuscripts. Who knows what she was really doing? In hindsight, it was probably something terrible. But all I wanted when I was young was to be able to travel just like her. To see the world."

Lucien tilted her chin up with his fingers, looking deep into her eyes. "That desire may be the only genuine gift she gave me. And lucky me, I get to do it with the love of my life. So, no. Leaving is not running away or trying to avoid the memories of her betrayal. It's being set free."

Helena slid her hand over his heart. "If that's the case, then by all means let's go see the world."

His answering smile was small but potent. Intimate. "Tomorrow is soon enough. Tonight...tonight I want to see Heaven."

He rose with her in his arms, carrying her to bed.

This time their passion wasn't the explosive conflagration of encounters past. It burned slowly as skin slid against skin and hands explored and stroked.

Lucien covered her with kisses, taking her mouth with searing intensity. But despite the heat, the gesture shared both desire and comfort...for a time. Then there was only their intense physical connection, the need that overrode thought.

He needed that tonight, and she was determined to give it to him.

Helena could feel Lucien's tension in the grip of his hands. He might leave marks he'd feel ashamed of on the morrow, but she didn't care. Helena wasn't about to douse these flames Lucien was hanging by a thread tonight, but she'd be doing him a disservice to reel him back. She was going to push him over and make him channel all that justified anger he was feeling into a different kind of fire.

So she coaxed him like a siren of old, rising over him and using her hips and hands to guide his cock into her hot sheath.

Lucien's surprise at her seizing the reins was almost as satisfying as the feeling of his shaft parting her folds. She moaned aloud as he slid against the slick walls of her channel. He overfilled her, stretching her to her limits. His manhood felt larger and thicker in this position, but Helena was determined to worship Lucien with her body, riding him, trying to make him feel everything he was to her.

And because he was always in tune with her, he responded in kind.

Not content to simply accept pleasure, Lucien soon flipped them over, covering her and using his sculpted form to give as much as he took.

He surged with her, grinding until she shook helplessly beneath him, moaning and crying out with each peak. Only once she was lying helpless and spent did he finally let go.

Lucien pulsed and throbbed, flooding her with heat as he gasped her name, whispering words of praise and love, promising forever.

EPILOGUE

*L*ucien sat back on the carriage and closed his eyes so his wife and Tomas wouldn't realize how nervous he was to meet his mother-in-law.

As far as Tomas was concerned, Lucien had already passed the greatest hurdle yesterday when they had arrived at the *Locanda Promessi Sposi* coaching inn to find the Conte Santa Fiora, Helena's father, waiting for them.

Matteo Garibaldi was not what Lucien expected. Not after all the dire predictions Tomas had made about the chilly reception he expected Lucien to receive. But the Conte surprised them all by embracing him and calling him son.

Lucien might have preferred being called out to the spectacle he'd made of himself, nearly bursting into tears.

But no one had so much as batted an eyelash. Apparently, excessive displays of emotion were acceptable in Italy—encouraged even.

According to Tomas, they were almost required in his family. Helena certainly hadn't restrained herself, leaping into her father's arms and weeping copiously before the pair broke into rapid-fire Italian in the middle of the inn courtyard.

Tomas had an equally emotional reunion with the man he called father. That had unsettled him more than anything. After all, the visible demonstrations of love and care between Helena and her father were not unexpected.

No, it was the open and effortless affection between Tomas and Matteo that made a lump rise in his throat and stay there.

"That went far better for you than it should have," Tomas sniffed once they had a moment to speak alone—after the tears and hugs finally wound down. "Father seems to think you two have a great deal in common given that he too was once victimized by magic."

"Sorry to disappoint you. I know you were looking forward to the fisticuffs," Lucien drawled into the grappa Tomas insisted he try. "Perhaps you can toss a few rocks at my head later to make yourself feel better."

"Oh, I won't need to do that. After all, you still have to make mother's acquaintance tomorrow."

"She'll love me," he insisted. But it got him thinking. He did not have the best history with mothers, did he?

But he pushed that thought away. He was in gorgeous, sunny Italy in the company of his beautiful wife and her family.

After the unexpectedly warm reception, he, Tomas, Helena, and the Conte had retired to a private dining room to eat, drink, and talk themselves hoarse.

Helena's new brothers were walking now.

"I have more grey hairs thanks to those two," Matteo had joked with great affection.

They in turn had regaled the man with the many sights they'd seen.

They had come to Italy via a circuitous route, stopping first in London for several weeks. There they had met a frail but still formidable Moira as well as Nigel senior at a meeting designed to appear like a chance encounter at the National Gallery.

Moira had been beside herself. She had been thrilled to meet her grandniece of course, but there had been a great deal of guilt under the surface. Moira regretted letting Isobel believe she was dead.

"My mother will understand, as do I," Helena assured her,

LUCY LEROUX

embracing the older woman. They spoke in whispers, letting the crowd conceal them and their secrets.

Lucien and Nigel were determined to find a way for his parents to meet Isobel and Helena again, without compromising anyone's safety, making plans within plans. Eventually, it was decided that in a few months' time, Nigel would escort his parents to the coastal town of Saint Tropez, where the entire Garibaldi claim would be waiting.

In the meantime, they were carrying several letters Moira had penned for Isobel, including a lengthy explanation of what had happened to her and no doubt several dozen superfluous pages of apology.

After London, they had taken a steamship and crossed the channel to the French port of Marseille before swinging up to Brussels. That was the beginning of a meandering course that took them to the great cities of Amsterdam, Antwerp, Belgium, before crossing into Luxembourg. From there they had made leisurely progress into France, spending many long sunny days enjoying potent wine and gorging on entirely too many heavy duck dishes and savory sausages.

Then came the Italian cities of Milan and Venice. Lucien would never forget his first sight of the Grand Canal or the Rialto Bridge. Genoa and Florence also held great charm. But now they were here near the Lake Bolsena estate where Helena had spent most of her life. And he was about to meet her mother.

Helena's pleasure in being home was palpable. She was constantly pointing out familiar sights, entertaining him with tales of her and Tomas's childhood mishaps, her face glowing with happiness and excitement. Her joy was infectious, but Lucien couldn't help feeling some trepidation.

Why the idea of meeting Isobel was more nerve-wracking than meeting her father, he couldn't say. All he knew was that his heart was beating a little too fast, his fingers downright clumsy as he threw the carriage shutters wide at Helena's request to show him the lake in all its bucolic glory.

They arrived at the manor house shortly before mid-day. Helena climbed out of the carriage without waiting for assistance. Tomas, who had been riding alongside the carriage with his father, let out a great whoop at the sight of the elegant older woman holding the hands of two squirmy boys at the front door of the handsome home. He dismounted and ran to her.

Helena had shown slightly more restraint, waiting for the conveyance to come to a stop before leaping out of the carriage with a cry of *"Mamma, mamma."*

Lucien hung back, following slower to let the siblings have what privacy he could give for their reunion.

The energy generated by the two women embracing surprised him.

The Conte paused to admire the pair, standing next to where Lucien was patiently waiting. "Now you see where Helena gets her looks."

"And quite a bit more it seems," he observed.

The Conte acknowledged this with a knowing smile. A tug on his pant leg made Lucien look down. He was surprised to see a dark-haired cherub with devilry in his eyes smiling back up at him.

"The twins went from crawling to running," the Conte said, giving the boy a loud smacking kiss that made him giggle.

Lucien couldn't resist reaching out to touch the boy's hair. "I believe you are going to have your hands full with this one."

"He's only half of the equation. Double the troublemaking and you'll have a picture of my future."

Lucien grinned. "You're looking forward to every hair-raising moment."

Matteo Garibaldi's laugh was big and hearty. "You know, I think you're right."

Swinging the giggling child over his shoulder, he grinned and went to join his family.

After more effusive hugs to her children, Isobel broke away from the group to face him.

Her smile faded.

She did not look unhappy, but the swift change in her expression was enough to make him wish his wife wasn't so occupied smothering her twin brothers with kisses.

Helena really was a younger copy of her mother. Both were built along the same elegant lines. Both had the same kindness and decency stamped into their features. But in Isobel's expression, there was a complex something, a layer of sadness that Helena lacked.

Yes, this was a well-loved woman and mother. That much was obvious. But so was the fact that Isobel had known darkness. She had known grief.

Lucien froze when she placed her hands on either side of his face.

"H-hello," he stuttered, his usual good manners in shambles at his feet.

Isobel studied him with eyes of flawless topaz. Helena's eyes. Except her mother's were potent with power and quiet wisdom, something Helena would only acquire with time.

It felt as if the woman was peering deep into his very soul. In fact, he strongly suspected this was exactly the case.

"Hello," he repeated, ignoring the sensation of being stripped down to his core. "I'm Lucien."

"Yes," she murmured, tilting her head. Isobel nodded, but it was less of a greeting and more as if she was acknowledging something to herself, confirmation of something she long suspected. "There you are."

She slipped her hand around his arm. "You probably know this house as well as any of us, but let's take the tour anyway."

Bemused, Lucien smiled down at her. Isobel had never seen him before today. But she had recognized him.

Helena materialized next to them. She took his arm with a bright smile.

Warmth and magic enveloped him from both sides. "Welcome home, Lucien."

"Thank you," he told them both. "It's nice to be here."

The End

AFTERWORD

Thank you for reading this novel! Reviews are an author's bread and butter. If you liked the story please consider leaving one.

Read the FREE short story The Hex, a Cursed Prequel
Available Now on Amazon and other major online retailers.

Subscribe to the Lucy Leroux Newsletter for a *free* full-length novel!
www.authorlucyleroux.com/newsletter
or keep up with her L.B. Gilbert releases
www.elementalauthor.com/newsletter

TO HELL AND BACK

THE SEVEN FAMILIES BOOK ONE

He will follow her to HELL AND BACK...

Orphaned and on the run, Valeria will do all she can to save herself from the enemies who want to steal her power *and* her life. Trusting nobody, she keeps to herself and refuses to let anyone into her life—or her heart. But when she ducks into a store for sanctuary, everything changes. Suddenly, Valeria is faced with the future she's always feared. Is she destined for an eternity of pain and suffering?

Draconis Imperia leader, Rhys lives with his clan on earth since God was a boy. Losing his one soulmate destroyed everything Rhys ever wanted and believed in. And when he encounters Valeria, it's like seeing a ghost. But the fiery and mistrustful witch is nothing like the innocent and angelic woman he remembers in his dreams.

Valeria refuses to succumb to the temptations of the irresistible Rhys. She's hellbent on protecting herself—and he's determined to uncover the truth. But when her enemies drag her to Hell, Rhys will do anything to rescue her. Can one dragon fight like Hell to save the witch he loves?

Read it on Kindle Unlimited or in paperback now.

ABOUT THE AUTHOR

A 7-time Readers' Favorite Medal Winner. USA Today Bestselling Author. Mom to a half-feral princess. WOC. Former scientist. Recovering geek.

Lucy Leroux is the steamy pen name for author L.B. Gilbert. Ten years ago Lucy moved to France for a one-year research contract. Six months later she was living with a handsome Frenchman and is now married with an adorable half-french 7 year old who won't go to bed on time.

When her last contract ended Lucy turned to writing. Frustrated by a particularly bad romance novel she decided to write her own. Her family lives in Southern California.

Lucy loves all genres of romance and intends to write as many of them as possible. To date, she has published twenty novels and novellas. These include paranormal, urban fantasy, gothic regency, and contemporary romances with more on the way.

Subscribe to the Lucy Leroux Newsletter for a free full-length book!
www.authorlucyleroux.com/newsletter

facebook.com/lucythenovelist
twitter.com/lucythenovelist
instagram.com/lucythenovelist

Manufactured by Amazon.ca
Acheson, AB

12277567R00155